COLLECTING THE DEAD

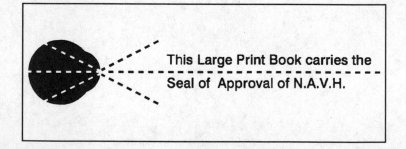

This Large Print Book carries the
Seal of Approval of N.A.V.H.

COLLECTING THE DEAD

SPENCER KOPE

THORNDIKE PRESS
A part of Gale, Cengage Learning

Farmington Hills, Mich • San Francisco • New York • Waterville, Maine
Meriden, Conn • Mason, Ohio • Chicago

GALE
CENGAGE Learning®

Thorndike Press® Large Print Mystery.
The text of this Large Print edition is unabridged.
Other aspects of the book may vary from the original edition.
Set in 16 pt. Plantin.

LIBRARY OF CONGRESS CATALOGING-IN-PUBLICATION DATA

Names: Kope, Spencer, author.
Title: Collecting the dead / by Spencer Kope.
Description: Waterville, Maine : Thorndike Press, 2016. | Series: Thorndike Press large print mystery
Identifiers: LCCN 2016041097| ISBN 9781410495334 (hardcover) | ISBN 1410495337 (hardcover)
Subjects: LCSH: United States. Federal Bureau of Investigation—Fiction. | Serial murder investigation—Fiction. | Tracking and trailing—Fiction. | Psychic ability—Fiction. | Large type books. | GSAFD: Mystery fiction. | Suspense fiction.
Classification: LCC PS3561.O63 C65 2016b | DDC 813/.54—dc23
LC record available at https://lccn.loc.gov/2016041097

Published in 2017 by arrangement with St. Martin's Press, LLC

Printed in the United States of America
1 2 3 4 5 6 7 21 20 19 18 17

This book is dedicated to the rarest among us, the men and women who face constant threat, who are cursed at, spit upon, condemned and assaulted — and who willingly accept such consequences.

They are the guardians of civilized society, who confront fear so that others don't have to, who rush in when others rush out, and who too often make the ultimate sacrifice so that others may simply live.

They protect property that is not theirs, seek the missing, console the grief-stricken, recover the bodies, shield the abused, and find justice for the slain and the violated.

Their work takes them into the heart of misery, to walk among the wretched, yet somehow they find a smile for their spouse and children when they arrive home.

To those who have dedicated the most.

To those who protect and serve.

ACKNOWLEDGMENTS

Special thanks first and foremost to the three gifted people who helped bring this book to life: my editor, Keith Kahla; my assistant editor, Hannah Braaten; and my amazing agent, Kimberley Cameron. Their talent and dedication is beyond measure and I am eternally grateful for all they've done.

Special thanks to my unofficial team of editors and first readers at the Whatcom County Sheriff's Office: Cheryl Café, Kristin Lunderville, Nickee Norris-Oaks, Altavia Chatman, Al Cheesman, Wendy Jones, and Stephanie Sturlaugson.

And to Detective Kevin Bowhay and Special Agent Thom LeCompte, who provided plenty of insight and an unlimited amount of fodder for my imagination. You know a friend is a keeper when you can call him on the weekend to get his opinion on how bad a body would smell after four months in the woods. Just saying.

Finally, a special thank you to my wife, Lea, and my daughters, Mary, Katie, and Abby, who've been with me on this journey since the beginning.

CHAPTER ONE

June 15, 10:12 A.M.
She had small feet.

I say she *had* small feet because to say she *has* small feet would imply that she's still alive. She isn't. I know. I always know. It's my special ability, my burden, my curse. The others think we're searching for a missing jogger, perhaps hurt or lost but certainly alive. I can't tell them we're too late; how would I explain such knowledge?

They wouldn't believe me anyway.

People are reluctant to give up the dead.

I turn the shoe in my hand, looking at it from every angle. It's a random selection from her closet made prior to my arrival, standard procedure for a track like this. I scrutinize the wear on the sole, the indentations on the leather, the signs of strain on the strap, as if to do so is to unfold and expose the mystery of her walking style, the way she carried herself, the way she some-

9

times dragged her left foot ever so slightly, almost undetectably.

You get to know shoes in my line of work: women's shoes, men's shoes, and, sadly, kids' shoes. This one is an ankle-strap pump with three-inch heel and leather upper. Not high-end, but nice nonetheless. I know that she last wore it about two weeks ago . . . but that part won't be in my report.

"Can you track her?" Sergeant Anderson asks.

I nod, but say nothing, pretending to examine the shoe further for the sake of my audience, which now includes four deputies, a dozen Search and Rescue volunteers, and my partner, FBI Special Agent Jimmy Donovan. The truth is I don't need to know how she walked, what her gait was, or whether she favored the ball of her foot or the heel. But illusions must be maintained.

Newsweek once called me the *Human Bloodhound.* I'm sure it conjured up the image they were looking for, wrong as that image was. If only they knew. If only they could see what a fraud I am.

"You said her husband reported her missing?" I say to the sergeant.

"Last night," Anderson replies. "Said she went for a run after work, as she always does, and never returned. That was sometime after five P.M."

"And there's nowhere else she would have gone? No other trails she runs?"

"None that the husband was aware of. She mostly stuck near home."

"Where is he? The husband?"

"He's in the house, resting."

"Resting?"

"He walked the loop four times last night looking for her before he called it in."

"Four times, huh?"

"Yep. And he walked it again this morning with us."

Taking off my glasses and securing them in their leather case, I stand for a moment and study the back of Ann Buerger's modest two-story home. My eyes follow her footsteps out the back door, across the lawn, and to the dirt and gravel trail at my feet. The steps lead north, quickly widening from a walk to a steady jog within the first twenty yards.

"The trail's a three-mile loop," Anderson says, "though you can turn off after the first mile and take the shortcut back just before the trail starts rising to Bowman Summit. SAR has walked the whole thing three times." He lifts his chin toward the Search and Rescue team. "They also checked the shortcut. There's no sign of her."

11

I nod. "Let's do it, then, step by step."

The trail starts off level as it skirts the western edge of Crest View, a community of ninety-seven single-family homes thirty miles west of Portland and just northwest of Henry Hagg Lake. The houses are a random mix of ranches, colonials, and the occasional split-foyer. It's considered an upscale neighborhood in this part of Oregon, and without exception the lawns are neatly cared for and the sidewalks are clean; a nice neighborhood by any standard.

Jimmy and I lead the way and set a brisk pace. The gentle trail around Crest View soon morphs into a steady incline that surreptitiously sucks the breath from your lungs. After the first mile at a ten-degree incline, I'm breathing hard and getting pissed at Jimmy, who's whistling the theme from *Mission Impossible* and looking like he's having the time of his life. It's not that I'm in bad shape, I can run ten miles with the best of them; I just prefer to do it a half mile at a time with twenty-four-hour breaks in between.

Turning, I wave Sergeant Anderson up from the back of the caravan. He looks like he's spent a fair amount of time donut-diving at the office, and right now I need an anchor to slow Jimmy. The sergeant's huffing pretty hard when he reaches us and I stop to let him catch his breath. *Mission Impossible* falters and then stops.

"What's up?" Jimmy asks.

"Just taking a breather," I say casually, tilting my head ever so slightly toward Anderson's sweaty face while trying to look unscathed by the hike.

Jimmy nods and takes a pull of water from his Camel-Bak, then asks Anderson, "What's the summit like?"

"I know what you're thinking," the sergeant pants, nodding his head as if he's been waiting for this question. "We looked over the side and couldn't find any evidence of someone falling." He gulps for breath from talking too fast. "It's not a straight drop, either, so if she lost her footing and went over" — *gulp* — "she would have left gouges in the dirt, uprooted plants, that sort of thing." *Gulp, gulp, gasp.* "Besides, the path is wide enough that she wouldn't have had to get near the edge."

"So if it doesn't drop straight off, I assume you can't see the bottom very well from the summit?"

"Not unless you tie off and rope out a bit."

"Has anyone done that?" Jimmy takes another drink from the CamelBak, a long one this time, and then secures it.

"Scott Johnson and Marty Horvath," Anderson replies, wiping his forehead and neck with a soiled ivory handkerchief. Stuffing the damp rag into his back pocket, he turns and quickly scans the faces of those behind us, then points at two of the younger and more athletic SAR members toward the rear. "That's them. Scott's the skinny one on the right. They both know how to rappel and couldn't wait to hook up. Fools wanted to start in the dark, but I made them wait until first light this morning. They had a pretty good look but didn't see anything. Course, the summit covers a good quarter mile."

"How high is it?" Jimmy asks, but he doesn't look all that interested in the answer, nor is he watching the trail, me, or Sergeant Anderson; his eyes are wandering from the twisted trunk of a deformed tree, to a chattering squirrel calling out a warning from a nearby branch, to a red-tailed hawk circling overhead, silhouetted against a powder-blue sky with the sun ticking slowly toward noon.

Jimmy's a hiker. He's also a pretty good tracker in his own right. I don't know what it is about him and the wildlands: the hills, the game trails, the isolated lakes in hard-to-reach valleys. I don't think even he knows, not really, but you can see it in his

14

eyes and hear it in his voice every time we hit the trail: he loves the forest.

I hate it.

Every time we end up in the bush it seems a body is involved. It started off as missing hunters who succumbed to the elements, and out-of-shape hikers who put too many demands on their hearts. These days it's mostly homicide victims and suspicious deaths. That's not what bothers me, though. The forest and I have history. And not the good kind, either.

I've often wondered if I'm the butt of some cosmic joke. Why else would God take a kid whose favorite saying was, "Homey don't camp," and make him the world's greatest tracker — and not even a *real* tracker, but someone who has to pretend?

Jimmy says he wouldn't.

But we live by the lie, Jimmy and I. The truth is a deep secret kept only because it would be too hard for most to believe. It's my life and even I have trouble with it.

God lovates me.

That's the word I came up with when I was fifteen as I struggled to decide whether God loves me or hates me, and settled on both. *Lovate.* I like the word; it's schizophrenic. As I grew older, however, I realized that God didn't really hate me . . . much . . .

and that my special tracking ability is really a gift, like when the Greeks left that nice horse for the Trojans.

So here I am, once again in the woods. It's the third track this week. The other two were easy; in and out within hours. One was on the outskirts of Atlanta. The stabbed and beaten body of a twenty-three-year-old male was found in the bushes next to a playground. The trail was strong and led us to a gang house three blocks away. It was amazing how quickly the gang members turned on one another when detectives started talking about murder charges.

The other track was in the dilapidated ruins of old Detroit. The PD thought the guy had been beaten to death, but it turned out he fell from the roof of an abandoned warehouse, hitting several obstructions on the way down and landing in the middle of the alley. It was a high price to pay for a couple dollars of stolen copper.

All in all it had been an easy week. No trees. No forests. No juggernaut of mosquitoes, ticks, flies, spiders, and gnats.

I won't be so lucky this time around.

As we start off again, Sergeant Anderson says, "So . . . *Steps,* huh? How'd you get a nickname like that?"

A couple responses immediately come to

mind, but Jimmy keeps telling me I get testy when we're in the woods and that I need to relax and be nice. He says I need to think about what I'm saying before I say it . . . which is what I thought I was doing.

He got his master's in psychology before joining the Bureau.

What the hell does he know?

"My real name is Magnus Craig," I say to Anderson, "but everyone's been calling me Steps since I was about fourteen, even Mom. That's the summer I did my first Search and Rescue."

"Missing hiker?"

"Worse. Two boys, aged five and eight. They wandered away from a campsite and it was already getting dark by the time I showed up. Someone said, 'How you gonna track them in the dark?' and I just said, 'Step by step.' Thirty minutes later I found the boys huddled in the hollow of a mossy old stump, scared to death but otherwise unharmed."

I pause and crouch on the trail, bringing the whole caravan to a halt. My eyes dance over nonexistent evidence on the ground, feigning curiosity at imaginary signs of passage. *Appearances,* I remind myself, *must keep up appearances at all times.* It's simple, really: a pause here and there, the occasional puzzled look, fingers working in the air as they help "read" the trail. *Appearances.* I learned that the hard way.

Standing, I start forward once more, the caravan lurching along behind. "By the time we reached the campground that night," I tell Anderson, "everyone was saying it was like I could see the boys' footsteps painted on the ground. Crazy, right? Then one of the deputies tossed me a bottle of water and said, 'Step by step, huh? Well, here's to steps.' As you can imagine, with a group like that it wasn't a huge leap before everyone was calling me Steps."

I neglect to tell Sergeant Anderson that I wasn't a member of Search and Rescue at the time and that my father brought me to the campground when he heard of the missing boys. He knew about my special ability, knew that I could help. Now, years later, there are three who know my secret: Dad, Jimmy, and FBI Director Robert Carlson.

"How long have you been with the FBI's Special Tracking Unit?" Anderson asks.

"I've been with the STU for five years now, since it was founded."

"I bet you help a lot of people," he says, and I can tell there's admiration in his words. But I don't answer. I average about two and a half call-outs a week, and these days they don't send me on the easy ones. There's always something unusual, unexplained, or sinister involved, which means the bodies pile up pretty quickly.

A slideshow of dead faces begins to play in my mind, unbidden and unwelcome. I force it to stop and replace it with the smiles of the living . . . but they're outnumbered and soon we're back to dead faces and dead eyes and dead gaping mouths.

Help? I think. *Not so much these days. I'm just the undertaker's front man.*

Bowman Summit is just as I pictured it: a high, dirty ridge lined by a gentle downsloping of trees to the east, generously mingled with the crude upthrusting of sedimentary rock, and to the west a crescent-shaped cliff dropping to the forest floor two hundred feet below. It's absolutely hideous!

"Now, *that* is a breathtaking view," Jimmy says, coming up beside me.

Putz.

I love him like a brother, really; he's quick to laugh and always the first to find the better half of a bad situation, but sometimes . . .

"Come on, Steps," Jimmy says, fakepunching me in the kidney, "even you have to admit that that's a gorgeous view. The way the mist hangs on the trees —"

19

I thrust the index finger of my right hand into the air, and Jimmy knows my meaning. We have one sacred rule: when in the woods, we don't talk about the woods.

He denies that I have hylophobia, the unreasonable fear of forests. I argue that, of all people, I should know whether I have an unreasonable fear of forests. But, apparently, because I don't go into a total meltdown on the trail, somehow that proves that I don't have it.

Psych majors.

"Hold it, Jimmy!" I bark, stopping dead in the path, my arms shooting up and out as if to block those coming up from behind.

The swath of trail ahead is little different from the rest of the summit, but etched forever upon it is the last paragraph of the last page of the last chapter of Ann Buerger's life. I see it as clearly as I see Jimmy standing next to me, though there is scant physical evidence.

An exceptional tracker would see some of it.

I see it all.

A shiver trembles through my body as a warm breeze comes in from the south.

You don't get lost on a three-mile trail that runs through your backyard, a trail you've

20

walked or run hundreds of times. It just doesn't happen. I didn't know the details of the search when the call came in at 6:23 this morning, but by 7:30 we were wheels-up out of Hangar 7 at Bellingham International Airport and southbound to Portland on the STU's Gulfstream G100 corporate jet.

Hangar 7 is both a home for the jet and an innocuous secure facility from which the Special Tracking Unit operates. The open bay is large enough for the Gulfstream's almost fifty-five-foot wingspan, with room enough at the back for a two-story row of offices.

Downstairs is a comfortable break room on the left that includes a sixty-inch LCD TV on the wall, several chairs, and a couch suitable for sleeping, which I can personally vouch for. In the middle is a kitchen area with a full-sized fridge (ice and water dispenser included), a sink, a dishwasher, and plenty of counter space and cabinets. To the right is our conference room: a glass-enclosed, soundproof room with a long and no-doubt-expensive mahogany table running down the center. The table is surrounded by a retinue of overstuffed, over-comfortable chairs.

The room doesn't get much use.

The chairs are well greased, though, and Jimmy and I like to spin around in them as fast as we can to see who gets sick first. We're professionals.

The second story is less complicated: Jimmy's office to the right, mine to the left, and Diane Parker's right in the middle, poor woman.

Diane's our "intelligence analyst," which basically means she's a walking encyclopedia of both useful and useless information, a secretary, a records specialist, a computer technician, a travel agent, and she's the only one who can unclog the garbage disposal in the kitchen.

Diane's the puzzle master, the one who digs through databases and finds the missing pieces and lines them up to tell a story. We won't need her on this one. The story is easy to read.

"He hid over there," I say, pointing to the right of the path, "in the outcropping, behind those bushes. He waited; bastard! Waited until she was almost past and then came at her. Maybe she saw him in her peripheral vision, maybe she didn't. He knew she'd be wearing headphones, so she wouldn't hear him coming until it was too late." I stop in the trail. "Her footsteps end here."

"Wha— Did he take her?" Sergeant Anderson breathes.

Jimmy knows. His eyes are already scanning the edge of the summit.

"He pushed her," I say. "Hard enough that she flew at least seven or eight feet before coming down. By that time she was over the side." I walk over to Jimmy and point. "Her left hand landed first and she tried to grab that root, but she had too much momentum." I shake off a shiver and continue, now in a quiet voice. "She fought hard, grabbing, clawing, wedging her heels. . . ." My voice drifts off as my eyes follow Ann's trail, until it disappears over the side and I gasp weakly, involuntarily, sadly. I didn't know her, but she deserved better. Not this.

The base of Bowman Summit is a hardscrabble of debris sloughed off by the mountain over generations, centuries, and millennia, mostly the result of slides and erosion. The castoff is eight to ten feet deep about the base and inclines sharply from the valley floor beginning some twenty feet out from the cliff wall.

A legion of trees populates the valley, fed by a network of small streams and creeks that no doubt empty into Henry Hagg Lake several miles away. The largest of the streams passes within a hundred feet of the summit base, providing clear, cool water to splash upon sweating faces. The forest is quiet today. The birds are about, but there's little singing and even the river's murmur seems muted.

She's waiting for us there, broken and quiet, sprawled upon the ground, empty eyes looking skyward, legs contorted unnaturally behind her: Ann Buerger. Two hours of hard trails, guided by GPS, and this is our trophy.

I'm tired of collecting the dead.

Their faces look back at me from the slideshow in my mind, as if to ask: *Why didn't you save me?* Even though they were dead long before I knew their names.

I feel Jimmy's hand on my shoulder as I kneel near the body. "We save the ones we can," he says quietly. *Our words.* After years of doing this they're almost a catchphrase. Their original intent was to remind us that we have a job to do, to get us back on task even under the most grisly of circumstances.

We save the ones we can.

Then his hand is gone and it's down to business. He begins to document the scene: photographs, GPS coordinates, measurements. It's murder. Everything has to be in the report . . . or most everything. What won't be in the official report are photographs of the places on her right forearm and right upper back where he shoved her. There's no way of capturing that information, no camera or film that sees what I see. My head hurts as I look and my eyes feel tight and full, like grapes on a vine ready to split from too much rain.

The signs are there like a beacon, a light in the darkness, a neon billboard. So clear they might as well be words on a page. I can almost feel the force of the hit, Ann flying through the air, the emptiness of falling.

From the pocket of my Windbreaker I retrieve the leather case and the glasses within. Unfolding the earpieces, I slide them onto my face. The relief is instantaneous as the crushing tightness in my head lets go and washes away. I can almost feel it draining out the bottom of my feet as I wiggle my toes.

It's a strange sensation. I've never gotten used to it.

My eyesight is twenty-twenty; the glasses have more to do with my sanity than my vision. They're very special glasses with thin lead-crystal lenses. I had them custom-made in Seattle, which wasn't cheap. I also have a pair with tinted lenses that pass for sunglasses, but I left them at home this trip.

The Canon PowerShot S95 is buried at

the bottom of my backpack and I have to dig past an extra pair of socks, an Oregon map, some bottled water, a box of granola bars, a thermal blanket, and my toothbrush before I find it. Powering up the camera, I go through the ritual. This photo isn't for the report. I click the button just once, and then check to make sure the image isn't blurred or washed out by the sun. I stare at Ann for a moment.

She won't leave me be.

Like the others, she'll haunt my memories. In one month I deal with more murders than most cops see in a decade. It's starting to take its toll.

"We gotta find the guy who did this," Sergeant Anderson says, breaking my trance. I didn't hear him come up, but he's standing next to me, just staring up the side of the cliff, his eyes searching for . . . what? A clue? An explanation?

I watch him a moment. I've seen that look before: anger, anguish, a sense of helplessness. I've seen it on thousands of faces at hundreds of crime scenes. I've seen it in the mirror.

My hand finds his shoulder; I don't know why. "We save the ones we can," I hear myself say. The words don't mean a thing to him. How could they? I just don't know what else to say.

I'm not good with people, not really.

Dropping my hand, I say, "Don't worry, I already know who did it." Stowing the camera, I take one last look at Ann Buerger and walk away.

The door is dandelion-yellow, with frosted glass inserts and a brushed-nickel handle. The doorbell chimes for the second time — a cheerful five-note chorus that's out of sync with the dreadful news about to be delivered.

Footsteps pad to the front of the house and a blur pauses motionless on the other side of the frosted glass. A dead bolt slides open, a door handle turns, and then there's a face pressed through the narrow door opening: red eyes, a red nose, a downcast, twitchy mouth — all the bitter qualities of sorrow. Seeing Sergeant Anderson, Jimmy, and myself, Matt Buerger opens the door wide and takes a step forward.

As I pull my glasses down an inch and peer over the top, my eyes consume Matt in an instant, telling me all I need to know. In the world of man-tracking the term *shine* refers to a hard-to-see impression left in vegetation or on a difficult surface, usually caused by crushing or pressing, such as a foot on a leaf. The only way to bring the track out is illumination. You can use sunlight, but most trackers pack a flashlight so they can get close and control the angle of the light.

That's not me.

I don't use man-tracking methods because I don't have to. Though we're in the shadow of the porch and I have no flashlight, I see the shine: it's on the door, on the floor, everywhere Matt Buerger walks and on everything he touches.

The shine.

It's the only track I need, and it's abundant and everywhere; overpowering. It can't be hidden or washed away. It can't be disguised and it can't be confused with another. It's not the same shine used by man-trackers, though. This shine is exclusively mine, or at least I think it's exclusive. Maybe God blessed someone else with this curse.

"Did you find anything?" Buerger chokes.

Anderson nods. "We found Ann," he says softly, but before he can continue, I blurt, "She's hurt, but alive and conscious."

Out of the corner of my eye I see Jimmy quickly grab Anderson's elbow from behind. His grip is firm and Anderson catches on quickly; smart man. Normally I'd warn the

28

locals if I'm going to try something like this, but I tend to be spontaneous, and this one just crept up on me as we ascended to the porch. I can imagine the sergeant's shock, however, and I can tell he's none too pleased. As far as he knows, Matt Buerger is the grieving husband, and what I just did is unforgivable.

"They're taking her to Adventist Medical Center in Portland," I continue, not wanting to give Anderson time to think things through. "She had some interesting things to tell us before she left, though." I fall silent and let the statement hang in the air. To the innocent, such words are intriguing and beg questions. To the guilty, they're accusatory, condemning.

Buerger's face goes blank, and then turns hard as stone.

"What'd she say?"

Without a word, Jimmy reaches around to the small of his back, snaps the button on the leather case secured to his belt, and produces a pair of nickel-plated handcuffs, which he dangles by one end.

"No." Buerger's mouth hardens. On his face and in his eyes the transformation is instantaneous and startling, like pudding turning to granite as you watch. He tries to slam the door, but Jimmy's too quick and launches into the dandelion-yellow field. There's a loud *crack* as the door slams open. Buerger lands on his back — hard. He lets out an involuntary *ummph* and flies across the polished hardwood floor, gasping, cursing, clawing against the momentum.

Jimmy's on him.

Watching my partner at work is like watching a tie-down roper at a rodeo — it's almost a thing of beauty — only instead of binding the legs of a calf together with a pigging string in three seconds flat, he hooks the suspect up with a pair of metal bracelets. If they ever come up with a police rodeo for restraining and cuffing, my money's on him.

No sooner does Buerger get his breath back than he spits it out again in a tirade of prolific profanity, capped off by, "Stupid bitch! She can't even die properly."

Close, but not quite a confession.

"I should've drowned her in the river instead of pushing her."

That'll do.

CHAPTER TWO

June 16 — too early

"Go away!" I say, burrowing deeper into the couch and pulling the blanket tightly about my shoulders. "I need sleep. You're supposed to have my back."

I know it's Jimmy.

The staccato *knock-knock-knock* repeats, echoing off the floor, the ceiling, and the giant picture windows of my sparsely furnished living room.

Of course it's Jimmy.

It's always Jimmy.

I need to get a life.

"Come on, Steps. Open up. You've got court in Seattle at three-thirty."

Pulling my hand free from the blanket, I fumble for my watch on the nightstand and slip it onto my wrist before raising the black dial to my face and squinting. "It's seven A.M. What kind of FBI agent is out harassing people at seven A.M.?"

"It's one-thirty in the afternoon," Jimmy replies. "You put your watch on upside down again."

"Damn!" I whisper under my breath, unclasping the black Movado and flipping it around. Sure enough, the dial reads one-thirty P.M. *Traitor,* I think, giving the watch a scathing look, as if its gears and springs are somehow to blame. "Well . . . it feels like seven A.M.," I say softly.

The knocking persists.

"All right, I'm coming."

My home is nestled on a hill overlooking the Puget Sound just north of Larrabee State Park and south of the Bellingham city limits. From the massive wall of windows in my living room I have a hundred-and-eighty-degree view of the myriad islands anchored in the Sound's deep waters. To the left, which is south, is Samish Bay, then Padilla Bay, Guemes Island, and behind her is the bustling city of Anacortes with its refineries, marina, and Washington State ferry terminal. Moving north you'll see Cypress Island, the San Juan Islands, and finally Lummi Island, with the fifteen-hundred-foot-high Lummi Peak standing sentinel.

It's inspiring.

My house has a name.

Odd, I know.

I felt a little uncomfortable about it until I discovered there are entire web sites dedicated to naming your house. Who knew? I always thought that for a house to have a name it had to belong to some long-dead patriot, some quirky industrialist, or have some unusual characteristic, such as being haunted. Places like Mount Vernon, Monticello, and the Winchester House come to mind.

Knowing that others are *intentionally* naming their houses makes it somehow less ostentatious, less snobbish. Kind of like naming your car. (Yes, my car also has a name, it's Gus.)

My house is called Big Perch, I'm guessing because it sits on the side of Chuckanut Mountain like some great aerie perched above the world. I didn't name it, but love it or hate it the name's not going anywhere. It's carved — and carved deeply — into a three-ton boulder at the end of my driveway. I've considered using dynamite on the boulder, but I don't want to cause a slide. I'm already on touchy ground with the neighbors down the hill. (One wayward bottle rocket causes one small fire and you're marked for life.)

Big Perch is twenty-four-hundred square

feet split between two floors; it has extensive decking on three sides that includes a hot tub and an outdoor fireplace, neither of which I've used in the last month. I've come to realize that I'm in a Catch-22 situation where I have the means to afford such things but not the time to use them.

I also own the adjoining lot to the south, which has a matching thirteen-hundred-square-foot house called Little Perch — again, I know what you're thinking, but I didn't choose the names, they came with the property.

Ellis Stockwell also came with the property.

He's the former owner, a retired Customs and Border Protection officer who lost the property in foreclosure. After retiring from CBP about ten years ago, he started a security consulting firm that quickly grew into a multimillion-dollar international operation. Ellis says he had a lot of luck growing the business, but I suspect the fourteen-hour days and seven-day work weeks had something to do with it.

Within four years he was living well. He had Big Perch custom-built, bought a Corvette, and managed to find a new wife along the way. That would be Vanessa, twenty years his junior, with a champagne-

and-diamonds appetite.

Almost immediately Ellis began constructing Little Perch for Vanessa's divorced mother — the two were inseparable. No one was more surprised than Ellis when two years later Vanessa emptied the business bank account and various investment accounts to the tune of $1.7 million. Hiding the money in a series of offshore accounts while Ellis was on a business trip, she hopped a flight to Cincinnati and shacked up with some guy she knew in college. They'd been Facebook friends for three years after reconnecting online. Go figure.

Ellis returned to an empty house. All Vanessa left behind was a single cup, a single plate, and a single knife, fork, and spoon. And one half-used roll of toilet paper in the guest bathroom.

The business was ruined.

Ellis was ruined.

When the bank foreclosed I must have visited the property a half dozen times before making an offer. On every visit, there was Ellis, still tending the flower beds, pressure-washing the sidewalks, touching up the paint. He was always cheerful, despite his troubles. He still has his federal retirement, which is substantial, but you could tell he loved the property.

On my first visit we talked a little; on other visits we talked a little more. He was intelligent, interesting, and had an endless supply of seemingly far-fetched stories. His bushy mustache and strong British accent seemed to fit him — though I remember wondering how it was that a British citizen could work for U.S. Customs and Border Protection. Six months later I learned that Ellis wasn't British at all, he was born and raised in Philadelphia. He just likes the British accent.

He's odd like that.

In the end we came to an arrangement that served both our purposes. I let him live in Little Perch rent-free and he looks after the property, making repairs when needed and keeping the landscaping under control.

You would have thought I'd given him back all the money his ex-wife had stolen from him, he was that happy. It's been four years and I have no regrets; he's as good as family now . . . bizarre, odd, sometimes Dr. Seuss–like family, but family nonetheless.

Jimmy gives me the quick rundown on the Buerger case as I shave and then scrounge a clean suit from my brother's closet. Jens is five years my junior, but we're about the same build — okay, he's a couple inches longer in the torso, but other than that we're mostly the same.

Jens is a postgraduate student at Western Washington University. I asked him once why he wanted to study anthropology and he said, "Because people are funny." I couldn't agree more, though he meant in the queer and unusual way, whereas I think people are funny in the dark and sinister way.

I like having him stay with me.

I'm gone half the time anyway, so someone might as well enjoy the view, the hot tub, the fireplace, the multiple large-screen TVs, the game room, and the endless flow of college girls that seem drawn to the place . . . though I'm pretty sure Jens has something to do with the latter.

Finding a striped gray jacket and matching slacks, I dress. Jimmy's telling me how pissed Matt Buerger was when he found out Ann was indeed dead. By that time he'd already been Mirandized and had given a very detailed written statement summarizing how he'd planned the attack for weeks (something us law enforcement types call *premeditation,* which is usually redeemable for copious amounts of high voltage or a needle in the arm and some bye-bye juice). He even admitted to failing on a previous attempt when he lost his nerve as Ann jogged by.

When I ask why Buerger had a beef with his wife, Jimmy's response comes as no surprise: The self-indulgent weasel had a girlfriend on the side and didn't want the hassle and monetary loss of a divorce. It's so much easier to pitch the wife over a cliff. With any luck his prison girlfriend will be a three-hundred-pound butt-squeezer named Meat, who likes sharing his boy toy with the other guys on the cell block.

Jimmy blathers on about some new case law we need to read up on, and a possible serial killer in Tulsa that may end up on our plate.

I like Tulsa — except for the weather. It doesn't really matter, though; as Jimmy often says, "We're not tourists." Jet in, jet out. Wheels up, wheels down. Get the job done as quickly as possible, and come home. Then do it all over again somewhere else.

"I'm good to go," I announce as I swing the jacket on, then I remember something. "Actually, I need three minutes." Grabbing my backpack, I scoot to the master bedroom as Jimmy looks with disdain at his watch.

Digging out the Canon PowerShot S95, I plug it into the computer and quickly download the single image from the disk.

Thirty seconds of trimming, sizing, and correcting in Photoshop, and I send it to the printer, which kicks out a beautiful, sharp, yet terrible photo. With scissors in hand, I cut the image from the photo paper, leaving a five-by-seven picture.

A small shelf is mounted to the wall above the computer, a shelf that holds but two items: one is a photo album in black, the other is an identical album but in white. Retrieving the black album, I flip it open toward the back. I try not to look at the other images as I find the next empty space. A couple strokes of a glue stick and the image is set on the page. I close the album and return it to the shelf.

I'll need to buy another black album soon, probably within the next two months. The white album's probably good for a few more years. I never look at the pictures in the black album, not intentionally. The white album's different. I like those pictures. They smile back at me; happy, relieved faces. Mother faces, child faces, husband, wife, and sister faces. Sometimes they're waving, eyes beaming and so alive.

I don't look at the black book.

The Gulfstream G100 — we call her Betsy — is a dream on wings, and one of the perks of the job that I really enjoy. Forests may make me quiver, but put me in the air and I'm in heaven. Les and Marty, our pilot and copilot, have banned me from the cockpit. Apparently I ask too many questions and touch buttons I'm not supposed to.

They were nice about it, though, and fortunately the G100 only seats four passengers, so there wasn't an air marshal on board to tase me. That wouldn't be fun. I went through training three years ago so I could carry a Taser, thinking it would be cool to have one if I ever needed it. No one told me that to complete the course I had to get *shot* by a Taser.

When they asked me if I wanted firearms training I said, "Hell, no!"

The King County prosecutor has me scheduled for three-thirty — last witness of the day. It should be interesting. I rarely have to go to court, which is good, since I get nervous with the whole process. Not from being in court, in front of people. That's easy. My *testimony* is what gives me fits and starts. It's too close to a lie, not that I'd lie in court, I just don't tell the whole story . . . and I have a guilty conscience, which eats at me. The jury hears about shoe size, trekking poles, stride length, shine, toe digs, and directionality.

But I'm not a man-tracker.

I don't need a good trail. I don't need a fresh trail.

All I need is essence and texture . . . which I can't talk about in court.

Most suspects fall apart in the early stages of the investigation, usually right after I find the body. They give a full confession long before it ever gets to court; it's pretty hard not to, when someone can tell you everything you did, where you walked, and what you touched. Most know when they're caught and are smart enough to work out a plea.

All but the sociopaths and the psychos . . . the Jonathan Quillans of the world.

Eighteen months ago, in a meth-induced journey into paranoia, Quillan killed his doper girlfriend's eight-month-old baby boy in a butcher-fest that gave me nightmares and day tremors for months. After a nine-day meth binge, his mind had descended into a wicked hell of frightening-awful hallucinations: snakes dripping from trees, spiders nesting in his ears, voices whispering in the walls, bugs under his skin that he had to pick at, and pick at, and pick at, but they'd never go away. There were terrible whispering voices that he wanted to block out but couldn't because he was afraid of the spiders in his ears.

The report reads like a modern-day horror story.

The cops are watching, the voices whispered. *There's a camera in the baby's belly.* He couldn't see the camera. Squeezing, pinching — the baby screaming — poking. It had to be deep.

Deep, said the voices.

When his girlfriend Nancy woke, the sound was no doubt still in her ears, a sound that she couldn't quite understand or place. The same sound had invaded her sleep and bullied her dreams, forcing itself upon her, screaming at her.

Screaming.

Pushing the empty Bacardi bottle off the bed, she stumbled to the bedroom door, holding the wall a moment with her right hand as the world righted itself. I remember staring at her handprint on the wall for the longest time: *ivory essence with a sandy texture.* When she stumbled into the living room, Quillan was bloody to the elbows, digging, digging, digging.

He killed her, too; poor, wretched, ignorant girl.

Like unzipping a zipper, he opened her throat from side to side in the kitchen as she tried to arm herself with a carving knife.

The voices told him to.

When they found Quillan the next afternoon, he was sleeping like a baby on the couch. Nancy's sister pounded on the front door for ten minutes without response, growing ever more frantic as her eyes fixated on the thin trail of blood leading across the porch and down the steps. When the police arrived and booted the door, they detained Quillan and did a cursory examination of the bedrooms, the bathroom, and the kitchen, finding nothing. There was no sign of foul play, only the telltale sliver of red trailing across the porch, but even this disappeared by the bottom step.

Quillan did his work well.

But the frantic scrubbing and washing of a tweaker nine days gone is no match for solid forensics . . . in this case chemiluminescence. That's the use of chemical agents, usually luminol, to illuminate trace elements of blood. It's a favorite among crime scene investigators because it reacts with the iron in blood to create a temporary blue glow. You can wash, scrub, and scour to your heart's content, but it's nearly impossible to fool the luminol.

They found a dead pool in the kitchen, a nasty patch of neon-blue where a river of blood had emptied onto the tile, splashing upon the cabinet facings, the fridge, the stainless-steel dishwasher, like so much water over a fall: too much blood to survive the loss. What had been a white and yellow kitchen and dining room now shimmered blue; every swipe of the cleaning rags was revealed, every attempt to destroy blood evidence was placed on display.

But no bodies.

That's where I came in.

Ivory essence . . . sandy texture . . . my special gift.

I see the hidden; I see the shine, every touch, every footfall, every cheek on a pillow, every hand on a wall. Some might call it an aura, I just call it life energy; either way it leaves its soft glowing trace on everything we come in contact with, radiating even from the blood we leave behind. Sometimes it's chartreuse with a wispy texture, or muddy mauve, or flaming coral, or a crimson baked-earth. Every shine is different and specific to a person, like fingerprints or eye scans or DNA.

This time it had an ivory color — what I call *essence* — and a sandy texture.

Landing at SeaTac, Seattle-Tacoma International Airport, Jimmy leads the way to a waiting car driven by an FBI staffer from the Seattle office, who takes us directly to

44

the King County Courthouse.

We're still early, so we kill some time in the cafeteria. The Quillan case was more than a year ago, so I review my notes for the third time before handing the file back to Jimmy. He stuffs it into his Fossil soft-side portfolio briefcase as I say a prayer that I'll never have to look at it again.

The courtroom is similar to others I've had the ill fortune to attend, though without the individual theaterlike seating found in newer buildings. Instead, family members, observers, and reporters sit upon hard church-type pews, lacking only hymnals and prayer kneelers.

The jury box sits at the front of the room on the right side: twelve overstuffed chairs, six to a row, with the back row elevated slightly above the front, surrounded by hard oak railings stained in dark cherry. At the front of the room, elevated above all others and brooding over the courtroom, stands the judge's bench. Made ornate with carvings and a marble top, it, too, is dressed out in undergarments of oak with a handsome, silky suit of dark cherry stain draped over the top.

My place is less ornate . . .

. . . and not so high.

Taking my seat in the witness box to the judge's left, I shift on the hard chair and try to find a comfortable position; it's not to be had. Perhaps it's just me, but I find witness chairs to be strikingly similar to the medieval Judas Chair, or Chair of Torture, a terrible invention embedded with a thousand or more piercing spikes rising from the seat and the armrests and protruding from the back. Its singular purpose, like the witness chair, is to encourage one's tongue to flap about in a productive fashion. Though in the Middle Ages the truth was less relevant than the confession.

I glance at the jurors and envy them their stuffed chairs. They look to be a decent group, with not a mouth-breather or drooler among them. The oddest of the lot is an older woman in a lime-green suit, big-framed glasses, and a 1950s-style beehive hairdo.

Seriously, I don't know if she's going for the retro look or if she just came from a Marge Simpson look-alike contest, but it's freaking me out.

Okay, maybe the beehive isn't *that* large, but I'd wager if it caught fire it'd take her a few minutes to notice . . . and several extinguishers to put out . . . and maybe a ladder truck.

I glance quickly from face to face, making eye contact with some, even sharing the edge of a smile with Marge Simpson. These will be the men and women who decide Quillan's fate. *I may not be able to tell them everything,* I think, *but I won't be false; the world has enough liars.*

"Do you swear to tell the truth, the whole truth . . ." *bla blah, bla blah, bla blah.*

I say, "I do," while thinking in my head, *All except for that "whole truth" part.*

"Good afternoon, Steps," King County Prosecutor Tully Stevens says as he approaches and shakes my hand. I've met Tully twice before. He's abrupt and, some would say, humorless, but he's a man of integrity and principle, a scarce combination these days, particularly among attorneys. He's not a handsome man, but he's not spare parts, either. At fifty, he still has a full head of salt-and-pepper hair that gives him a distinguished look and earns respect from juries . . . plus it balances the jut of his oversized ears.

"Steps, could you please explain to the jury why you were called in to this case and what your role was." His eyes direct me toward the seven women and five men in the jury box. I give a nod, thinking, *Here we go,* and dive in.

"The King County Sheriff's Office contacted the FBI's Special Tracking Unit after Ms. Moongood and her infant son went missing and investigation revealed a large amount of blood at the residence that suggested foul play. While the house had been cleaned, deputies found a blood trail on the porch" — I gesture toward a large photo on an easel to my right — "that terminated three feet down the gravel walkway.

"I picked up the trail where the blood ended. Directionality initially suggested the suspect was heading west, toward a parking lot in front of the apartment complex, but then the trail turned south and led to the trunk of a 1996 Chevrolet Caprice parked on the street about a hundred feet from the victims' house."

"And you checked the trunk?"

"I did."

"What did you find?" Tully asks, knowing full well the answer.

"Nothing." One of the jurors lets out the smallest of gasps, unnoticed by all but myself and perhaps Tully. I force myself not to smile. "The trunk was empty, but signs on the ground indicated the suspect then entered the driver's seat of the vehicle."

"Was this the defendant Jonathan Quillan's car?" My eyes follow his gesture to where Quillan sits smugly in a suit, his head shaved bald and his shirt buttoned to the top, concealing the white supremacist tattoo around the front of his neck. Even if the shirt had been laid open and the tie removed, the jury would see little more than unintelligible lines of no significance. The tattoo, which reads *White Power,* is written in Elder Futhark, a Norse runic alphabet used by the Vikings between the second and eighth centuries. Viking symbols and motifs are all the rage with neo-Nazis, skinheads, and white power punks these days, punks like Jonathan Quillan.

"No," I say. "The car is registered to the defendant's neighbor, Bakri Saaed, and was parked in front of his apartment."

Tully holds up his finger; whether to stop me there or to get the jury's attention, the result is the same. "And Mr. Saaed has already testified that he *does not* know Jonathan Quillan," he says to the jury, "*nor* did he give him permission to use his vehicle." Nodding to me, he says, "Continue, please."

"The track would have ended there," I say, "if it wasn't for Mr. Saaed's GPS. When we contacted him, he advised that the unit keeps a log of the vehicle's movements, speeds, and times."

Tully stops in front of me, his stone face

unreadable. "And you reviewed this log and discovered . . . what?"

"The log indicated that the car left its parking spot at one-seventeen A.M. and drove a couple miles to I-5, then south to Highway 90, where it headed east for about thirty minutes before turning off near North Bend. The GPS led us to a spot on Rattlesnake Mountain just west of North Bend, where the vehicle parked.

"The suspect exited the vehicle and removed Ms. Moongood from the trunk —"

"How do you know that?" Tully interrupts, cutting off an objection from the defense.

"There were heel marks where he dragged her off the road, as documented in photos number thirty-two and thirty-three," I say, indicating the pictures on display to my right. "He likely held her under the arms, faceup. If he held her facedown, her knees likely would have dragged, leaving additional marks. Plus, her toes would have left a wider drag than her heels."

Drag marks lined in lavender.

"And where did those drag marks lead?"

"To a spot less than thirty feet off the road, where both Ms. Moongood and her baby were found under a blanket covered in leaves and dead brush. That ended my involvement with the case."

Except for a single picture I snapped. . . .

"Thank you, Steps." Tully's voice is monotone, still giving nothing away. Turning to the defense, he says, "Your witness."

Defense Attorney Robert Baumgartner glides silently across the floor and hovers in front of me, his used-car-salesman smile firmly in place and his slicked-back politician's hair glistening. I can tell right away that he and I are not going to see eye to eye.

"You must be an impressive tracker, Mr. Craig —"

"Steps," I say.

"Right," he replies with the smile-that-isn't. "To track a man across concrete and gravel and a dozen other difficult surfaces, why, I'd imagine there can't be too many trackers in the world capable of such a feat, am I right?"

"You are."

"And most of these supposed *signs* you followed that day don't even show up in the evidence photos. Why, I've had several *professional* man-trackers look at the photos, and none of them can see your signs."

"Objection," Tully cries. "Lack of foundation."

"Sustained," the judge replies, giving

Baumgartner a withering look.

"So how is it you can track across surfaces that others can't?" he shoots at me.

I shrug slowly — *I can't tell them everything, but I won't be false.* "There are always signs," I say, "you just have to see them. If I touch the rail here next to my chair" — I place my hand upon the wood to demonstrate — "my fingers disturb any dust present; they leave minute traces of body oil and perspiration behind; they may even leave transfer, if, for example, I have mud or paint or blood on my hands."

"Come on, Mr. Craig! On concrete? On gravel? You're stretching the limits of my very active imagination."

"Shoes leave scuff marks," I say. "They displace gravel. They leave dirt and mud behind. Perhaps . . ." I leave the word hanging and can almost feel the jury leaning forward in their seats. "Perhaps, with the court's permission, a demonstration is in order."

"We're not taking the jury to the woods so you can point out boot prints in mud," Baumgartner spits.

"I didn't say we have to go to the woods," I snap back. "I can demonstrate right here, in this courtroom."

Baumgartner studies me silently for a moment, eyes searching for a trick, a trap, a hidden clause, and finding only my exaggerated smile hanging below bright, taunting eyes. It's too much for him. Slowly, a smile seeps out from his tight mouth, spilling to the left cheek, then the right — a genuine smile this time. Like a circling shark, he smells blood in the water; what better way to discredit me than to have me fail in front of the jury?

"I have no objection, if it pleases the court," he says in a controlled voice.

Neither does Tully.

I take a moment to explain the parameters of the demonstration, and then the bailiff escorts me to the hall and the doors close behind us with a solid *thud* that echoes through the tiled passageway. Beyond, Baumgartner is laying a trail for me to follow, no doubt trying to be clever and using what little he knows of man-tracking against me, poor fool.

I'm thinking about sushi.

Not that I like the stuff, it's disgusting; my brother Jens eats it by the plate. No, I'm thinking of sushi because it's tightly bundled with seaweed, and, like sushi, I'm going to wrap this testimony up with seaweed.

Robert Baumgartner is seaweed . . . at least his essence and texture are that of seaweed, dark green and slimy-wet, his tracks and touchings not unlike the clawings of some nefarious sea beast risen from surf and slouching ashore for some ill purpose. I find the essence and texture appropriate, since seaweed's slippery and disgusting and some people actually swallow it, much like Baumgartner's theories and hypotheses.

The courtroom door opens. *Too soon,* I think. Either Baumgartner is not as clever as I thought, or he's overconfident.

Walking to the front of the courtroom, I see the jurors have moved to the front of their chairs, where they perch like expectant vultures. Whether they plan to feast on my carcass or Baumgartner's is not so clear, though Marge Simpson manages a small smile as I pass. Stopping in front of and slightly to the left of the judge, I turn to Baumgartner and point to the floor with both hands. "This is where you were standing when I left."

He nods, but it was a statement, not a question.

Jimmy's parked on a pew in the third row on the right. He sees me — *sees* me like I see life energy, *reads* me like I read essence and texture. My loathing for our esteemed defense attorney is as clear as the tracks he left around the courtroom. Jimmy's looking right at me and shaking his head slowly from side to side. I can almost hear his voice in my ear: *Don't do it, Steps.* He's afraid I'm going to lose control and toss aside the part of my job where I *pretend* to track, and instead brazenly walk through the courtroom and point out everywhere Baumgartner walked and everything he touched. It's tempting. I'm tired of living the lie . . . but then I hear Jimmy's unspoken words in my ear again: *Remember, you're a man-tracker, not some mystic or superhuman aura reader.*

I take a deep breath, hold it a few seconds, and then release it in a long stream, letting my angst go with it. Today I'm a man-tracker.

On my hands and knees with a borrowed flashlight, I illuminate the carpet and pretend to find signs and directionality. I follow the trail up to the bench, and then back down, over to the Washington State flag at the right, then back to the U.S. flag at the left, then around the outer edge of pews on the left side of the courtroom, up the center aisle, a pause at the jury box, and then down the pews on the right side. As I reach the back of the room I stop, a smile coming to my lips.

Baumgartner's trail disappears and I kneel

to conduct a faux-examination of the final print, suppressing a chuckle as I picture him trying to fool me. After a moment, I rise and examine the area around the back pew, a seemingly random scan in search of signs. After toying with Baumgartner for a few minutes, I suddenly discover a right-shoe track — or so I say — on the seat of the back pew, then the left-shoe track on the pew in front of it, all the way to the front of the courtroom, where I get down on my knees and examine the attorney's shoes up close, saying, "I think I found him."

The courtroom explodes with laughter and one of the jurors actually claps. I stand, brush my pants off, and take my seat back in the witness box. The judge bangs his gavel and bangs it some more until the room settles.

Silence.

More silence.

Ticking-clock silence.

"Mr. Baumgartner —" the judge begins.

"No further questions."

CHAPTER THREE

June 16, Seattle

We're wheels-up out of SeaTac just after five P.M. and just a twenty-minute flight from home. The Puget Sound is large, blue, and beautiful out the left window; enchanting. Ferries like the *Kaleetan,* the *Kittitas,* and the *Tacoma* shuffle passengers and cars east and west between Seattle and Bainbridge Island, Edmonds and Kingston, Mukilteo and Clinton, while freighters run north and south as they come and go from the ports of Seattle and Tacoma. Islands dot the Sound, both big and small, some with roads and busy cities, others with little more than private piers and rough airstrips.

Island living.

It sounds quiet and serene. Might be kind of nice, though I think I'd want to be somewhere more tropical . . . but without humidity or bugs . . . and no monkeys screeching all night and pooping on my

57

deck . . . for that matter, no seagulls, either. They can be just as messy. And no sharks. What's the point of living on the water if you can't go *into* the water?

Actually, Big Perch is sounding pretty good right now.

"Seriously, what's wrong?" Jimmy says, leaning forward in his seat, his hands clasped together on the table between us. When I don't answer, he continues, "You did good work today . . . you do good work every day. Bad guys go to jail for a long time and victims' families get closure and justice."

"There's no justice for what Quillan did," I say flatly.

"Why? Because the death sentence is off the table? He's off the street for the rest of his life. There won't be any other victims, except for maybe Quillan himself if he crosses the wrong person in prison."

"We can hope," I say, my eyes still on the Sound. Jimmy just watches me. "I've thought about it, you know."

"Thought about what?"

I look him straight in the eye. "Quitting."

He plays it cool, conversational, but I can tell he's upset.

"What would you do?"

"I don't know," I say honestly, slowly

twisting my fingers into knots. "Maybe find buried treasure, or Jimmy Hoffa, or Bigfoot; whatever I can do to make a living that doesn't involve death . . . well, except for Jimmy Hoffa."

"Bigfoot's an animal; shine doesn't work for animals."

I long-shrug and stare at my hands. "Buried treasure, then."

"You think you can find buried treasure using your tracking ability?" Jimmy's skeptical but intrigued. "Like, say, Blackbeard's treasure?" Lowering his voice and leaning closer, even though there's no way the flight crew can hear, he says in a conspiratorial tone, "You'd have to know what Blackbeard's shine looks like, right? How could you know that? How could his energy still be around after, what, three hundred years? You're good, but that's a lot of layers of shine to sift through."

He knows better.

Once I've seen someone's shine, I can concentrate on it and block all the others out — for the most part — even if it's been three hundred years and a hundred thousand people have walked the same path . . . provided the path is enduring, like stone. If someone walks across a field of leaves, or crosses a wooden bridge, the shine survives only as long as the leaves or the wood. Often the leaves blow away and the wood rots, taking the shine with it.

"I was actually thinking of the Lost Dutchman's Mine," I say with a half smile.

"Really?" Jimmy's voice is subdued, but his eyes widen noticeably and he leans in closer. He's read all the stories about the Lost Dutchman's Mine and even spent two weeks looking for it after college.

We both know it's just a dream, though.

If I quit, the STU ceases to exist; what's a Special Tracking Unit without the Human Bloodhound? Jimmy would be reassigned, most likely to a counterterrorism position. Diane would be transferred back to the Criminal Justice Information Services (CJIS) complex in Clarksburg, West Virginia, which would break her heart, since her daughter and two young grandsons live in Seattle.

Les and Marty don't actually work for the FBI; they're on contract. In addition to their base monthly salary, they get bonus pay based on their flight hours, and government-rate per diem to cover food and lodging whenever we have a layover. Jimmy and I draw per diem, too. The difference is when Les and Marty draw it in, say, New York or Fresno or Boulder, they're out seeing the sights, tasting the local fare, and taking advantage of all the natural and man-made attractions.

Jimmy and I rarely stay at the nice hotels; we never eat a $30 breakfast, a $40 lunch, or a $60 dinner; we don't sightsee. Jimmy and I spend our time following *shine* down back alleys, across fields, and through forests . . . all the least desirable places.

Les and Marty would miss the per diem more than the job.

"It's just a thought," I say, pushing dreams of the Lost Dutchman's Mine to the furthest alcove of my mind, saying good-bye to Edward Teach's treasure, and rest-in-peace to Mr. Hoffa. I can't ask Jimmy to quit and come with me. He has a family and a good career.

Pushing forward in my seat until I'm perched like a bird at the very edge, I look at my partner, then reach across the table and snatch the folder from his briefcase — *the* folder — the one decorated with gruesome photos of a young mother and her baby, the one with surreal images of a glowing blue kitchen, a blood trail, a heel drag.

"I'm tired of *this* haunting my dreams, even my waking dreams," I say, slamming it down on the table. "Doesn't it ever get to you, Jimmy? You're with me every step of

61

the way. You see the same blood, smell the same decomp. How do you deal with it?"

Jimmy doesn't answer; he just lifts the folder from the table, his movements slow and measured, not in a caring manner but in the way one would treat a toxic chemical, an infected animal, or unstable explosives. Closing the file with equal care, he slides it back into the briefcase.

"Magnus" — *he never calls me that* — "you've got to stop dwelling on the dead and remember the living. How many more would be dead if you didn't stop these monsters? And I'm not talking about Quillan. He's just another messed-up tweaker who went over the edge —" He shoots up a hand to stop me as I open my mouth to interrupt. "Let me finish.

"When we started, the FBI had a long list of unsolved murders believed to be the work of perhaps hundreds of serial killers, and that list was growing by about two hundred murders a year. How many are you up to?"

"What do you mean?"

"You know exactly what I mean. Aside from the hundreds of killers like Quillan and Buerger that you've identified, how many *serial* killers are behind bars today because of the work you've done over the last five years?"

"I don't know."

"Liar! You remember every one of them. You dwell on them, just as you dwell on the dead. It's seventeen, seventeen of the sickest bastards that ever walked the earth. How many more victims would be dead now, I wonder, if you hadn't stopped them? Most of them were averaging one every year or two; Plosser was good for three a year himself, and his victims didn't die quickly or well. He dragged them through hell itself before he finished them. No one deserves that, Magnus." *There it is again.*

"So just suck it up and live with it, that's what you're telling me," I snap. "Just ignore the nightmares that wake me dripping in cold sweat, leaving me shaking for the better part of an hour before I can calm myself, before I can breathe normally." I stand and take a few steps to the back of the plane — I like to pace when I'm thinking or fretting or making a point, but the plane's just not large enough. I pause and turn in the aisle, my hands resting on the backs of the chairs to my left and right.

"I come from a great family, Jimmy. We all get along like families should but rarely do; I love my mother; I love my father; I love my brother. I've got no childhood traumas weighing me down, no hidden scars, no unresolved issues."

"Except the forest, when you were eight," Jimmy interjects.

"I think we can both agree that that was an unusual exception. The point is I should be the most grounded, sane, and stable person you could hope to meet, yet I feel like I'm going crazy, like the stuff in my head's just swirling around and beating against the side of my skull trying to get out, only it's the most horrific . . . the most . . . it's evil . . . and it plays like a movie in my head over and over again . . . so awful you just want to hug your knees to your chest and cover your ears and close your eyes and just scream."

Warm water lands on my cheeks and I look up at the ceiling . . . then realize the source; embarrassed, I brush the tears away.
I really am losing it.

Jimmy's silent; he's not even looking at me now, just staring at the table, picking absently at its scuffed corner, pondering. After a long moment, he lifts his chin and studies me. What can he say? There is no brilliant solution to my dilemma, no pill I can take to feel all better. The only solution is to walk away from it all, to just up and quit, but, much as I talk, I'm not ready to do that yet. Even if I did quit, it would take a hundred lifetimes to forget the things I've seen.

"What do I do?" I whisper.

"You take that damn black book of yours and you burn it," Jimmy says without hesitation, pushing forward in his seat. "You burn the pictures and the memories with it; you let the dead go. You let them rest in peace, the peace that *you* gave them."

I plop down hard in my chair.

"And then you take the pictures from the white book and you hang them on the wall, hang them where you'll see them every day, in the bathroom, in the kitchen, in the hall, so you'll remember they're alive because of you. They live and breathe and hug their children because of you. They're the ones you dwell on."

He pushes back from the table and looks to the window. "That's what I do," he adds in a soft voice. His eyes find mine for the briefest moment. "It helps with the nightmares."

CHAPTER FOUR

June 18

Jens is standing at the kitchen window, a cup of coffee in his hands, when I emerge from the master bedroom still drying off from a steamy shower. He's staring at something in the yard to the southwest and it doesn't take much of a guess to figure out that it's Ellis.

I smile and walk over to the calendar on the wall next to the fridge. "What's he wearing?" If Jens was staring out the south-facing window in the den, this might be a loaded question, since Ellis likes to sunbathe nude on the deck outside his bedroom. That's why we keep the blinds closed on the south side of the den during the summer.

We've had a few unfortunate mishaps.

Jens's face and voice are emotionless when he says, "The deerstalker."

I look at the box on the calendar for June

18, which has two entries scratched out in blue ink: *Jens — AS* and *Steps — PH.* Neither two-letter code matches the one for the deerstalker hat, which is SH. Of course, DS or DH might *seem* to make more sense when labeling the deerstalker, until you realize it's the style of hat worn by Sherlock Holmes, hence SH.

We have to use codes so that Ellis doesn't know we have an ongoing competition to guess which hat he'll wear on any given day. It's a ritual for Jens and me, one we've grown rather fond of. Even if he did find out, Ellis wouldn't mind. He'd get a good chortle out of it and run off to buy a couple dozen more hats just to make things difficult.

Ellis already has hundreds of hats in his collection.

Most are highly collectible and displayed with great care in his den. These include Civil War kepis, slouch hats, and Hardee hats, an authentic tricorne from the Revolutionary War period, spiked Prussian helmets, even an assortment of early leather football helmets. Most of his hats are at least a hundred years old, and none of those are handled, let alone worn.

There are thirty-seven much newer hats, however, that Ellis wears on a regular basis.

Sometimes he'll wear two or three different hats in a single day. The AS that Jens guessed is for the tan ascot that Ellis seems to favor over all the rest. I guessed he'd wear the pith helmet (PH), a rigid safari-type hat worn in the tropics in the 1800s.

Jens actually keeps a spreadsheet to track the frequency with which each hat is worn, including the season, day of the week, etc. I just go with my gut. I know that Ellis is full of bluster in the late spring and frequently talks about big-game hunting in Africa — he's never been — and the pith helmet seemed a good choice.

We were both wrong, but the day is still fresh and full of promise.

Opening the fridge, I rummage through the second shelf looking for a blueberry yogurt. *Peach, no; cherry, no; peach, peach, no and no; vanilla — definitely no.* I settle for the cherry. "So what was this big question you wanted to ask me?" I push the fridge door closed and peel the aluminum foil off the top of the yogurt.

Jens grimaces — *hard.* I don't know if you can really grimace hard, or smile hard or frown hard, for that matter, but when you grimace and it looks like you're either in pain or constipated, I call that hard. He sets his coffee on the counter with slow deliberation.

"Promise you won't be mad?"

This doesn't sound good.

"How can I promise not to be mad when I don't know what I'm *not* supposed to be mad about?" I say guardedly.

"It's just that . . . well . . ." He throws his hands up in the air, flustered. "That was a week ago! I told you I needed to talk to you a week ago. Seven days." He holds up seven indignant fingers — I know they're indignant because they're glowering at me. "It was kind of time-sensitive," Jens adds.

"It was six days ago, and I asked you if it was urgent and you said no."

"*Urgent* means I need an answer immediately."

"I think that's open to interpretation," I reply, taking a mouthful of cherry and turning the spoon upside down in my mouth as I raise an eyebrow at him.

Jens crosses his arms. "Excuse me. I didn't have my *Magnus Dictionary of Ridiculous Definitions* or I would have known that. In any case, it's too late. They needed an answer, so I just jumped in with both feet — but I don't regret it. She's just the coolest, and I know you're going to love her . . . but I know how you can get . . . so . . ."

"Wow!" I bark. "Now I'm totally confused. She? Did you get married or something?" I tease. "I know you're not shacking up with someone. You're the one who's always giving me lectures about integrity —"

The look that crosses Jens's face makes me pause and do a double-take.

"You've got to be kidding me." The words gush from me like so much air rushing from a punctured tire. Pushing my spine ramrod-straight, I teeter on the balls of my feet a moment, then slouch over and lean in close to Jens, hissing in his ear, "You *are* shacking up!" My arm shoots up and an accusing finger is pointing down the hall toward his bedroom. "Is she in there right now?" Strangely, I'm more curious than mad.

"No," he snaps instinctively. "Well . . . yes."

My head rattles back and forth. "What does that mean?"

"It means of course I'm not shacking up, but, yes . . . she's in there, and she's a dog."

"Shhh," I hiss. "She'll hear you. And that's just rude, by the way."

Jens looks at me for a long moment, shaking his head. "Wait here," he says curtly. "I'll get her." Like *he* has any grounds to be curt.

I could be curt. I could even be terse or

abrupt; I'm not the one shacking up in my brother's house. By the time I think it all the way through he's across the kitchen and down the hall.

I hear some muffled words — *reassuring words?* Maybe words like, *No, sweetie, you're pretty.* And, *No, babycakes, I didn't say you're a dog, don't be ridiculous* — and then Jens is back in the hall carrying her purse cradled in his right arm. My eyes aren't on Jens, though, they're on the door . . . waiting . . . patiently . . . still waiting.

Nothing. She's taking her sweet time.

"Magnus," Jens says as he walks up beside me, "let me introduce you to Ruby. And Ruby," he says in a cuddly-wuddly voice that's just revolting, "this is Magnus."

I'm still waiting . . .

. . . and then the purse barks . . . and my yogurt goes airborne.

"It's a dog," I say, pointing at the blond bundle in his arms.

"That's why you're with the FBI," Jens smirks. "You don't miss a thing."

71

Chapter Five

June 20

I'm wearing uncomfortable shoes.

When I say I'm wearing uncomfortable shoes, I'm not talking figuratively, as in the proverbial "walk a mile in his shoes." I'm not even using a psycho-figurative version of the proverbial, a version where I'm walking in the shoes of a phony man-tracker or, worse, I'm wearing the shoes of an FBI agent who has a badge but doesn't normally carry a gun, and who feels more like a pizza delivery guy than a Fed.

While the figurative and the psycho-figurative might be true, when I say I'm wearing uncomfortable shoes I'm *really* wearing uncomfortable shoes, the tangible, physical, tying-type of shoes: pinching, squeezing, binding, uncomfortable shoes.

A certain blond Yorkie named Ruby peed in my Nikes last night.

It's true.

She had ten thousand other places to pee both inside and outside the designated peeing areas, yet she chose my Nikes, my *new* Nikes, the ones that fit so well. So I'm stuck with an old pair of off-brand clogs disguised as tennis shoes. They're a size too small and the left heel has a hole the size of Jupiter's storm, and not nearly as pretty.

Jens told me the dog will grow out of it.

She's just nervous.

But he said the same thing yesterday after Ruby peed on my car keys . . . which were on the coffee table. See, to me that smells like premeditation. The little rodent didn't just stumble upon a comfortable shoe that time, she first had to find the car keys, then she had to get her little wiggly body from the couch to the coffee table — no small trick — after which she had to navigate around, through, and over all the myriad obstacles on the coffee table so she could hover precisely over my keys like a B-17 bomber launching an aerial assault.

Do you know what happens to electronic key fobs and chipped keys when they marinate in piddle for nine hours?

I do.

Luckily I had a second key fob hanging next to the door.

Too bad I don't have a second pair of

sneakers.

Now, instead of striding across the asphalt parking lot in front of Hangar 7 with a brisk *step-step-step,* I'm slouching along with a *step-stump-step-stump* as the hole in my left heel sucks up every piece of loose gravel or debris in my path.

When I scolded Ruby — this was *after* I put my foot into a cold wet shoe — she just fell to the floor and looked up at me with bared teeth. Jens tells me that means she's smiling, but if a lion smiled at me like that I'd be running for the door. I advised Jens that henceforth I'll be referring to Ruby as *the Rodent,* or simply *Rodent.*

He just smirked at me and waved it away. The Rodent smiled some more and I'm pretty sure I heard a low growl, vicious little schemer.

Down days — or DDs, as we like to call them — are the days in between missions, the slow, quiet days when we're really not expected to do much, and rarely do. The first day after a mission, DD1, is usually the best. I catch up on sleep, relax a bit, maybe shop online for a book to add to my collection — I've been looking for a first edition, first printing of *The Hunt for Red October,* but they're not easy to find in good condition, nor are they cheap.

Once or twice a week I go to the health club with Jimmy; he lifts and I pretend to lift. Eventually he coerces me into doing reps with him until my arms and legs are solid iron — and I don't mean strong like iron, I mean heavy like iron: battleship-heavy, with a couple frigates thrown in for good measure. He's like all the PE teachers I've ever had rolled up into one and sprinkled with Nazi dust.

I've never been much for working out; I always thought the term *health club* was a bit of a misnomer, since every time I leave the place I'm winded, sweaty, and fatigued, like I'm coming down with the flu. Fortunately, I'm blessed with good genes, so I don't have to exercise much to have a good physique.

Jimmy says it's unfair.

I think he's just jealous of my abs.

On DD2 we're usually in the office about half the day. Well, not in the *office* part of the office but in the break area downstairs watching a movie, or in the hangar playing ping-pong or foosball.

By DD3 Les and Marty start popping in and out, checking the plane and lounging around the break area, while Jimmy and I kill time with Nerf guns, exploding soda

75

bottles — we like to experiment — and marathon sessions of *CSI, Game of Thrones,* or *The Walking Dead.* Three days is our average downtime.

Today is DD5.

"Heather Jennings called for you," Diane shouts from the railing outside her office as soon as I step foot in the hangar. She's waving a piece of paper in her hand, no doubt Heather's phone number, which I'm supposed to dutifully call. Diane should know better, but she has that smug, motherly, the-polite-thing-to-do-would-be-to-call-her-back look on her face.

Heather's the hack reporter who wrote the article for *Newsweek* last fall, the same article that labeled me the Human Bloodhound. I guess I shouldn't call her a hack reporter, she's actually very intuitive and thorough; the problem was she saw *everything* and understood most of what she was seeing.

To say I let her get too close is probably an understatement.

She was embedded with the team for three weeks and went on seven searches, amassing enough notes to write a book. I did my best imitation of a human tracker: looking for signs, getting down on my hands and knees with a flashlight — *in the mud!* —

documenting shoe size and stride and pausing studiously at just the right moments. I thought it an Oscar-worthy performance.

I was wrong.

On her last day with the team she took me aside and called me a fraud in the nicest, most polite way imaginable, complete with a kiss on the cheek. She admitted that she didn't know how I was doing it but knew that it wasn't man-tracking. Still, we parted on better-than-good terms, and over the next month there were a number of dinners together, and several movies. Things were just starting to get, well, comfortable . . . and then the article came out.

"Don't even start on me, Diane. I'm not calling." She's still waving the paper.

"Why not?"

"You know why. She stabbed me in the back."

Ripped my heart out.

Shredded my soul.

Diane sighs. "Right. She stabbed you in the back. Why don't you just admit that you won't let *anyone* get close to you?"

"What are you talking about?"

"You know exactly what I'm talking about. How many dates have you been on since we've been working together? Who was that girl that Jimmy set you up with? The fitness coach?"

"That was Emily, and she wasn't —"

"Right. Emily. After three dates you stopped calling her. Why? Because she wanted to know more about what you do for a living. I've got news for you, Steps. That's normal. That's the stuff people talk about when they're getting to know each other."

Diane knows nothing about my *gift;* how could she possibly understand?

"And about Heather 'stabbing you in the back' " — she uses air quotes to frame the words — "you have no idea what you're talking about. You've never even bothered to ask for her side of the story, have you?"

"Her side of the story was published in *Newsweek* for all the world to see."

"She has editors, you know. You could at least hear her out. She's called you every couple weeks since November; I think she deserves a little of your time."

"I don't think so," I mutter, more to myself than to Diane. Turning, I exit the hangar just as quickly as I entered: *step-stump-step-stump-step-stump.* A trip to Bellis Fair Mall suddenly sounds appealing; better than sticking around the office while Diane *peck-peck-pecks* at me in that relentless manner of hers. If I didn't love her, I'd hate her . . . okay, I'd strongly dislike her; Diane's a little hard to hate.

A couple hours should give her time to put this Heather thing out of her head.

Besides, I need shoes.

Evil exists.

Many dismiss it as a relic of our superstitious past, or view it as a religious phenomenon and don't buy in to good and evil, heaven and hell. Psychologists explain it away as chemical imbalances, genetics, or nurturing.

I know evil exists — *real* evil — because I see it from time to time.

I'm looking at it right now.

I came to Bellis Fair Mall to buy a new pair of shoes, and instead find the recent shine of my nemesis, the elusive one, the killer I call Leonardo. He's been here before — just a couple times over the years, but it's enough. He always parks in the same spot. And not the same general *location* but the exact same parking spot. Maybe he's OCD or a creature of habit, it really doesn't matter. It just means that whenever I come to the mall, I check that parking spot.

Sometimes I think he's taunting me.

But that's impossible.

Eleven years have come and gone since that cold February morning. Four thousand days, spent and discarded, falling away one by one like leaves from the great tree that measures the weeks, months, and years of our lives. Into great moldering piles they gather, those leaves, surrendering to time and corruption until nothing remains but the memory of the leaf, the memory of the day. Eleven years; so long, yet I still know the shine: a dark oozing pitch, black as the heart that made it. There are no metaphors for darkness that suffice.

It was my sixteenth birthday.

Who goes on a Search and Rescue mission on their birthday? I almost refused but then learned it was Jessica Parker — Jess — who was missing. Cheerleader, Girl Scout troop leader, track star, honor student, Jess Parker. The worst thing she ever did was take a hit off a joint after a football game, and then only once. She was a senior and I a mere sophomore, one step above a maggot freshman, but who didn't daydream about Jess? It wasn't possible.

She walked down her hundred-yard driveway to get the mail and never came back. She was there, and then gone; it was that fast. And of all the countless times my special skills served me well, this was not

80

one of them. There was no track to follow; Jess's trail ended at the mailbox. I could see where she'd landed on the ground, could see a tiny spot of blood on the weeds by the ditch, could see the black tracks exiting the vehicle, scooping her up, and putting her in the back.

I pointed out the blood; it was so minute the deputies hadn't seen it.

That was the extent of my usefulness; that, and the knowledge that she hadn't wandered off or run away. This was an abduction; the news hit everyone hard in the gut and immediately changed the tone and urgency of the investigation.

Two days later they found her in a small clump of forest seven miles away. Her partially nude body was laid out on the ground, empty eyes staring at the sky, feet together, arms extending from her sides. His darkness was on her and around her and I saw what he'd done, how he'd posed her, how he'd used her.

She's burned into my soul, Jess Parker is, seared and smoldering and raw, a hurt that everyone in the community felt and one that I could do nothing about. She's just gone and the world is unjust and I have to look at the human wreckage floating in the wake of such monsters. Over and over and over I have to look, and I fear the monsters are looking back. They're with me in the lonely watches of the night, when sleep has fled and all that remains are the images. And Jimmy wonders why I want to quit.

I named the evil Leonardo because he wants to be called that . . . he left signs.

Jess Parker was posed as Leonardo Da Vinci's Vitruvian Man. The detectives working the crime scene only saw her lying on the ground with her arms outstretched pointing east and west and her feet together pointing south.

I saw the rest.

I saw Jess's shine where he'd first placed her arms in a raised position and her legs wide before moving them to their final pose. I saw the black circle he'd walked around her body. The only element missing is the square; why it's not included remains a mystery, as does everything else about this case.

I've seen Leonardo's track four times since the murder of Jess Parker, and always at Bellis Fair Mall. I beat myself up over it every time, wondering, why this mall? Why haven't I seen his track elsewhere in the county? Does he only pass through from time to time? Is he heading to a vacation spot, a job, a reunion? Is he Canadian? After all, the border is less than twenty miles away. Is he a student at the university, or a visiting professor?

No answers come.

All that remains is the puzzle of footsteps; footsteps that always start in the same parking spot in the same far corner of the mall parking lot. He visits two or three stores, always pays cash, and leaves as quickly as he came. In the handful of previous sightings, not a single clerk has been able to provide a compelling description of Leonardo.

When I'd ask his height, they'd say, "Average."

When I'd ask his weight, they'd say, "Average."

When I'd ask his hair color, they'd say, "Brown," or "Black," or "Sandy blond," or "Average."

Pointless.

Useless.

Still, I follow Leonardo's track; I go through the routine. This time it's just two stores. Then I walk the path from the mall to his parking spot and back again, looking for anything out of the ordinary. There's nothing.

I find my way to the security office.

"I need surveillance video of the southwest

parking lot for the last three days," I tell the security officer monitoring the cameras. A quick flash of my FBI badge dispels any objections and I wait patiently for forty-five minutes while they look for someone who knows how to copy video from the system.

I can't see shine in pictures or video, it's just not something that can be captured, even with the most sensitive equipment. But I *can* see what kind of vehicle Leonardo was driving . . . maybe. The southwest parking lot gets little use, particularly in the summer, so there's a good chance I can narrow down the selection to just a few vehicles. After all, I have an advantage: I know exactly where he parked.

"I'm sorry, Mr. Craig," the young security officer says, hurrying up to me. His shine is a pleasing ginger essence mottled with French lilac, I note, with a slow bubbling texture, much like a lava lamp. "We can't get the DVD burner to work. It tries to copy the file but then gets hung up."

"I've got a thumb drive," I say, digging in my right front pants pocket.

"It doesn't work with those," he insists, eyeing the drive in my hand. "Chet will be in later. He can usually figure out the system."

I don't bother arguing.

There are two truths I've learned about surveillance video: one, no one ever seems to know how to download the file, and two, the picture quality is usually so bad the offending camera should be considered legally blind — banks and casinos excluded.

Pulling a business card from my wallet, I scribble a word on it and hand it to Ginger-mottled-with-French-lilac. "Give me a call when it's ready. If I'm not available, ask Diane to come pick it up." I tap her name where I've written it on the card.

"Special Tracking Unit," Ginger reads off the card. "That sounds cool."

I make my exit before he can ask me how to join up.

CHAPTER SIX

June 21, 5:57 A.M.

Betsy descends from the clouds and banks left as Les lines her up for a landing at Redding Municipal Airport. The early morning sky is clear and blue, promising a beautiful and hot California day.

Sleep eludes me on these short flights, but sleep tends to keep its distance from me anyway, as it did last night; as it did the night before. The only gifts the Sandman chooses to bestow upon me these days are nightmares, and nightmares of nightmares. Jimmy studies the bags under my eyes but doesn't say anything.

The call came in at 7:35 last night, halfway through a recorded episode of *Jericho,* and just as we were winding down DD5. It was more of the same: a woman's body found by a hiker at the Whiskeytown National Recreation Area just west of Redding. Foul play suspected. Details are few and sketchy, but the Shasta County Sheriff's Office had secured the scene overnight pending our arrival, keeping everyone out but the crime scene investigators (CSIs), who, in this case, were not full-time CSIs but cross-trained deputies.

Betsy kisses the runway at 6:05 A.M. and taxies to the U.S. Forest Service hangar; the USFS has graciously allowed us to use their facilities while here. When the door opens and I start down the ladder to the tarmac, I breathe deep and take in the dawn; it's crisp, almost tart. The sun has been up less than twenty minutes and night's chill is still in the air. Broken fragments of dissipating shadow cling to the west side of the hangar, the airport terminal, and the hills to the north. The sounds of morning are everywhere.

I'm already tired and the day has just begun.

A dark blue Ford Expedition pulls up as our hiking boots touch the runway. While it's unmarked, it's clearly a law enforcement vehicle, evidenced by the collection of antennas on the roof and the hidden lights in the grille and windshield. As the driver swings the door wide and steps out, I see the uniform of the Shasta County Sheriff's Office, complete with four stars on the shoulder boards. He's a large man, at least six-four, in his fifties, with shoulders like a linebacker and size-fifteen shoes that actually look small under him.

"Sheriff Gant, I presume," Jimmy says as we meet halfway between the plane and the SUV. Jimmy's hand is dwarfed by the sheriff's bear paw as they shake.

"Call me Walt," the sheriff says in a strong, rumbling voice.

We do the whole small-talk thing for about five minutes and I learn that Walt has a deep, genuine laugh and a love for his job and the people he serves. It's refreshing and I find myself wanting to help this guy as much as I can . . . if I can.

That depends on the body and the crime scene.

Two identical folders are waiting on the front and rear passenger seats. Sheriff Gant's people are nothing if not efficient. Each folder contains a complete case synopsis, maps, a half dozen eight-by-ten glossies, and a one-page directory of hotels and restaurants in the Redding area. They even marked the hotels that offered a law enforcement discount. I climb in the back and let Jimmy ride shotgun.

"A nice couple named Jim and Valerie Bartowski found her," Walt says as we turn off Muni Boulevard onto Knighton Road, heading for I-5. "I've never met them until last night, but I recognized the name when I heard it. Valerie trains dogs and has quite a reputation; very well respected."

"Dogs?" I say.

"Cadaver dogs," Walt clarifies. "They happened to have one of their pups with them on the hike and he led them off-trail to the body."

"How far off-trail?" Jimmy asks.

"Maybe thirty feet, but it's pretty overgrown in that area. Doubtful anyone would have found her anytime soon if it wasn't for the dog."

"If she's been dead two or three months," I say, "how come no one smelled decomp and reported it?"

"I'm sure plenty of people smelled it, but most would have likely written it off as a dead deer or squirrel. If time-of-death is accurate, she's been there since sometime between mid-March and mid-April. Not as many hikers out there that time of year." Leaning over, he taps at one of the eight-by-tens in Jimmy's lap. "Not much left, I'm afraid; mostly skeletal. We couldn't find the skull. Probably some animal ran off with it."

"Is there an incline where the body was

found?" I ask without looking up, my eyes busy dissecting the photos one by one.

Walt breathes a long drawn-out *hmmm.* "I believe there is," he says at length. "Hard to be certain with the trees and underbrush, but the whole area has its ups and downs, so I'm guessing it does."

"Skulls tend to roll downhill after detaching," I say in a matter-of-fact voice. "We should be able to find it, provided the killer didn't take it as a souvenir." Walt chuckles, and then realizes I'm serious.

"You're sure this is female?" Jimmy says.

"Pretty sure."

"How do you know?"

Walt hesitates. "There's one photo I didn't include in your folder."

"Why?"

He just shakes his head. "Better you see it with your own eyes."

Buck Hollow Trail is a pleasant stroll through hell; an oppressive chaparral thick with mossy oaks, rotting logs, and pollen. Jimmy loves it. The trail follows an old logging road north, passing streams, belching frogs, and a forest floor untidy from deciduous decay. A musty wet flavor taints the air; I taste it on my tongue, smell it in my sinuses, feel it in my throat.

Dead leaves.

Dead earth.

Worms.

Three hundred yards up the trail we come across an armada of deputies, detectives, and U.S. forest rangers corralled by yellow crime-scene tape. Two small generators and a dozen portable lights sit idly to the side, no longer needed with the coming of dawn. A trail, now well worn, has been hacked through the thick scrub to the west, leading some thirty feet to where a man in slacks, dress shoes, shirt, and tie stands juxtaposed against the wild.

"Steps, Jimmy, I'd like you to meet Dr. Noble Wallace, our coroner."

"Call me Nob," the doctor says without emotion. "Noble is too regal and Dr. Wallace makes me think you're talking to my father."

After the traditional round of palm-mating and arm-pumping, Jimmy asks, "What do you know so far?"

And then I see her.

On the other side of the good doctor, dumped unceremoniously on the ground, is a sad stretch of bones. Most of the flesh is gone, and several of the ribs with it. Other bones have been pulled away from the body and gnawed upon by teeth of every size.

I pull my lead-crystal glasses off, and the

crime scene suddenly erupts with neon shine. If I paid any attention, the flood of color would be exhilarating: like static electricity pulling at every hair follicle on my body. But I don't pay attention. Even the coolest sensation dulls after ten thousand repeats. Folding the metal earpieces down one by one, I slip the glasses into their leather case before turning my attention back to the body.

The skeleton is problematic.

As the flesh surrenders to rot and rodent, so goes the shine. On the ground around the corpse are no less than two dozen distinct shines, any one of which could be the killer. I need to find something that sets him apart from the others.

"Female," Nob begins. "Based on bone fusing, I'd place her age at around twenty-four, give or take a year. I'll be able to firm that up once I take X-rays. Height was between five-two and five-four and she was fairly trim. We don't have the skull, so dental records won't do us any good, but we can run DNA." Looking at Walt, he adds, "All the physicals seem to match your missing person. Oh, and she was a natural blonde but dyed her hair brunette."

"How do you know that if you don't have a skull?" Jimmy asks.

The doctor remains silent, but points through the trees to the north. His jaw is set and the muscles of his face are taut. Our eyes meet briefly and I see the horror in his expression . . . the haunted stare . . . the same look I see in my bathroom mirror in the long hours of the night.

"I'll show them," Sheriff Gant says softly, waving us along as he starts picking his way through the brush.

The tree is unremarkable from all the others along Buck Hollow Trail, giving no clue as to why he chose this particular trunk to make his statement. Perhaps he had no preference and this one was just convenient. Regardless, the killer took his time decorating it, as if bestowing special favors upon the forest sentinel.

I look at the display.

Brilliant amaranth — almost crimson — with the texture of rust.

His hands are all over the tree, all over her bra, her shirt, her panties. Each is nailed to the tree. Her shirt is at the bottom, fastened lengthwise with three nails near the center and equal portions drooping off each side of the tree. Above the shirt the panties, barely recognizable, are held by a single nail. Then the bra, its straps wrapped around the trunk as if the tree were wearing it.

Above all this, as if crowning the display, is mounted a tangled mass of faux-brunette: a scalp peeled from the poor girl's skull. I can see where he grabbed her hair, wrenching her head back as he went to work on her.

I pray she was already dead.

"This one's killed before," I say to no one in particular. But as I say it my mind is grinding, grinding, grinding. *Brilliant amaranth and rust.* Why do I know that? Why does it seem so familiar?

Turning suddenly, I snatch up my cell phone. Her number's on speed dial and Diane answers on the first ring. I don't even wait for her to say hello.

"I need you to do something."

By 10:45 A.M. Dr. Wallace identifies the victim as twenty-three-year-old Alison Lister. "As suspected, the skull was found not far from the body, under some brush," the good doctor explains, "though it didn't find its way there due to predation." He leaves the words hanging, begging for explanation.

I raise a curious eyebrow at him — after a two-hour plane ride and hours in the woods, it's the most I can manage without some caffeine . . . and maybe a scone; a blueberry scone.

"How do you mean, Doctor?" *Jimmy to the rescue.*

"Your perp — that's what you Feds call them, right: perps?"

"Only on TV," Jimmy says.

"Well, then, it appears your suspect separated the skull from the spinal cord right at the occipital bone, probably with a hacksaw, if I had to guess. The exterior has mostly been picked clean — that part was predation; crows and rodents and such — and, of course, the flesh from the top and back came off with her hair when she was scalped. Despite the damage from both man and beast, the teeth are still intact, and Alison's dental records were already on file. She was reported missing four months ago, which means either she was kept alive for a while, or our estimated time of death was a bit off."

"Local girl?" Jimmy asks.

"Born and raised. No drugs, hardworking, pretty, just your all-American girl." He shakes his head slowly. "She didn't deserve this."

None of them do, I think. *The world is filled with monsters, Doctor.*

The world is filled with monsters and some of us hunt them. Some of us wallow into the nightmare and track the beasts to their lairs. We pay for our successes with happy thoughts and well-slept nights and sanity, for we give up a little of each with every monster we capture.

Is it worth it?

I don't know.

Ask me as I shiver in the darkness at midnight, freshly woken from a vision of blood and unspeakable horror.

Ask me then.

Little is known about Alison's disappearance. She worked the evening shift at a Redding take-out pizza joint — not one of the chains, but a local start-up called PizzaZ. She finished her shift at eleven P.M., said good night to her coworkers, and headed home. The next day she didn't show up for class at the community college, then was a no-show for work that night; highly unusual for Alison.

Her parents, also residents of Redding, filed a missing persons report the next morning after a long night checking with friends and relatives and searching for Alison's car, which was absent from the parking space in front of her apartment. In the four months since Alison's disappearance, the only real evidence came from the discovery of her car in the Walmart parking lot three days after she went missing.

"An analysis of the store's surveillance video showed Alison parking her car and entering the store shortly after eleven the night of her disappearance," Walt explains. "She bought several small, indistinguishable items from the cosmetics section and the freezer and then exited the store at eleven-fourteen P.M." He inserts a DVD into his laptop and queues up two video files.

"This first video is a minute and seven seconds and shows Alison as she leaves the store and returns to her car." The nighttime images are washed out and grainy and show the whole abduction . . . yet show nothing. Still, the video was enough to convince the Shasta County Sheriff's Office and Redding PD that this was a kidnapping, not just someone who didn't want to get found or was suicidal.

While the video is poor quality, we can see Alison as she approaches her car — appearing only as a multipixel blur. As she pauses by the driver's door, a shadow moves in behind her. With startling speed he's on her, and they both drop from view, falling to the asphalt between Alison's Honda Accord and an older white pickup parked next to her.

The shadow pops up near the truck's tailgate eleven seconds later, lingering; there's a blur of activity, and then it moves to the other side. The headlights flash on and splay across the empty parking lot as the truck pulls slowly out of the parking space; in seconds it's gone, giving no clue to final direction.

"That's all we have to go on," Sheriff Gant says. "Redding PD tried identifying the truck, but there's just not enough detail."

"Can you burn us a copy?" Jimmy says. "We might be able to come up with something." He's thinking about Dex, which is fine by me. I have a piece of Leonardo video I was going to have him look at anyway.

"This next one has us puzzled," Walt says, queuing up clip number two. "This is right after Alison went into the store. We didn't catch it at first because we were too focused on her and the cameras inside."

When he presses the play button, images of the parking lot begin to unfold but from a different angle from the first video. Alison's car is in the upper portion of the screen, nestled among shadows broken only by the soft glow of the parking lot lights.

There's little activity on the screen for almost three minutes, but Walt lets it play out. "There it is," he says, pointing to the white truck as it drives purposefully through the parking lot — not up and down the rows but across them — and parks next to the silver Accord; the lights turn off; nothing.

A minute passes.

Two.

"He's waiting for her," I say, mesmerized.

A light appears in the cab, just briefly, almost mistaken for the reflection of a headlight sweeping past the windshield. In seconds it's gone, leaving an ember behind, a small orange glow that flares up, then settles down, flares up again, then settles down.

"He's smoking."

"Did your detectives find any discarded butts?" Jimmy asks.

"That would be Redding PD," the sheriff replies, "and I already checked the report and there's no such documentation. Ooh. Here we go. Watch closely."

A shadow exits the driver's seat and walks around the back of the truck to the Honda, cigarette still in hand. He stands there for several minutes, taking pull after pull on the cigarette before flicking the glowing ember into an empty parking space. When he moves to the back window it looks as if he's leaning over the car, maybe peering inside.

"What's he doing?" I say to no one in

particular.

"That's what we were wondering," Walt says. "The car doesn't appear to have been tampered with. In fact, it was still locked when they found it."

"I'm assuming Redding PD impounded it?"

"We did," Sheriff Gant clarifies. "There's some ambiguity about jurisdiction on this one, so we're treating it as a joint case between Redding PD and the sheriff's office. The car's locked up tight in our evidence building a couple miles down the road." Walt anticipates my next question. Standing, he says, "I'll drive."

The Shasta County Crime Lab and Property Room on Breslauer Way in Redding, California, is like every other evidence building or property room I've seen: too much property from too many cases with too few investigators to work the cases and too few leads. It's always a case of funding, or lack thereof. It's the same reason DNA from a stranger-rape takes more than a year to analyze in some states; meanwhile the suspect may be out committing additional offenses instead of sitting behind bars where he belongs.

"Some of the case vehicles we keep outside," Sheriff Gant says, pulling the Expedition into a no-parking zone by the front door and pointing to a number of cars parked behind a chain-link fence to the left of the building. "Only major-case vehicles stay inside. We just don't have room." He leads the way through an alarm-equipped door and into a large open-bay warehouse.

Alison Lister's Honda Accord is in the corner.

Even now, after four months, the car is nearly spotless inside and out, but as I slip my glasses off I see him at once — *brilliant amaranth and rust.* I walk around the car and check for more shine before returning to the driver's-side rear window.

"Can you give us a minute, Walt?" I say. The sheriff nods and walks across the warehouse to a small office, where he pours himself a cup of coffee.

"What is it?" Jimmy says.

"I think he pressed the side of his face to the window here." I circle an area with my finger, being careful not to touch the vehicle. "I couldn't make it out at first, but I'm pretty sure I see his jaw and his nose."

"Like he was looking inside?"

"No, that's the thing; the side of his face is completely flat on the window." I shrug. "It's almost like he's using it as a pillow, resting his head on the glass."

Jimmy's face is grim. "He's imagining her, getting close to her through her car, building up his courage . . . or excitement."

I know he's right. As soon as he says it I know it, and it sends a shiver through me. I tease Jimmy about his psychology degree, but I've seen him dissect the minds of too many sociopaths, identifying their motives, their traumas, their fetishes, for me to doubt him. He reads people, particularly bad people, like I read shine. He should be at the FBI's Behavioral Analysis Unit, but instead he's stuck with me.

"That's not all," I say. "Before he pressed his face to the glass, it looks like he drew something with his finger. I can barely make out a circle with . . . I don't know . . . maybe some dots and lines on the inside. The facial imprint is fuzzy at the edges; these lines are sharper, but they're being blocked by the larger print."

"You don't have any idea what it is?"

"No," I reply, "but it's important to him. It means something."

It means something.

CHAPTER SEVEN

June 21, early afternoon
Diane calls at 1:32 P.M. and by 1:49 we're in the air heading for Carson City, Nevada; more specifically, we're heading for Washoe Lake State Park, just north of Carson City.

Brilliant amaranth and rust: now we'll see how good my memory is.

Landing at Carson Airport, we leave Les and Marty to figure out where to park the plane and make our way to the terminal looking for our local contact. He's already there, a big grin on his face, his eyes hidden behind dark aviator glasses.

"You boys look like hell!" he bellows, pumping my arm and slapping Jimmy on the back. Detective Bobby Decker of the Nevada Highway Patrol looks impeccable in his suit and tie; his obsidian hair is perfectly and precisely in place and I detect a Goldilocks portion of Stetson aftershave — not too much, not too little, but just the right

103

amount.

Bobby's nickname around the office is GQ and he earns both letters. Buried under the pretty exterior, however, is a smart, ambitious cop with a head for details and a memory like a titanium lockbox. Bobby was with us two years ago for the Natalie Shoemaker homicide; it only seemed fair to give him a heads up.

Besides, we need a ride.

"Diane told me what you're up to," Bobby says as we get into his unmarked Dodge Charger. "She didn't tell me why, but then I remembered that she's really good at playing dumb when it suits her."

"Yes, she is," Jimmy and I say in unison.

"So, are you gonna fill me in?"

"It's this case we're working in Redding," Jimmy says. "Steps thinks it's connected to the Shoemaker homicide."

"Really? How?"

"It's just a hunch," I lie, letting the words settle where they fall as I stare out the window. Bobby takes the hint and doesn't push the issue. We make our way to Interstate 580 and then head north. I let my mind wander, grounded only by the slow count of the mile markers as they flash by in green and white.

The more I think about the Lake Washoe

case, the more I'm convinced the shine is the same. We've handled maybe two hundred cases since then, but I remember shine — I have to — and if Redding isn't a match, it's uncannily close. Plus, there was something odd about the Lake Washoe case, something I can't yet remember, something that didn't mean anything at the time, but that's now nibbling at the ragged edge of my mind . . . like a rat let loose in a pantry.

I *need* to return to Lake Washoe.

The signs along the freeway tell me we're close, and then I see sunlight dancing on water: Washoe Lake. It's a bit of a misnomer, as the lake is actually a marriage of Big Washoe Lake, Little Washoe Lake, and the marshy Scripps Wildlife Management Area that connects the two. The lakes are shallow — no more than twelve feet deep — and during severe droughts they've been known to dry up completely. Almost daily winds beat and flay the shallow waters into a turbid broth.

Washoe Lake State Park, established in 1977, extends to the south and east of the lake and sprawls across more than eight thousand acres, offering miles of trails and abundant wildlife: mule deer, coyotes, hawks, eagles, even pelicans.

We turn onto Eastlake Boulevard and

travel the short distance to the park entrance. It's hot when we get out of the car; the stygian-black asphalt of the parking lot soaks up the sun in scorching gulps and belches it back in waves of shimmering heat.

It's June in Nevada; what was I thinking?

The average summer temperature here is hell, with a 25 percent chance of purgatory. I console myself with the knowledge that our hike will be short, mostly level, and through high-desert grasses and shrubs . . . no forests. The fact that the park sits more than five thousand feet above sea level should help: the temperatures tend to be slightly cooler than, say, Reno to the north, or Las Vegas to the south. Like when you preheat your oven to 425 degrees and the beeper hasn't gone off yet because it's only at 350.

Kind of like that.

The thermostat on the dash of the Charger reads ninety-four degrees, which is boiling point for anyone from the Pacific Northwest — and I forgot to bring water. As I ponder the sea of scrub and sagebrush beyond the parking lot, I wonder what spontaneous human combustion feels like. Is there a warning? Do you feel a tingling sensation first — a growing heat at your fingertips and toes — or do you just burst into flame with a big *wooomp* that sucks the air out of the room?

Let's hope we don't find out.

From the visitors' center we strike north along the equestrian trails. The path is completely deserted as we trudge over sunbaked earth, and for a moment I imagine that all the other hikers have already burst into flames and added themselves to the sand and dust at our feet. Or, wisely, they've all retreated to cooler areas during this, the hottest part of the day. Really, it's a toss-up.

Memories flood back in the form of familiar landmarks.

We're getting close.

The Sierra Nevada Mountains are to my left, rising majestic, silent, and eternal over the desert valley, their crooked backs cutting into the sky. The wind is absent this afternoon, leaving the lake unmolested and looking like so much polished glass. A stunted pine, twisted by the desert winds, stands to our right, no more than a bush, but stubborn and determined.

I remember it.

Turning off the path, we pick our way through the low brush. A roadrunner darts from the bushes at our feet, startling other birds to flight. I remember the birds, so many of them, so many different kinds and colors.

Then we're upon it, a small outcropping in the middle of flat scrub; memories and images muscle themselves to the front of my mind, escapees from my subconscious where I try to contain them.

I remember it all; unwillingly.

On the other side of the outcropping was Natalie Shoemaker; her body, ravaged by coyotes and buzzards, was shoved up under the lip of the jutting rock. Unceremoniously deposited like so much garbage or an unwanted toy cast aside.

That, too.

I remember.

Circling around the mound, I feel my left hand rising to my glasses and then slipping them off before dropping back to my side. I see Natalie's silhouette upon the rocky ground: *prussian blue and bubbles,* still beautiful. Time, wind, and rain have blurred the image to a weathered and diluted stain. Other shine surrounds her; I see Bobby and Jimmy and myself among them . . . and one more, the one I came for: *brilliant amaranth and rust.*

And now I remember something else.

Cursing, I search the ground a moment, and then I'm walking briskly north, away from the formation, twenty feet, thirty, fifty feet. And then it's before me upon the ground, exactly as I remember it, undisturbed. I fall to my knees and feel the scorched sand burning through my jeans, but all I can do is stare. It all makes sense now, the tree, the shirt nailed below the scalp, the smudge on the car window.

From the ground a face looks up at me, a face made from the wind-worn rocks of the high desert: Two eyes, a nose, a dark, down-turned mouth — all enclosed by a circle of rocks. It's not the have-a-nice-day face of pop culture. No, it's just the opposite.

"I should have remembered," I say to no one in particular.

A hot breeze kicks up from the east.

CHAPTER EIGHT

June 22, 12:45 A.M.

It's late when we land at Bellingham International Airport and ease Betsy into Hangar 7. It's been twenty-one hours since we left for Redding yesterday morning. Since then we've been in the woods, in the desert, and in the air four times — all that on little food and less sleep.

I'm spent.

Still, the revelations of Washoe Lake have cast this case in a new light: two bodies dumped two years and two hundred miles apart, a single suspect confirmed through shine, and a calling card in the shape of a face with a downturned mouth. It's horrifying and intriguing at the same time.

After discussing the case with Walt and Jimmy late into the evening, I thought I'd be able to sleep on the flight north, but it wasn't to be. Every time I closed my eyes, visions of rock formations and scalps hanging from trees pushed them open again. Jimmy didn't say much during the flight, and after landing we barely muttered good night to each other before piling into our cars and making for home.

The quiet of my bedroom finds me restless.

Time drifts by in the darkness.

I'm staring at the glowing red numbers of the digital clock at 3:08 A.M. and somehow I imagine a downturned face hidden among the block-shaped numbers. Some cases get under your skin like that. They crawl into your brain and start pushing buttons and pulling levers. This is going to be one of those cases; God help us.

Eventually exhaustion takes me.

I sleep . . . but I don't sleep well.

The night, dark.

The body, cold.

A hard moon rises above an aegis of restless clouds, lifting the black of the forest and replacing it with a lesser shade just beyond twilight. In the distance a mountain squats mean and hard, like a slate-blue troll leaning against the night sky. Its massive shoulders bend and sag under a blanket of cold white snow.

Where am I?

Where's Jimmy?

A keening gale is in the treetops, a harbinger, sending the branches into a frenzy of snapping wooden screams as they claw at one another, tossed about in the unforgiving wind. And as I watch, the tempest falls upon the mountain, breaking over the dome and spilling down its slopes, chewing snow and rock and tree, turning the slate-blue giant into a boiling sea of gray.

The body remains, neither noticing the storm, nor caring.

I can't see him from where I'm standing, but I know he's there, this young boy of eight. *How do I know that? Jimmy? How do I know he's eight?* The boy is tucked under the snow-covered log twenty feet in front of me, his small body curled into a fetal position, huddled against the cold. I know he's there because I saw the remnants of his last breath only moments ago, a weak white smoke in the dark; just a puff, and then it was lost in the wind.

Eight years old; he's too young to die alone in the woods at night.

He lies still now, without breath, without life.

Where's Jimmy?

I want to run to the boy, to wrap him in my coat and blow warmth, blow *life,* into

112

his lungs, but my legs are frozen, my feet immobile, trapped. I can do nothing for him but watch and wait.

I am the eyes in the woods; he who waits.

There's a change in the wind, a change in the howl and the roar of its blustering temper tantrum, something hidden within the cacophony. I strain to hear, leaning forward, then back, twisting my head from side to side to find its direction. It's elusive because it's all around me. There it is again, more distinct, separate from the wind if only for a second, but what was it?

Wolves?

It sounded like the remnant of a howl, just a scrap of sound: there and then gone. My eyes turn back to the log, to the hollowed-out snow and to the soil beneath it, to the darkness over and around the body. I feel like I'm waiting for something, trying to understand something, but it's just beyond the edge of remembrance.

There it is: a howling or baying, louder this time. It comes from behind me, where the trees march off into miles of darkness, through valleys and up hills, across rivers and away from mountains.

Where's Jimmy?

A blanket of shadow presses in on me and I should feel fear, but I don't. I should run from the wind, away from such sounds and such sights and such horrors, but I don't. I should feel cold . . . but I can't.

The wolves are near.

I hear wailing, howling, barking.

Barking?

Not wolves — dogs!

Jimmy, if that's you, hurry.

There's still time.

The dogs are closer now and coming on fast.

I hear voices muffled in the wind, and shouts snatched from the throat and tossed high among the branches. There are at least four distinct voices, but the wind continues to murder their words as they draw near. The dogs are baying constantly now, louder and louder. The voices follow behind, urging them on, and there's something else, something I can't make out. The dogs break through the underbrush and race past me, finding the log and the cold hollow tomb below. They pace back and forth before the fallen fir; their tone is now different, more urgent.

The voices are close: yelling, shouting, calling. I finally see them as they emerge from the forest behind me, seven, no, eight men, exhausted, struggling forward, calling.

There's that word again, only this time I hear it.

"Maaagnus."

The man in front is shouting my name; again and again he shouts it. "Magnus. Maaagnus." As he nears I wave my arms and yell, "I'm here, Jimmy, I'm here!" but he runs right by me without seeing.

I recognize his face as he passes. His features are hardened by fear, desperation, and fatigue; still, he's younger than I remember. It's not Jimmy, though.

"Dad!" I shout as he passes, but he doesn't hear. He's at the log now, pulling the snow back with shovellike hands. He reaches in and pulls the small body out, pulls the young boy from the darkness into the night, and cradles him in his arms.

"I'm here, Magnus. I'm here."

I remember the cold, the wind, the dark.

I remember I was eight.

I remember I was dead.

Wake up.

At first I think the forest is speaking, but then I recognize my own voice.

Wake up.

Wake up.

Wake up.

I'm sitting up in bed, my right hand trembling ever so slightly; it's barely noticeable anymore. Nineteen years have passed since that night in the forest. The eight-year-old boy is long gone, replaced by a twenty-seven-year-old man. The dream is the same, though, always the same. As time passes, it visits less frequently, maybe once every month or two.

I tell myself it's because I'm finally getting over it. The truth, I fear, is that there are now too many nightmares competing for my sleeping hours. The bodies are stacked like cordwood outside the door to my dreams, each with its own horrid tale, and each with its own monster.

Now there's a new monster among the woodpile.

CHAPTER NINE

June 22, 9:35 A.M.

The hangar appears deserted when I pass through the outer cipher door, but so often appearances are deceiving. I've barely stepped inside when I hear them from across the open expanse of the cavernous hangar. Two voices — female — having a raucous good time, it would seem, laughing, squealing, and talking back and forth faster than a Wimbledon tennis match.

Stranger still, this cacophony is coming from Diane's office.

As I cross the hangar floor and skirt around Betsy's right wing, I can just make out someone's head as she leans back in the chair facing Diane's desk. More laughter, and then the head is gone again. The overgrown ficus tree just inside Diane's door and the elevated deck outside our row of second-story offices obscure the view.

Foresight and hindsight.

Most people think they're opposites or at least that they're quite different from one another. They're not. They're actually the same thing, only separated by time. When I started walking up those steps, had I had a little foresight I could have run, but by the time I pause in front of Diane's office, it's too late.

In hindsight I realize I *should* have run.

See what I mean? It's all in the timing.

Rising from her desk, Diane says, "Good morning, Steps," in the warmest of voices; she's devious that way. "Did you get some breakfast?"

I hold up a half-eaten granola bar in one hand and a Diet Pepsi in the other.

"Oh," she says pointedly. "That's healthy."

"This," I say, thrusting out the granola bar, "is healthy. This" — I wave the soda bottle — "is caffeine. I didn't sleep well. We didn't land till sometime after midnight."

"Twelve thirty-seven A.M., I saw." Then she drops the hammer. "Since you're here, let me introduce you to Miss Heather Jennings . . . but . . . wait . . . I believe you two already know each other, don't you?"

Evil.

Devious.

Heather swivels in her seat and gives me a generous smile.

She smells good, like coconut and citrus; all tropical-island-like. Suddenly the hangar is stuffy and hot, and my cheeks are flush with warm blood as my palms begin to sweat. She's beautiful, smart, sweet; impossible to hate. Damn her.

"So," Diane says, turning back to Heather, "I've made reservations at the Hearthfire Grill for six o'clock, if that works?"

The Hearthfire? That was our restaurant.

"That's perfect," Heather says, rising from her chair and hitching her bag up onto her shoulder.

"Do you need a ride?" Diane asks.

"No, I drove my Honda up."

"The convertible?"

Heather nods, a grin on her face.

"I just love that car," Diane trills. She's practically pawing Heather's arm; it's disgusting. "Do you remember how to get there?"

"Sure, I can find it. I've got my GPS. Besides, Steps took me there a half dozen times." Turning, she eyes me from top to bottom, a coy smile on her face, neither approving nor disapproving. "Is it still his favorite restaurant?"

"They know him by name. I'm surprised he doesn't have a reserved parking spot."

"I go there *maybe* three times a month," I

say in protest, but then realize I'm really not part of this conversation.

"Thanks, Diane," Heather purrs.

"My pleasure, hon."

Then, just like that, she's down the stairs, across the hangar, and out the door, taking the coconut trees, oranges, limes, and the tropical breeze with her.

"Nice to see you two are still so chummy," I say, wiping my brow and pouring on the sarcasm in my very best how-could-you? voice. "Dinner at the Hearthfire Grill? That's nice. Special."

"It is, isn't it?" Diane replies, her eyes all a-twinkle.

The surveillance video from Bellis Fair Mall is sitting on my desk when I flip on the light: a single disk in a white paper sleeve. I expected more, but a note attached to the disk indicates that mall security reviewed five days of video and copied only those segments where there was a car parked in the spot I indicated. "Thank yooou, buddy," I say softly as I slide the DVD into the computer. Instead of spending hours scanning through irrelevant video, my search has been reduced to seven short clips.

The first video shows a mother and her daughter in an eighties-style station wagon with wood-grain siding. Wagons, vans, SUVs, and the like are always good vehicle choices for killers, but I know from previous video that Leonardo is a dark-haired male, average in every way.

Clip two is what appears to be a teenage boy in a beat-up red and white Bronco, and this is followed by a family in a motor home, a man in a black sedan, another man in a burgundy sedan who parks for a while and then leaves without ever stepping foot out of the car, two women in a Subaru with bikes on the roof, and lastly, a white fifteen-passenger van loaded down with boys on some kind of outing. The top of the van bristles with canoes and pixelated lumps that might be suitcases; more gear is strapped to the back.

I watch each clip carefully, dutifully, before going back to number four — the man in the black sedan. I watch him exit the vehicle and point his arm at the hood; the lights flash briefly as the car locks. Starting at the driver's door, he walks around the front of the car, down the passenger side, and back to the driver's door, where he checks the door handle.

Hello, Leonardo.

There's no doubt it's him. Each time I've seen his shine at the mall he does the same

121

thing before leaving his car: he walks in a slow, methodical circle around the entire vehicle.

Is it a ritual? Some type of protection circle? Is he checking the car; the tires? Or is he just obsessive-compulsive, driven by his own mind to go through strict, repetitive routines before doing anything? Jimmy and I have discussed it a dozen times, but we're still not any closer to an answer. As for me, I'm betting on the obsessive-compulsive disorder . . . with a little bit of psycho wack-job thrown in.

The car is too far away to make out the plate. That's the joke when it comes to security cameras; in almost every case they're either too far away or too cheaply built to show any real detail. Casinos and banks invest in better-quality equipment and generally have better placement, but they're the exception to the rule.

After transferring the video to my thumb drive, I swap disks and start working on Alison Lister's kidnapper. The video is bad and I'm not optimistic we'll be able to identify the make, let alone the model. The truck is just too far away, the resolution is too poor, and the only view is from the side. A portion of the front and rear can be seen at an angle, but few details are revealed. Regardless, I transfer the video.

Plucking the thumb drive from the USB slot, I pause just long enough to check my voice mail: two messages, Mom reminding me about the family picnic in July and my optometrist telling me I'm overdue for an exam.

"I'm heading to the S.O.," I tell Diane as I pause in her doorway. "I need to see if Dex can ID Leonardo's car, plus I have the video from Redding."

"It's the sheriff's office, not the S.O.," Diane replies without looking up. "Just because we work for the government doesn't mean we have to assign acronyms to everything."

"S.O.," I whisper. "S.O."

An eight-by-ten color photo sits on top of a manila folder at the edge of Diane's desk. I recognize it immediately. I should; I took it two years ago at Washoe Lake. Picking it up, I stare at the pattern fashioned from rocks in the high desert soil. "I see Jimmy already talked to you."

Diane nods. "I should have a list for you later this afternoon."

I place the photo back on her desk, on top of the manila folder. "We have two. I'm betting we find more, making this guy a serial."

"I hope you're wrong."

I tap the photo twice. "He left his calling card; what kind of sick bastard does that? He's marking his conquests, maybe keeping score." Diane meets my gaze and I give a curt nod. "He's a serial; you'll see."

Dexter Allen's office at the Whatcom County Sheriff's Office is a cluttered hole in the basement of the crumbling county jail. Half-buried in the ground with only a handful of windows that look up at the sidewalk outside, the administrative offices of the sheriff's office are decrepit and worn. The walls are worn, the structural concrete is worn, the floor tiles are worn — even the air is worn, stagnant from poor circulation.

The texture of the ceiling tiles is mismatched due to their constant replacement as various liquids leak down from the jail above: gray water from the jail shower, soapy water from the jail kitchen, and questionable water from the jail toilets, which are frequently and intentionally stuffed with jail toilet paper to cause an overflow.

These internal rainstorms are frequent enough that the shelves in the archives room down the hall are carefully and constantly covered in heavy plastic to protect the original case reports. Sometimes the liquid is clear, other times it's brown. In one case, brown chunks spilled out onto a desk in the Detectives Division, prompting several detectives to collect the sample for analysis, convinced that the inmates were now defecating on them by proxy.

Dex pays little mind to the crumbling edifice.

Surrounded by his monitors, he crunches data, reviews case reports, and sips Diet Pepsi. The only decoration in the bland office consists of several Civil War paintings on the wall and his diplomas from the Defense Language Institute in Monterey, California, and the Naval War College in Newport, Rhode Island. He laughingly calls himself a relic of the Cold War, but after seventeen years as a Russian linguist, then intelligence analyst, and finally as a project manager for various "operations" at the Office of Naval Intelligence, he somehow landed this unlikely position as a crime analyst with the sheriff's office.

He's on the phone when I walk into his office and plop down in a chair. I only half-listen to the call, something about a wanted burglary suspect hiding out in a house near Maple Falls. No doubt he's talking to one of the deputies, maybe a detective, but certainly someone keen on getting their hands on the suspect.

The call ends and Dex shoots me a grin.

"Diane said you'd be stopping by. So . . . how's Heather?"

"Oh, shut up."

He chuckles; I'm glad my misery provides joy for so many people. Handing him the thumb drive, I say, "I need a little FVA."

Forensic vehicle analysis, or FVA, is an analytical process developed by Dex over years and made real in the form of a photo database. The idea came to him after too many blurry surveillance images crossed his desk: an armed robbery showing only the vehicle's taillights, a rape where the only clue was the image of the front corner of a truck as it pulled into a parking space just off-camera, a homicide with only nighttime images of a passing SUV.

Faced with this onslaught of consistently bad imagery, he did what every good analyst does: He changed the game. Dex doesn't think outside the box, he redefines it.

When I first heard about FVA two years ago, I called him an out-of-the-box thinker, meaning it as a compliment. He smiled and shook his head. "There is no box." When I gave him a questioning look, he said, "The idea of thinking machines was once way outside the box, right? Yet now computers are as mainstream as TV, radio, and the printing press — they're right in the middle of the box with everything else we take for granted day in and day out; therefore there is no box, just vision and actualization."

He tapped the side of his head with his index finger: "Computer visualized" — then he tapped the CPU on the floor next to his desk — "computer actualized."

I remember telling him he sounded like a Zen version of Tony Robbins; he just laughed.

Plugging the thumb drive into the USB port, Dex starts a frame-separation program, then selects the video from Bellis Fair and opens it in the program. "Say when," he murmurs as he fast-forwards through the video clip.

"Stop!" I say fifteen seconds later as the black vehicle first rolls on-screen. He tags the first frame and then tags another frame after Leonardo parks. With the parameters for the beginning and end of the frame separation identified, Dex clicks a button and starts the extraction. Within seconds the segment of video is dissected into almost six hundred separate still-frame images showing angles of the front, side, and rear.

Dex is already lost in the hunt, almost

oblivious to my presence. His hands work the keyboard and the mouse at a furious pace as he views one photo after another, enlarging some, sharpening others. He selects a dozen of the best images, including shots of the front, side, and rear of Leonardo's car, and then opens the forensic vehicle analysis database.

"See here," he says, drawing my attention to the rear of the vehicle with his index finger, "the little flash. That's the third brake light. That's what I call a 'window-high' position because it's at the inside top edge of the back window. You'll also notice the license plate is not down on the bumper, but up between the taillights; that's a 'center-high' position. The picture quality is about average for surveillance video —"

"Which means it sucks," I say.

"Which means it sucks," he replies. "Still, there's plenty to crunch through the database." He moves his finger to a dark spot behind the rear door. "There's some kind of reflection here, looks like a window behind the door — hard to be certain with the car being black. Let's take a look from another angle."

Pulling two side shots and a front angle to the top of the image stack, he immediately taps the screen and with an I-told-you-so tone says, "There it is! See the reflection? There's definitely a window behind the rear door. That narrows our search considerably."

"How so?"

"It's just not that common, particularly with the newer cars. Let's run it and see what we get." Pulling up a query screen, he selects each of the identified criteria, then adds two more, pointing out that the taillights are configured in a "horizontal sweep" and have "bleed," a term he uses to identify taillights that extend into the trunk. After checking boxes next to each criterion, he hits the query button and the database instantly returns thirty results with links to photos for each one.

"Volvos, Audis, Hondas, and Hyundais, but none appear to have what I'm looking for," Dex hums as he clicks methodically through the pictures. "Oh, wait. Here we go." Tapping the screen several times, he points at the array of images on display. "That's it. No doubt whatsoever. It's a first-generation Saturn L-series sedan, which was manufactured for model years 2000 through 2005 . . . though it looks like this one is a 2000-through-2002 model."

"How can you possibly know that?"

"Look at the front. The L-series got a

face-lift for 2003 that included a much larger grille and a redesigned front fascia. That," he adds emphatically, "is the pre-face-lift model."

"So we're looking for a black 2000 to 2002 Saturn L-series sedan." I roll the information around in my head a minute, digesting it, turning it inside out. "Too old to be a rental," I say to myself; the words come out as a mumble. "That's good. Good." I'm pacing now, something I do when I'm thinking. It drives Jimmy up the wall. Sometimes I do it just for fun.

Dex is at my back when the thought comes to me and I snap around so quickly I trip over my own feet and have to catch myself on the corner of a file cabinet. When my mother called me graceful while growing up, she didn't mean it as a compliment.

And tripping over my own feet was the least of my concerns as a teen; the real damage came from walking into walls, poles, mailboxes, and doors, particularly in public, and worse when it happened in front of classmates, which was often.

For years I blamed it on puberty and its corresponding growth spurts, but I had to give up that excuse in my early twenties and finally admit that I get distracted. Often. Of course, it doesn't help that layer upon layer of shine covers everything I see. I can turn some of it off for short spurts, but it's hard to turn it all off without my glasses.

Righting myself with as much dignity as I can muster, I plant myself in front of Dex's desk. "You have access to DAPS, don't you?"

He just smiles and swivels one of the monitors in my direction. The Washington State Driver and Plate Search database, also known as DAPS, is on the screen. "I pulled up every Saturn in Whatcom County with current registration," he says. "It should be printing right about now." As if on cue, the printer hums to life and quickly kicks out several pages of data.

"I'm also going to print a statewide list," Dex says, "in case your theory about him being from out-of-county is true."

Dex knows the Jess Parker homicide as well as I do, probably better. He wasn't at the sheriff's office at the time of the murder, but quickly got up to speed when he was hired a few years after, organizing the vast four-thousand-page case report into a searchable database that scored every single document, tip, or follow-up report by relevance. He did the same for the 137 identified suspects, most of whom have since been eliminated from the list, either because their DNA didn't match, they had strong, verified alibis, or, in one case, they were dead at the time of the homicide.

Dead is *always* a good alibi.

Dex is as frustrated by the case as I am. And I know he's suspicious of my claims that Leonardo has been visiting the mall. He's not a tracker, but I can tell from our conversations that he's done some research since Leonardo's first shopping trip a number of years ago. He knows that human tracking doesn't work on asphalt, or on the frequently polished floors of Bellis Fair Mall. To his credit, he doesn't ask too many questions.

Other than my father, Jimmy, and FBI Director Carlson, Diane and Dex are the only ones I've considered sharing my secret with. I still might. It depends on Leonardo.

Collecting the statewide printout of Saturn L-series sedans from the printer, we next tackle the mystery truck from Redding . . . and immediately derail. "It's just too far away and too poor-quality," Dex says. The most he can pull from the image is that the truck is a standard-cab, and there's a slight reflection on the front fender that might — *might* — be a badge, but fender badges on trucks are so common that it only narrows the search by half.

"Here's one thing," Dex adds, pointing to an image of the truck as it almost exits the screen. "See that hint of red?" I follow his finger to the upper back edge of the cab, just above the rear window.

"Third brake light," I say. "Like on the Saturn."

"Exactly, and those weren't introduced into the U.S. until 1986; that means your suspect truck is '86 or newer."

I give him a defeated smile. "That's ninety-eight percent of the trucks on the road."

"Oh, less than that if you factor in the standard cab and the fender badge," Dex replies in a chipper voice, "but, yes, you're still looking at thousands of trucks, perhaps tens of thousands, depending on the location and size of your search area."

"Tens of thousands, is that all?" I say sarcastically. "No problem. You've been a big help, Dex."

He just grins.

Hangar 7 is a regular hive of buzzing activity when I return. Les and Marty are tinkering with Betsy . . . which is a little disconcerting considering neither of them are mechanics and they have the left engine cover cracked open. Marty's poking around inside with a screwdriver as Les looks on.

I try not to look or listen as I pass. The less I know, the better.

Jimmy's in the break room plopped down on the couch next to his wife, Jane, looking through some catalogs and magazines. Their son, six-year-old Pete, is by himself at the foosball table on the hangar floor. He's wearing a blue hoodie with the hood pulled up over his head so far you can barely see his eyes.

The conversation in the break room smells like a remodel. Jane's been talking about a makeover on their kitchen for the last year and recently told Jimmy that she's tired of waiting. Worse, she's under the impression that I'm going to help — so I make a beeline for the foosball table instead.

"Hey, Petey," I say, eyeing the rows of miniature plastic soccer players. "You want to give your Uncle Steps a foosball thrashing?" His face is in shadow, but I see the eager smile. "Hey, what's with the hood, buddy?" His smile turns instantly to grimace as he hesitates, then walks up close to me. Looking around quickly, he pulls the hood back a few inches, just enough for me to see that his thick curly hair is gone. Not gone as in shortened, but gone as in nearly bald; the kid's got barely a quarter inch of hair left, just fuzz. My eyes go big and I give him a sympathetic look as he pulls the hood back in place.

"What happened, big guy? You get some gum in your hair or something?"

He corkscrews his mouth and says in his husky little voice, "We went to the barber shop and I got to pick which piece I wanted to go on the hair cutter." He looks up at me with big eyes. "I didn't know the red one makes you bald."

Trying not to smile, I tell him, "You look very handsome. A bald head is the sign of a tough man, a strong man, someone not afraid to be who he is." I poke him softly in the belly. "But not every bald man is tough *and* handsome." I study him for a moment. "I'd be careful if I were you, Petey. The girls are gonna want to run their hands all over your head."

"Eeewww!"

"Give it a couple years; you might not mind it so much."

We play two rounds of foosball, with Petey winning both rounds. Jimmy doesn't like it when I let him win. He says that losing is a character-builder and that when Petey finally *does* win a game, he'll know it was a real win.

Ppppfth! Fathers. What do they know?

135

Besides, I'm his Uncle Steps — even if we're not technically related. I'm supposed to spoil him, teach him how to throw knives and juggle kittens, jack him up on sugar, and send him home as a six-year-old nightmare incarnate.

That's what uncles do.

When I poke my head into the break room, Jane is holding up two color samples, one of which Jimmy is less than happy with, comparing it to the inside of a baby's tainted diaper. Catalogs are spread out over the coffee table: cabinets, countertops, sinks, tile, paint, faucets, appliances, pretty much anything you'd need if you wanted to build a kitchen from scratch.

Jimmy is holding three separate catalogs uncomfortably, like a new father holding an infant. His shoulders are slumped and he has an exhausted look on his face, but his eyes suddenly light up when he sees me. "Steps!" he says with surprising enthusiasm. "You're back . . . finally. Look, honey," he says to Jane, "Steps is here. Oh, that means we've got to get back to work."

"Hi, Steps," Jane says, throwing me a smile and shaking her head patiently as Jimmy dumps the catalogs on the table and makes for the door. "So we've settled on a thirteen-by-thirteen porcelain tile called

Mountain Slate Iron," she tells me. "It's a darker tile with stone texture and coloring; very pretty."

"Sounds nice," I say absently, trying to be polite.

Jane stares at me a moment. "You've forgotten already, haven't you?"

"Forgotten what?" *This can't be good.*

"Last Christmas; you said you'd be happy to help with the makeover. We need someone with experience."

Crap.

"That was probably the Baileys Irish Cream talking," I say, screwing on a grin. "Besides, my tiling experience amounts to one hall closet and half a bathroom."

"Did any of the tiles crack?"

"No." *Not yet.*

"Well, then, you must have done it right."

"I have to say," I begin, choosing my words carefully, "I'm a little shocked at how cavalier you are about the qualifications of your remodel crew. One poorly laid tile can absolutely ruin a remodel. I even read that if you don't —"

"Stop! You're not getting out of it, Steps," Jane says in rapid-fire. "Jimmy doesn't want to pony up and hire a licensed and bonded expert, which is fine. I get it. It's a lot of money. But if I'm letting amateurs work on my kitchen, I want at least two brains trying to figure out how to spread the mortar and hang the cabinets. Between the two of you, I should get a usable, perhaps functional, maybe even a beautiful, kitchen."

Silence.

"Wow," Jimmy mumbles. "I feel so emasculated."

"Harsh," I say. "Just give me the word, Jimmy, and I'll go all spider monkey on her. I'm pretty sure I can take her."

"I'm pretty sure you can't," Jimmy replies.

"Wow," I whisper. "I feel so emasculated."

CHAPTER TEN

"Eleven possible victims," Diane says. "Seven bodies recovered so far, that includes Alison Lister. The other four are listed as missing persons, but their physicals and the MO appear to match."

All but three of the chairs have been removed from the conference room and pushed out into the hangar. Eleven stacks of paper of varying heights line the elegant mahogany conference table, stretching in single file from one end to the other. One of the stacks, the second from the door, I recognize immediately from the photo resting on top: the Alison Lister case.

The other stacks appear to be in reverse chronological order with a summary and photo on top — courtesy of Diane's meticulous attention to detail. In front of Alison, in the number one position, or number eleven depending on which way you ap-

139

proach things, is twenty-four-year-old Lauren Brouwer, a brunette who went missing in Oroville just two months ago. The police report contains scant information spread out over a couple dozen pages. As I glance down the line, I note that all of the women are in their late teens to early twenties; all are brunette, with hair color ranging from the darker brown tones to black.

But Alison Lister was a natural blonde.

Two photos grace the top of Alison's stack: one is her driver's license, issued two years ago, which clearly shows her shoulder-length blond hair. On top of this, however, is a second photo, a more recent photo.

"Where'd this come from?" I ask Diane.

"The Redding *Record Searchlight,* February third of this year; I pulled it from an archived article. The photo's not that great."

"It's good enough," I say.

The four-hundred-word article from the business section of the *Record Searchlight* trumpets the recent announcement that PizzaZ, Alison Lister's employer, planned to open two new stores, one in Redding, another in Anderson. More importantly, Alison's name and picture are attached to the article. She's smiling at the camera as she tosses pepperoni onto a large pizza, her distinctly brunette hair pulled back into a ponytail behind her. *Brunette, not blond.*

"Did any of the other victims dye their hair?"

Diane hesitates. "I don't think so."

"We have their driver's license photos," Jimmy says, gesturing to the case files on the table. He starts going down the line, reading from each printout. "Brown . . . brown . . . brown . . . black . . . brown . . . wait, here's another blonde. Tawnee Rich out of Susanville."

"She's one of our missing persons," Diane says immediately. "I think she's also one of the anomalies."

"Anomalies?" I say, but Diane is already punching keys on her laptop.

In less than ten seconds — which is a lot longer than you'd think, especially when you're watching someone who types at ninety-plus words per minute — she says, "Here it is," and turns the laptop to face us. On the screen is a chart of the dead and missing girls, along with some basic biographical information and a column listing the times between abductions. The first victim, Valerie Heagle, went missing fifty-seven months ago. Thirteen months later Jennifer Green went missing, nine months after that it was Tawnee Rich, but only a month later the fourth victim, Leah Daniels, was kidnapped out of Eureka.

"One month," Jimmy says. "What didn't he like about Tawnee?"

"Her hair," I say. "He was expecting a brunette. When he found out she'd dyed her hair, my guess is he scalped her and cut off her head with a hacksaw, just like he did Alison Lister."

"Then he went hunting for a natural brunette and Leah Daniels caught his attention." Diane taps the laptop screen, saying, "It's almost the same pattern with Lauren Brouwer, who was kidnapped just two months after Alison."

"Of the seven bodies found," I say, "were any others scalped?"

Diane shakes her head. "No, just Alison."

"How is it we never got called in on any of these?" Jimmy says.

"We did," Diane replies. "Natalie Shoemaker. Lake Washoe. Remember?"

"Aside from that." There's an edge to Jimmy's voice. "Nobody noticed that nearly a dozen women had been kidnapped and murdered in less than five years?"

"The crime scenes are spread out over three states and nine counties," Diane says. "This guy's no dummy. My guess is he's done some serious time, and probably for something where the evidence ensured his conviction. He's not taking any chances this time around and is spreading the crime scenes around, which means he also knows that law enforcement has a poor track record of sharing information between jurisdictions."

"Great," I say with a sigh. Circling the table once, I glance at each stack in turn and then decide to start at the beginning: Valerie Heagle. Taking a seat, I pull her file close. "Anything else we should know before we start?"

Diane nods. "Valerie Heagle," she says, her eyes indicating the file. "She's the odd one out. The age, height, weight, hair, and most of the MO match, but there's one distinct difference."

"What's that?"

"She was a prostitute. Not the street-walking type, either. She advertised her services through various online forums — Craigslist, Backpage, the usual — and then met her clients at local motels."

I close the folder. "That . . . that doesn't make sense. Serials who target prostitutes generally stick to prostitutes; look at Gary Ridgway, Joel Rifkin, Lorenzo Gilyard, Jack the Ripper." Turning to Jimmy, I say, "That doesn't make sense, right?"

He's got a curious look on his face, as if

he's puzzling it out. "At first glance, no, it doesn't make sense. It's a complete change of victimology." He starts pacing slowly up and down the table, his eyes never leaving the stacks. At last he stops and turns to Diane. "Valerie was the first, you're sure of that?"

"That's what it looks like, at least in this part of the country. I haven't extended the search beyond northern California, southern Oregon, and western Nevada."

He paces to the end of the table, turns, looks at me, shrugs his shoulders. "She was practice."

"Practice?"

He nods. "I think Diane's right. This guy's been locked up somewhere, probably for a while. Valerie was an easy target, someone to cut his teeth on, so to speak."

"Bad choice of words," Diane scolds.

"How so?"

"You'll see when you start going through the files."

"What makes you so sure she's one of our victims?" I ask.

Diane walks over to the folder and flips it open in front of me. Leafing through the pages, she stops on an eight-by-ten glossy of Valerie's car and points to the rear window.

"Crap." I just stare at the image.

Instead of stones in the high desert scrub, as was the case at Lake Washoe, or clothes nailed to a tree, the pattern is drawn into the dirt and grime on the back window. Whether Redding PD intended to document the image or just got lucky while photographing Valerie's car, who could say? It really didn't matter.

"That's what he drew on the back of Alison's car, too," I say. "We just couldn't see it after he pressed his face all over it."

Jimmy moves around the table to take a look and the muscles around his mouth visibly tighten when he sees it. After a moment, he says what I've already thought.

"They'll call him the Sad Face Killer. Just watch."

At precisely four o'clock, Diane corners me in my office. I know exactly what this is about; Diane was kind enough to inform me an hour after Heather left. Since there are no windows to dive out of, I just sit behind my desk and smile politely.

"Don't forget you have a date at six," she says sternly.

"I forgot to go."

"What do you mean, you forgot to go? It's not till six."

"I'm planning ahead."

She gives me a scowl and then turns her disapproving eyes to my clothes, looking at them as if they just came off some syphilis-ridden leper. She doesn't need words; her downturned mouth and upturned eyebrows say it all.

Twenty minutes later I'm at Big Perch changing into "something more appropriate," which means another excursion into Jens's closet.

A date with Heather at the Hearthfire Grill.

I could kill Diane.

What makes this worse is that she's recruited Jimmy to make sure I actually show up. They're like a matchmaking Bonnie and Clyde, using a restaurant in place of a tommy gun as they march me off to my doom . . . though perhaps *doom* is too strong a word. . . .

"Technically, this is kidnapping," I tell Jimmy as he backs out of my driveway and throws the black FBI-issued Ford Excursion into drive.

"You don't have a drop of Viking blood in you, do you?" he shoots back.

"I'm Norwegian; of course I have Viking blood."

"Your mother is Norwegian. I think that

bloodline skipped over you somehow and just left the Scottish. Frankly, I'm disappointed."

"Because I don't want to have dinner with Heather Jennings I suddenly lack the Viking pedigree?"

"Yes!" Jimmy roars, his voice rolling off in laughter. "She's smart, she's funny, she's got legs up to here —" He smacks me with the back of his hand and I look over as he puts his hand at chest level and repeats, "Up to here." He wags his index finger at me, saying, "She's smoking hot in every way and you're like a third-grader at recess." He pauses. "You do like girls, don't you?"

"Don't be stupid."

"I'm just saying," he purrs, shrugging his shoulders.

I look at him hard. "Don't you remember what she wrote about me?"

"Something about gonorrhea . . ." he begins, laughing even louder as I throw my hands up in exasperation. "Come on, Steps. It wasn't that bad; some of it was actually pretty flattering. You're the only one who was upset with it."

"She revealed details that could have compromised us . . . that could have compromised several of the cases."

"You're just upset because she came a

little too close to the truth."

There it is.

I should have guessed that Jimmy would figure it out. He knows as well as I that Heather has this uncanny way of separating fact from fiction, even the fiction we build up around ourselves, say, to hide some secret ability we don't want anyone to know about.

I was mad about the article, that part is true.

She wrote about things she shouldn't have, things she promised not to. It was that dishonesty, that betrayal of trust that hurt the most; it wasn't like her. Or maybe I just didn't know her as well as I'd thought. In the end, though, the article was just an excuse; a means to an end. The real reason I pushed her away was raw fear. Fear of what she'd learn.

Heather Jennings.

I loved her.

I love her still.

But she only knows Steps the FBI tracker. What happens if she meets the other Steps, the real Steps? Will she be repulsed? Horrified? Intrigued? Will she put pen to paper and carve out an exposé eviscerating the Special Tracking Unit and laying bare the fraud of its chief tracker?

I'd rather not take that chance, so I'll bury my heart deep so it can't be found. I'll get through this dinner — somehow — and then get on with life. Alone. Maybe love is not meant for everyone. Maybe that's the price some pay.

She's waiting in front of the restaurant when Jimmy pulls up. Waves of dancing heat rise above her and around her, emanating from a flaming basin placed within the landscaping behind her, but they may as well be emanating from her. She's stunning, breathtaking, every inch the woman I remember, though more beautiful from her absence.

"Holy crap," Jimmy mutters as his eyes fix on Heather.

It's not really swearing, but still surprising coming from Jimmy's lips. He loathes profanity like I loathe forests, coffee, animals, and Styrofoam. This contempt doesn't prevent the occasional spontaneous utterance, however, which explains the *Holy crap* that just spilled out of his mouth. Fortunately, *crap* is on our list of acceptable words, so he gets a pass this time.

I've always been fascinated by word origins and find it interesting that the root of profanity, the Latin word *profanus,* translates to "outside the temple" and was taken

149

to mean something that desecrates what is holy. But what if you are in a wholly *unholy* environment? How can you desecrate the holy when there's nothing holy in sight?

I imagine that's why cops cuss more than librarians.

Jimmy's objection to foul language isn't based on his religious beliefs, though. He avoids such language out of respect for what he calls the "higher mind." He's told me repeatedly through the years that profanity is the refuge of a simple mind, and that people who swear excessively lack the imagination to think of anything better. He once told me that profanity *pushes the mind into the sewer of human wretchedness and drags the soul along for company.*

I've argued that in law enforcement you often have to speak the language of your audience. I've known detectives who could talk to clergy one moment, and then dive into a sea of the filthiest profanity with a heroin addict the next. It's an amazing process to watch, almost like they flip a switch and become a different person.

Of course, most deputies, officers, and detectives lack that unusual gift and have to muck around somewhere in the middle range, which means they occasionally drop the F-bomb in front of clergy or say *hal-*

lelujah to the heroin addict.

It's not that Jimmy *doesn't* curse, but it's a rare occasion, and shocking to behold. He's quite good at it when he wants to be. Over the years we've established certain words that are acceptable within our one-on-one conversations. These include *damn, dammit,* and *hell,* though he prefers the minced oaths *darn, darnit,* and *heck.*

The minced oaths *shoot, friggin', bull snot,* and *bull hockey* are also acceptable, though I've yet to use the latter two in conversation.

Ass is acceptable . . . surprisingly.

I had to argue for it, however, pointing out that it's the common term for a donkey and has historical precedence in the Bible and literature. Nevertheless, Jimmy was *not* happy when I uttered it in front of Petey one day. It was strictly by accident and my attempts to smooth it over where less than successful. I told Petey we don't call people *asses,* we call them *donkeys.*

A week later we were in the lounge at Hangar 7 watching some G-rated movie — I don't remember which one. It was just me, Jimmy, and Petey; Jane wasn't there, which is why I'm still alive. Halfway through the show, Petey points at the bad guy and says, "He's a real donkey-hole, isn't he,

Uncle Steps?"

Yep. Not one of my finer moments.

Heather cuts a demure pose, hands clasped together in front of her as if she's unsure what to do with them; her long hair is as I remember it, her face, her posture, her grace. She's wearing a breathtaking V-shaped silk blouse in soft lime with cascading ruffles that end at a point halfway between her waist and her knees in front and well past her knees in the back. This is complemented by black denim stretch jeans that empty into a pair of black high-heeled Michael Kors sandals.

I know my shoes.

When we first met, she was a twenty-three-year-old up-and-coming reporter, one year out of grad school, who had already made a name for herself with an online investigative news blog she founded and edited. *Newsweek* scooped her up before the ink was dry on her diploma and she soon found herself specializing in crime and criminal justice stories, including a major piece on the Porsche Novatny abduction and murder that had so captivated the public that year.

"Heather," I breathe.

"Steps." The corner of her mouth curls up

temptingly, teasingly. "You know you're almost late?"

I grin. "Almost late is right on time."

"Same old Steps," she says, shaking her head.

I study her a moment, devour her.

"It's good to see you," I finally say. "You look . . . hot."

She begins to smile, but then I hurriedly add, "Let's go inside where it's a bit cooler."

I hold the door open and she brushes briskly past. For a moment I wish she'd turn around and club me over the head; it would serve me right.

Let's go inside where it's a bit cooler?

I don't even know why I said it. What an idiot! Of course I meant the *other* hot. Why wouldn't I? She's gorgeous, always has been. I'm about to quick-step after her, spin her around, and apologize when it hits me like a two-by-four to the forehead: Stick to the plan; bury your heart; let her go. Thirty seconds in her presence and she's already turning me against myself.

It's not natural.

Just get through this dinner, I tell myself, *let her apologize for the article, say good-bye, have a nice life, and then put her out of your mind forever.*

Forever.

Uh-huh.

Our table is next to a massive picture window that opens onto the Puget Sound. A gull hovers against an otherwise spotless blue sky, a still figure riding a gentle breeze. Miles away, at the end of the world, islands rise from the deep in the shape of pyramids and plateaus, lording themselves over the Sound. Much closer, a discordant fleet of boats is tied up in the harbor like so many birds gone to roost. There are sailboats, motorboats, fishing boats, and yachts. Their sizes are as varied as their colors and shapes. A lucky few have managed to escape the coop and now ply the open waters of the Sound, long white tails trailing behind them.

It's breathtaking.

"I always loved this view," Heather says. "It's so romantic."

Great! That helps.

We make small talk between visits from Miguel, our waiter, who starts us off with a baked Dungeness crab, shrimp, and artichoke dip served with flatbread. For the entrée, I stick to my usual, char-grilled wild Alaskan silver salmon finished with wild mountain huckleberry sauce. Heather opts for the garlic herb chicken and Parmesan mashed potatoes; not a bad choice.

On the table, set intentionally off to the

side, is Heather's black leather portfolio. It's the same one she was using while embedded with us, so I know there's a note-pad inside, along with several pens and copious reference documents and other papers she considers important or relevant. She's waiting to spring it on me — whatever *it* is — but she wants to put it on display first.

Then it hits me like a hammer.

Maybe she's not here to apologize; maybe she doesn't feel bad at all about the article or the way we ended; maybe she really doesn't have feelings for me at all.

Maybe she's here to get another story.

As we work our way through ample por-tions of salmon and chicken and mashed potatoes and cornbread pudding, I find myself glancing at the folder with increasing frequency. She's up to something, I just know it, only she's too clever to just throw it out for discussion. She's trying to bait me.

Now I feel insulted.

Does she honestly think I'm that easy, that predictable? I couldn't care less what's in the folder. I couldn't care less about her agenda, or whatever angle she's trying to play.

It's just a portfolio.

Why would she need her portfolio for a dinner date?

I make it all the way to dessert before I can't take it anymore and blurt, "What are we doing here, Heather? What's in the portfolio?"

As soon as the words are out of my mouth, I think, *She just won. She broke me.*

There's a smug look . . . no, a confident look on her face, a look I remember so well, a look that says she knows something I don't. It's been nine months since she was embedded with the unit, but I remember how hard it is for her to hide her emotions.

The girl has no poker face.

Without a word, she opens the portfolio and extracts four sheets of typed and stapled paper. The pages are neither crisp nor clean and appear as if they've been folded and unfolded dozens of times. A coffee stain graces the lower edge of the top page, and every corner is dog-eared. She sets it on the table and pushes the stained and worried mess slowly across, her eyes intent on my face.

"What is it?"

"Something I want you to read." Her face is blank. There's no emotion in her eyes now and the corners of her mouth are unmoving, giving no hint either up or down. *She's*

156

been practicing her poker face. I feel my stomach ball up and my intestines go to water.

"Last time I read something you wrote, we didn't speak for nine months."

"*You* didn't speak for nine months," she clarifies. "I've called every couple weeks, or have you forgotten? If you don't remember, I could call Diane. She and I have become great phone pals." She gives a short shake of her head, truncated and abrupt. "It's funny, when I was embedded with the team, I didn't really get to know her. It took you, Steps, to help us get close. Did you know she went to Hawaii with me over Christmas — I'm sure she told you?"

"Hawaii . . . ?" I shake my head. "I remember she said something about a beach . . . was that when she showed up all tan? Or . . . or . . ." *Jimmy's right, I'm not a Viking.* I quickly slug down some water from my perspiring glass. *I'm drowning here; suffocating, choking.*

Setting my glass down, I cross my arms over my chest . . . then remember that Heather studied body language . . . extensively; she's like the Amazing Kreskin of reporters. I always thought that reading body language was the purview of law enforcement, a skill used to help decipher a suspect's guilt.

It never occurred to me that such a skill could also be useful to reporters . . . until I met Heather. Maybe it's something they teach at journalism school, or maybe Heather took it on herself to learn, realizing its great potential. In either case, she's good at it; I should have remembered that. In the short span we've been in the restaurant I've probably shifted my gaze from one eye to the other, then to her lips, at least a dozen times.

That's bad.

I quickly uncross my arms and take another drink.

The left corner of her mouth twitches up half an inch and her eyes smile, letting *me* know that *she* knows what *I* just remembered. *Damn!*

She gives the worn pages a push closer. "Just read it."

I hesitate . . . then hesitate some more . . . and then realize that the only thing that's going to make this go away — make *her* go away — is to give her what she wants. With my right index finger I spin the pages around so they're right side up and read the title aloud, " 'Signs of Passage: The FBI's Special Tracking Unit.' " Pushing it away, I say, "I've already read this."

"Has anyone told you you're stubborn?" she hisses.

"No one that's credible."

"This," she said, picking up the paper and shaking it in my face, "is what I wrote, not that tripe they printed."

Confusion.

"You're saying the article that was printed wasn't what you wrote?" I shoot back, disbelieving, wanting to disbelieve. "So . . . who wrote it?"

Heather pushes back from the table and studies me. "I explained all that in the very long phone message I left on your machine after the article came out," she says.

"Phone message . . . yeah —"

"You deleted it without listening; Diane told me."

"I was mad."

"You were stupid."

I'm speechless a moment, then my fingers reach out for the papers, and I pull them close, like a drowning man hugging a life preserver. "So who *did* write the article, if it wasn't you?"

"My no-talent editor. She stole my notes and hijacked my story. I quit the next day." She pushes back from the table and stands.

"Where are you going?"

"The ladies' room to check my lipstick."

159

She smiles. "You don't need me staring at you while you read, do you?" Without waiting for a reply, she spins and walks briskly down the aisle, dragging my captive eyes with her. I shake it off quickly and turn my attention to the worn pages of the article — and devour it. It's good, really good, the whole piece, and nothing like the published version.

Guilt washes over me; I should have known. I've read much of Heather's work, and the published piece lacked the luster and compelling prose, it lacked the picture-perfect detail and the heart, delivering instead the hurried, banal, and sophomoric sentences and paragraphs of a mediocre reporter on a deadline.

I'm a fool.

Before we agreed to let Heather embed with the team, we'd done our research. Jimmy was impressed with her interview style and the way she could ferret out the truth — we didn't find out until later that she could read body language like others read poetry.

For my part, I set out to read two or three of the articles from her blog — to get a feel for her writing ability — and ended up devouring everything I could find: hundreds of blog pages, articles from her college newspaper, even several short stories, one of which won the H. E. Francis Short Story Award.

She's a natural; Jimmy and I both recognized it and agreed that if the STU was going to get some media attention, as the director intended, we wanted Heather to write it.

I look up just as Heather turns down the aisle toward me. She's walking slowly, gracefully, and I have a hard time taking my eyes off her. I glance at the menus standing upright on the inside end of the table and wonder aloud if they offer crow as an entrée.

I may need a double serving.

More importantly, my excuse for not seeing Heather is gone, and my heart isn't eager to find a replacement. *Why not just tell her?* I think as she approaches the table. What harm could come from four people knowing my secret instead of just three?

I give her a conquered smile when she takes her seat, and say, "I owe you an apology. I should have known."

"You should have," she jabs back playfully.

I hesitate. What harm could it do?

"I have something to tell you; a confession, I suppose." My chair is suddenly uncomfortable and I fidget forward, then back again, but there's no good position. "I have this . . ." *Secret. Just say it!* "I have this problem with commitment." *Coward.* "It's because of the job," I add quickly.

Heather leans forward and just smiles. "Who would have guessed?" she says in the most serious of tones, giving her head a little shake of concern.

Tell her; it's not too late.

TELL HER!

I ignore my screaming inner voice and push it back into the id where it belongs. Right now I don't know if it's a foolish decision or a wise one; only time will tell. Time is an impartial judge.

We sit and stare at each other in silence; not the uncomfortable silence of strangers but the silence of kindred spirits reunited. The world continues on and passes by outside the window, unnoticed and unmissed for the moment.

"What now?" I say at length.

Heather picks up her glass and swirls the ice. "I'd say you owe me a walk along the water," she replies.

Her grin is contagious.

CHAPTER ELEVEN

June 26, 9:37 A.M.

"I've told you this before."

"I know, I just want to hear it again — it's interesting," Jimmy says.

I sigh, not impatiently, just in resignation. Betsy is at a cruising altitude of forty-one thousand feet, or "flight level four one zero," as Les and Marty would say. Her nose is pointed toward Redding, where a serial killer awaits.

We still have an hour before we start our descent, so Jimmy and I kill time the way we always do; it's routine . . . ritual. We call it Plane Talk; not *plain,* as in normal or usual, but *plane,* as in airplane. Plane Talk is reserved for Betsy, for those times when we're just trying to get through the hours that occupy the space between airports, between home and the job. Plane Talk includes everything under the sun but usually tends toward the more bizarre or un-usual.

Kopi Luwak is a good example.

It's a type of coffee.

Jimmy calls it monkey-butt coffee. It's a rare gourmet variety from Indonesia made from beans that have allegedly passed through the digestive system of a monkey. I say *allegedly* because, in truth, it's not a monkey, but a catlike creature called the palm civet that digests the meat around the beans and then excretes the beans whole — minus dung.

They say it's the best coffee in the world.

I've never tried it.

Then again, I've never licked the back of a Colorado River toad, either. The psycho-active toads and the associated rumors of people licking them to get high was another subject of our midflight conversations.

Regardless of the subject, Plane Talk is almost always stimulating.

Today's subject, life after death, is a repeat . . . times ten or twenty, but what else are you going to do at flight level four one zero in a flying aluminum tube when the pilot and copilot have banned you from the cockpit?

I push myself back into the exceedingly comfortable overstuffed executive seat, which is slightly reclined, and resist the urge to close my eyes. "I remember my grandfather's passing the best; Grandpa Samuelsen," I begin. "It was a couple weeks after my tenth birthday, almost two years after . . . well, after my experience in the woods. Two years after I started seeing the shine."

Jimmy knows not to push on this point.

"We were at the nursing home for a visit; I think we visited almost every day. Jens and I were playing with our Hot Wheels — Mom always brought along a bucketful to keep us busy — and I just remember a sudden commotion around Grandpa's bed. The last couple visits he'd mostly slept, and the last time I heard him speak was probably the week before, so all this sudden noise and activity had my full attention.

"Nurses started coming into the room and alarms were going off and as I watched I saw Grandpa Samuelsen's shine lift up out of his body and drift toward the ceiling, like a slightly inflated helium balloon floating slowly up. The colors and texture suddenly seemed more vibrant, and it pulsed with more energy than I'd ever seen. It was like the old shine — the body shine — had been coated in some hard grimy shell, which was now peeled away. I don't know if that makes any sense."

Jimmy nods but doesn't say anything.

"At the time, I didn't know what was happening. His body still had the essence and texture I was used to, but it looked shabby by comparison . . . and somehow flat and empty without that energy pulsing from it.

"When I looked back at the ceiling, there were other shines, maybe a dozen, though it was hard to tell because they were moving about, weaving in, around, and through my grandpa's shine, each just as vivid and distinct and full of energy. And the more excited they got, the brighter they glowed, until I couldn't even look at them.

"Then they were gone; just that fast. And . . . there was something else. . . ." My voice trails off and I suddenly wish I could take back the last words.

"What?" Jimmy's leaning forward in his chair, perching rather than sitting.

"It's something I never told you before," I say hesitantly. "I wasn't . . . I wasn't sure if you'd believe me." My shoulders shrug involuntarily.

Jimmy smiles, then chuckles. "I solve murders following invisible clues that only my forest-hating, slightly neurotic, anal-retentive best friend can see. What's to disbelieve?"

He has a point.

"Come on, spit it out," Jimmy coaxes.

Turning my eyes to the window at my left, I watch the wing shudder and float as we skim through the atmosphere at more than five hundred miles an hour. The sky is robin-egg blue in every direction and the clouds make a cotton-ball floor beneath us, so fluffy and soft-looking you just want to stretch your arms out and fall backward into them.

It's what I like best about flying: the view.

"It wasn't just Grandpa Samuelsen's shine that I recognized near the ceiling," I say to the clouds below. "There was another." Turning, I meet Jimmy's eyes. "It was my Grandma Samuelsen." His eyes go wide and I nod. "She died the year before."

Jimmy lets out a long low whistle.

Chapter Twelve

June 26, 5:40 P.M.

It's been a long day.

Long and filled with many miles both in the air and on the ground. Now the day is almost done, and we are far from where it started; far from that nondescript hangar in Bellingham, Washington.

Reflecting back, it seems like days have passed, but I know that it was this very dawn that found us descending into Redding. So much has happened since. On arrival, a four-seat Cessna 172N was standing by, and Les flew us some ninety miles to Susanville, California, leaving Marty with some free time on his hands. We had to rent the Cessna because the airport in Susanville was too small for Betsy, as were some of the other airports we passed through as the day progressed.

After promising to bring back copious amounts of Dungeness crab, Marty rented a separate Cessna and headed to San Francisco for the day . . . to spend some of that per diem.

Throughout the day my thoughts kept drifting back to him, imagining him at Fisherman's Wharf, Alcatraz Island, Pier 39, Chinatown, maybe even riding a cable car. I envied him.

Our path proved much darker.

The first stop of the day, Susanville, is — *was* — the home of Tawnee Rich, who went missing thirty-five months ago and has yet to be found. Police impound still held her 1999 Mazda 626 in covered storage and it took but a second to find Sad Face's shine on the driver's door, all over the driver's seat, the steering wheel, and the trunk. More importantly, the sad-face pattern is scrawled on the top of her trunk lid. Invisible to all but me, it glowed large and bright in unmistakable amaranth.

I surreptitiously indicated the area of the trunk to Jimmy while the evidence technician was distracted; he knew exactly what I was suggesting. We'd done this dance before.

"Do you mind if I dust the trunk lid?" Jimmy had asked, turning to the tech.

"The case detective has already gone through the vehicle inside and out," the tech answered stiffly. "There was nothing usable."

"I'm sure they did," Jimmy had replied, "but I'm not looking for fingerprints."

This seemed to spark the tech's interest and he nodded his approval.

After retrieving a brush and a round two-ounce container of powder from his backpack, Jimmy gently dusted the left side of the trunk with a steady twirling motion, then blew the powder clear, leaving the faint outline of a one-foot-diameter circle, two eyes, a dot for a nose, and a downcast mouth.

Without a word, Jimmy photographed the image from multiple angles using different filters. We'll need those images for court, to prove the case is linked to the Sad Face Killer. Without them, all we have is my word, and I can't exactly walk into court and say I saw a sad face on the victim's car, an image that everyone else missed.

"How'd you see that?" the tech had stammered.

"Lucky, I guess," Jimmy replied. "The light was reflecting oddly . . . just a hunch."

After Susanville, we flew to Medford, Oregon, where Dany Grazier was kidnapped eighteen months ago. Finding nothing on her car, we headed south again to Yreka,

California, and caught a ride with Special Agent Janet Portenga of the U.S. Forest Service. Fifteen miles into the Klamath National Forest we came upon a patch of dark forest where Dany's body was found. Sad Face's shine was all over the place, including a detour through the brush to a pine tree forty feet from the body dump where he had carved a sad face into the trunk.

Jimmy documented it with his camera, each click of the shutter sounding loud and inappropriate; offensive. It's one of many sounds left in the wake of a homicide. They grate on you after a while.

Then it was northwest to Brookings, Oregon, for Erica Overdorff — another of the still-missing. Then to Crescent City for Jennifer Green and south to Eureka for Leah Daniels, which had led us to this miserable patch of fetid-green northeast of Weaverville in the Trinity National Forest on a peak overlooking Trinity Lake.

The forest here is oppressive.

The warm June air has spent the afternoon baking last winter's leaves where they lie, brewing a musty, earthy stench of decay that settles between the trees and presses in from all sides. The heat sucks the moisture from my brow, my neck, my face, leaving my skin feeling slapped and raw.

Despite this, my mind is not on the forest. Instead, I stare at a lone tree at the edge of a high bluff that drops off steeply to the water below. It's a tree little different from the others around it, except this one has a special color of shine around its base.

There was something about Leah that Sad Face liked, I can tell that right away. She's still dead, of course, but he took extra care choosing a dump site and positioning her body. He could have just dumped her in the woods like the others.

He didn't.

I see where he leaned her up against the tree not far off the well-traveled trail, ensuring she'd be found quickly. He faced her toward the lake, perhaps so her dead eyes would have something pleasant to fix upon.

He sat next to her for a spell.

Maybe he leaned against her; maybe he held her.

The shine isn't all that clear.

Hikers found her early one April morning two years ago. Rigor indicated she had been dead less than twelve hours; lividity showed that she'd been killed elsewhere and had spent several hours on her side before being propped upright against the tree. She had on the same clothes she'd been wearing when she went missing eight months earlier, and her unmolested purse was resting in her lap.

Whatever goodwill she had earned with Sad Face, it only went so far. In the end, he choked the life from her just like the others.

It's a quiet flight back to Redding, Jimmy and I each alone with our thoughts. We wear headphones so we can talk back and forth above the rumble of the Cessna's engine, but few words are exchanged. Jimmy is working something out in a notebook that he's been scribbling in all day, and I spend most of the flight thinking about Heather and our dinner together just a few nights and so long ago.

Tomorrow's schedule should be easier.

CHAPTER THIRTEEN

June 27, 7:40 A.M.

Jimmy's reading the morning paper and eating scrambled eggs washed down with coffee while I nibble at a sesame seed muffin and sip orange juice. The food is good . . . for a complimentary hotel breakfast.

Halfway through my muffin, Marty bounces in, shoots me a big grin, and makes a beeline for the coffee. I pray he goes for decaf, but he plants himself in front of a dispenser of full-strength French ground and tops off his one-liter thermos, followed by a sixteen-ounce paper cup. Stirring cream and sugar into the cup, he plops down in the seat next to me, still grinning.

"How was San Francisco?" I ask politely.

Out of the corner of my eye I see Jimmy slump in his seat, burying himself deeper in the newspaper as he slowly lifts the top edge up to obscure his face. Jimmy thinks that Marty is too loquacious. Or, in his words,

He doesn't know when to shut up.

"Greeaat!" Marty purrs, smiling ridiculously like some kid on a candy binge.

I hope it was great, I think. *We didn't get our crab till almost eleven last night.*

He starts babbling on about how *amazing* the aquarium was, which doesn't surprise me since he's visited close to fifty in the time I've known him. He once told me his goal is to visit every major aquarium in the country. As he rambles on . . . and on . . . and on . . . I realize he's not talking about the Aquarium of the Bay by Pier 39, he's talking about the Monterey Bay Aquarium two hours south of San Francisco in Monterey.

"Whoa. I thought you went to San Francisco."

"I did." He smirks. "But I started in Monterey. I rented a little convertible, visited the aquarium, and cruised Seventeen-Mile Drive with the top down. *Then* I flew to San Francisco." He leans toward me. "That way I scored two aquariums in one day — and I still remembered to bring back crab," he adds with a wink.

Yeah, at eleven o'clock!

"The giant Pacific octopus exhibit was awesome," Marty blathers on. Then I hear all about San Francisco, the aquarium, Pier

39, and his misadventures with the panhandlers. He didn't make it to Chinatown or Alcatraz, but that doesn't seem to dampen his enthusiasm.

Les and Marty are switching places today, so I'm sure Jimmy and I will have plenty of time to hear more about Marty's trip on the plane. *Yay.* The Cessna is loud, but it's equipped with headphones for both the pilot and passengers. I'm not sure if they have a mute button.

Oroville, 9:23 A.M.
Burgundy.

It's a great color, deep and rich and regal. Not like other shades of red that can be too bright, begging for unnecessary attention like a spoiled toddler throwing a temper tantrum. No, burgundy speaks of the wine for which it's named, dark and luxurious. It looks great on Lauren Brouwer's 2004 Chrysler 300, a car that itself is dark and luxurious.

I always liked the styling of the 300 series. It looks like the offspring of an unnatural pairing between a Bentley and an English bulldog — beefy, yet elegant. An hors d'oeuvre of class and power and style wrapped up nicely in Detroit steel and garnished with leather.

Lauren loves her car.

I say *loves,* because her shine tells me she's still alive . . . somewhere. I know she loves her car because she posted more than a dozen pictures of it on Facebook when she bought it six months ago.

Someone else loves the car.

Or perhaps it's just that they love Lauren.

I know this because the car has been washed recently, and probably often. Where dust from the gravel driveway and the nearby fields has settled on the other cars in the driveway, Lauren's stands apart, clean and gleaming in the morning sun.

Loving hands have treated the tires, polished the wheels, and cleaned the windows to a squeaky shine. The pristine gem waits for Lauren's return; a sad vigil, a hard vigil, a hopeful vigil. A vigil shared by her parents, who wait for us inside the house.

When Lauren went missing, the Chrysler 300 was found parked at the grocery store where she worked swing shift. Neither Oroville PD nor the Butte County Sheriff's Office deemed it worthy of impounding because there was no indication it was involved in Lauren's disappearance.

A quick walk around without my glasses reveals no sign of Sad Face. No shine on the door, the seat, or the steering wheel; no sad-face image traced out on a window or trunk or bumper; no face print on the back window.

Sad Face didn't touch the car.

I catch up to Jimmy as he's ringing the doorbell.

"Anything?"

"No," I say. "It's clean."

Footsteps approach the door and I get the sense that someone's looking through the peephole. A lock clicks and a grim man pulls the door wide. The lines on his face belong to a man much older and there's a tic at the corner of his eye that probably wasn't there two months ago.

"Good morning, sir," Jimmy says gently, extending his hand in greeting. "I'm Special Agent James Donovan and this is Operations Specialist Magnus Craig."

"Martin Brouwer," the man says, shaking Jimmy's hand. As I step forward and extend my hand, our eyes meet and I see that same haunted, sleepless, vacant look that I've seen too often.

Souls bleed.

They bleed through the eyes, for it's in the eyes that you see the wound. Small wounds, great wounds, and sometimes terrible wounds that rip the soul asunder, some so awful they change the soul — and the eyes — forever.

It's the eyes that bleed out such sorrow; the sorrow of a parent wondering every minute of every day where their daughter is and what's happening to her — and at the same time not wanting to know, because the thought of it leaves them hollow and broken. It's the eyes that reveal the rents and gashes in the soul, the cracks along the edge, the empty hole where part of the soul has died and turned to shadow.

The blood of the soul is the teardrop.

Aside from tears and hopelessness and grief and desperation, there's something else in Martin Brouwer's eyes: gratitude. This, too, I've seen before, and it always surprises me that there's still room for it, that it hasn't been pushed out and discarded.

It's hard to imagine how gratitude could survive within the hostile, acidic environment of angst and sorrow and dread, but there it is. As long as there is hope, there is gratitude. It's easy to understand such an emotion when we find someone alive, but so many times it's the other way around. Yet, there's still gratitude, gratitude that we brought a loved one home, even dead. It's gratitude for the effort, gratitude that we tried, even if we failed. And in those cases, like Lauren's, where someone is still missing, and has been for too long, there is gratitude that someone is still looking.

Hope and Gratitude: the resilient sisters.

Martin's fingers twitch ever so slightly as he takes my hand and holds it for a long moment. *His eyes.* He's a beaten man, but not yet broken. Not yet.

Hope and Gratitude; they feed him.

I want to tell him right then that Lauren is alive, that I see her shine pulsing and vibrating with the rhythm of life. *She's just lost and we're going to find her.* But I can't give him that hope if there's any chance that Lauren won't come home; that would break him by parts and finish him whole. It's enough to tell him we're going to pour our hearts and souls into finding his daughter, and that we're the best at what we do.

I say the words, but they crumble as they fall from my tongue.

Martin has heard them before . . . again and again.

He just nods. Polite. Grateful.

Alice Brouwer greets us in the living room, a small mouse of a woman with big frail eyes and brown hair. She has a perspiring ice-cold pitcher of pink lemonade and a small plate of cinnamon rolls sliced in halves that she places on the coffee table before greeting us with a tepid smile and a hand-shake.

We talk for a half hour, seated around the coffee table. We have a few questions that Jimmy asks, but mostly we let Martin and Alice tell us about their daughter. Some memories bring smiles and even the occasional laugh, but more often it's the tears of the soul that pour out with the story.

Lauren is a gentle spirit, always smiling, a good daughter, never in trouble. She has a fiancé and a December wedding to look forward to, and a love of animals so deep that she had saved nearly $20,000 in the hopes of opening a five-star boarding kennel for dogs. She has the whole thing planned out on a five-year timeline and just finished year two ahead of schedule.

Her older brother, Larry, who's studying to be an architect, helped her design the three-thousand-square-foot building, leaving room for growth down the road. It includes an exercise arena, a playroom, and speakers in every room that play soft, soothing music while the dogs sleep in their people-like beds.

That is Lauren Brouwer — dreams and hope and heart.

Tears follow smiles follow tears.

I find myself holding Alice's hand, patting

her arm.

I think of my own mother, Lovisa. After decades in America, she still speaks with a strong Norwegian accent and gets cross with Jens and me when we mimic her. When we were growing up, she was often stern, demanding, and disciplined. She set the bar high for us and accepted no excuses. But she's also quick to laugh and to hug, and she leaves no doubt that she loves you with every ounce of her great Norwegian heart.

That's my mother . . .

. . . and it tears me up to think of the hell she would go through if Jens or I were missing or dead. I imagine she would be much like Alice Brouwer and too many mothers before her.

"No one said life is easy — or fair," she often told us. "Life is life. There's no scale to weigh out your days and make sure you get your share of the good." She's right, of course. We pass our years one yesterday at a time, hoping our days will be many but never knowing. In the end we strive for one thing: to make enough good days to outweigh the bad.

Alice and Lauren and Martin deserve some good days.

But life isn't easy, nor is it fair.

As we step to the door and say our goodbyes, Alice suddenly holds both her hands up. "Can you wait one minute . . . please?" She turns and hurries down the hall before either of us can reply, and we hear a shuffling noise, drawers opening and closing, and then she's hurrying back with something in her hand.

Taking my left hand, she turns it palm up and places a silver heart-shaped locket in the center. Slowly, gently, she closes my fingers around it. "Give this to my Lauren when you find her. We gave it to her when she graduated high school. She wore it constantly, but for some reason she wasn't wearing it the night . . . the night . . ." Her eyes go to water. "I just want to see it around her neck when I hug her and hold her."

"I will." The words lump in my throat and it's hard to swallow.

Lauren's shine glows through the gaps of my fingers.

Pulsing.

Pulsing.

Pulsing.

The rest of the day goes as expected; first to Red Bluff some sixty miles north of Oroville and home to Ashley Sprague. Or at least it *was* her home, until she went missing more than two years ago and hasn't been seen since.

Unlike the others, Ashley was a feral spirit — wild beyond measure — so it wasn't uncommon for her to drop off the grid for days or weeks at a time. So feral was her spirit that no one bothered reporting her missing for more than a month.

The report was taken reluctantly.

Red Bluff PD still hesitates to call her missing, believing instead the rumors that she tripped off to Mexico to bartend with some boyfriend in Cabo. Who can blame them? Ashley was the boy who cried wolf, only substitute *girl* for *boy,* and *partied hard and disappeared often* for *cried wolf.*

By the time she was eighteen — old enough to be booked into the county jail — she had been reported as a runaway fifteen times, had been booked into juvenile detention a dozen times, and had been through rehab three times.

Feral.

Capital *F.*

Her first stint in the county jail, exactly twenty-three days after her eighteenth birthday, was for DUI. It took her a few days to raise bail, which, as it turns out, wasn't fast enough. Corrections officers found her bleeding and unconscious next to her bed on the second morning. No one was talking, but the word was she mouthed off to the wrong gangster girl and got a broken jaw and a concussion in return.

After that, Ashley seemed to straighten out. She held a variety of odd jobs, tried community college — it didn't take — then, when she was twenty-one, she took a course in bartending and seemed to find something that suited her.

She was working her way through the legal maze to get her juvenile record sealed when she disappeared; she thought she'd have a better shot at getting a decent bartending job with better tips in Vegas or Reno if she could leave her juvenile baggage behind.

Every agency has their share of Ashley Spragues; scores and hundreds and even thousands of them, depending on the size of the agency and its jurisdiction. And every time they're arrested they talk about how they're going to change their life, how they have this plan, how they don't need the drugs or the booze or the destructive boyfriend anymore.

Almost none succeed.

Almost none try.

Ashley Sprague *did* try — and *was* succeeding — but her juvenile record was hard to shake. Many of the officers and deputies in the city and county knew her on sight and had too much history with her to believe anything she said, so much so that when her coworker reported her missing they glanced through the missing persons report, saw her name, and then disregarded.

Never mind.

It's just Ashley . . . again.

There was no search for Ashley Sprague.

No forensic examination of her car or her apartment.

She became one of the invisible missing, landing among the ranks of prostitutes and drug addicts. It wasn't fair, but life isn't fair.

There's my mother in my head again: *No one said life is easy — or fair.*

Sadly, Ashley was reaping what she had for so many years sown . . . and it was a bitter harvest.

According to the case report, Ashley's 1995 Hyundai was parked and locked in her numbered parking spot at Dorchester Apartments, a low-income housing project near the center of town. When she never returned, never paid the meager rent, and never picked up her car, it was towed and later sold at an impound auction for $325.

I'm not interested in Ashley's apartment or the dumpy tavern with the gaudy red neon sign where she worked. I just want to see her car. I want to see if Sad Face touched it, sat in it, drove it, used the trunk. I want to see if Ashley's shine is *in* the trunk.

Or did he just leave a sad-face circle on her window?

Perhaps Ashley *isn't* one of Sad Face's victims. It's possible. Perhaps her age and height and hair are just a coincidence. After all, she doesn't have much in common with the other victims — except Valerie Heagle, the prostitute.

Diane might be wrong on this one.

For Ashley's sake, I hope so.

The California Department of Motor Vehicles shows her car currently registered to Jacob Aase, five-foot-seven, 155 pounds, brown hair, brown eyes. His driver's license photo looks hollow around the cheeks and eyes. I recognize the look. His license is suspended due to unpaid tickets and his address is on the north side of Red Bluff.

Simple enough, right?

But when we pull to the curb in front of Jacob's house, simple becomes suddenly complicated, and complicated becomes, well, frustratingly typical.

Planted at the edge of the dead lawn, snug up against a cracked and weathered sidewalk, is a red, white, and blue FOR SALE sign that looks like it may have aged and

187

faded since being placed. The house itself looks naked: no blinds, no drapes, no ratty moth-eaten curtains. The large window to the left of the front door opens into a stark and empty house. The walls have a coat of fresh paint, but the lousy patch job on the abused interior walls leaves them looking pockmarked and worn.

Some would call it a quaint single-story bachelor's pad, which is, no doubt, how the real estate agency listed it.

I call it a shack . . .

. . . with an apology to shacks.

The house is barely nine hundred square feet, has a noticeable downward pitch on the southeast corner, and green paint on the exterior that's so far gone it looks like some faded, curling, alien fungus. The front door is off-kilter and even from the road I can see the frame is damaged at the latch where it's been booted open more than once — either by cops or crooks, maybe both.

And those are the better features.

The crowning glory is so redneck I don't know whether to laugh, cry, or scream: someone has stapled a giant blue tarp to the roof. Bright blue. Big. Yacht-sized. It covers most of the backside of the roof and drapes over the peak by several feet, giving the house a fluorescent-blue Mohawk.

"Safe to say Jacob Aase doesn't live here anymore," I say casually.

"Safe to say," Jimmy echoes.

We stand at the sidewalk a moment just staring at the house, wondering what our next move is. After a moment Jimmy says, "Tweaker TV," and points to the front door. My eyes follow his finger and I see it, hidden above the door and tucked up under the eaves.

"There's another one." This time Jimmy points to the right front corner of the house.

"Probably a couple more in the back and one on the other side," I say.

Tweaker TV.

It's a bit of a joke within law enforcement. Whenever you see a $500 house with $2,000 worth of surveillance equipment, it's a good bet you're dealing with drug dealers, meth cooks, or a nest of dope fiends. Sometimes it's just one monitor and a single camera at the front door. Other times it's a wall of monitors, each dedicated to a single camera.

The tweakers — meth addicts, so named because of their sudden, jerky, tweaky mannerisms — have a particular affinity for surveillance cameras, especially when they haven't slept for days on end and paranoia and hallucinations are starting to kick in. When that happens, Tweaker TV is the best show on the box.

"Looks like they left in a hurry," I say. "Didn't even take the cameras."

"Why bother?" Jimmy replies. "They can steal more."

Both Jimmy and I know what this means. It's not just that Jacob Aase has relocated, he's likely an addict or a dealer, which means tracking him down is going to be problematic. It's easy to get lost in the drug community. There are always flophouses, drug dens, motor homes, and transient camps to disappear into.

"What now?"

"Call Diane." Jimmy sighs. "See what she can dig up. I'll call the PD and see what they have on Jacob."

Sometimes it all comes down to luck . . . or good timing.

I'm still on the phone listening to Diane churn through one database after another in a high-speed digital pursuit of the elusive Mr. Aase when Jimmy taps me on the shoulder, grins, and says, "We caught a break."

Back in the car, Jimmy tries pulling a U-turn from the curb, but the rental — luxurious as it is — has the turning radius of a nine-legged pig. After three trips to drive and two trips to reverse we finally get straightened out, and Jimmy starts to fill me in.

It seems that Jacob Aase landed himself in the Tehama County Jail three weeks ago after multiple motorists called to report a naked man walking down the center of Manzanita Avenue swearing at cars as they passed by and sometimes cowering behind light poles talking to himself.

After a ten-day meth binge, Jacob was tweaking hard. The skin on his face and right arm was covered in red sores where he had repeatedly picked at the imaginary bugs under his skin — meth mites — until he was covered in scabs, then he picked the scabs. Then he picked some more.

By the time the cops found him on Manzanita he was in full meltdown. Recognizing immediately what they were dealing with, Red Bluff PD tried talking him down from his psychosis, but by this time the hallucinations were so vivid and frightening all he saw were blue devils with badges.

"They stole my clothes," he screamed over and over and over again as he picked and picked and picked. Meanwhile, officers discovered a two-block trail of discarded clothing, starting with a particularly foul piece of underwear — officers dubbed it *the*

underwear that crawls — that was unceremoniously draped over a fire hydrant. Working
backward they found socks, then jeans, then
shoes — a discount brand designed in the
fashion of the Nike Cortez but without the
quality. Farther on, they found his shirt
stuffed under the windshield wiper of a
Dodge Neon — he's a tweaker, they do stuff
like that — and his jacket was lying in the
middle of the road thirty feet west of his
backpack (which was filled with clothes
even more stanky than *the underwear that
crawls*).

He didn't discard the clothing, though.

He made that perfectly clear.

No.

They stripped him naked and *They* stole
his clothes.

Then, apparently, *They* — he was never
quite clear on who *They* were — laid his
clothes out behind him just to taunt him.

In the end it took four blue devils to
restrain him and carry him off to hell . . .
though in this case "hell" was the Tehama
County Jail. Not pleasant, but by no means
does it resemble the fiery abyss.

They even have ice.

And they only have three levels, not the
nine described by Dante — though the first
floor sometimes *smells* like the Malebolge,

Dante's eighth level of hell. It can't be helped. That's what happens when inmates paint the walls of their cell in their own feces.

Good times.

"His car was parked in the street a half mile away," Jimmy says. "When he ran out of gas he just started walking . . . and stripping."

"Okay, what's scary is that he was *driving* in the first place."

"Drug-impaired driving. Happens every day in every city across the country." Jimmy shrugs. "The only thing worse is the drunk drivers; they still kill more people."

"Yeah, but that's just numbers. There are more drunk drivers than tweakers."

Jimmy shrugs again but doesn't say anything.

"So the car is in police impound?"

"The meth pipe on the front seat was enough to get a search warrant. The shotgun in the trunk and the three small baggies of meth in a hidden compartment in the door were enough to seize it. It'll probably end up back at the same auction where Jacob bought it."

A Red Bluff officer named Danny Coors — like the beer — meets us at the impound yard with a ring of keys and ushers us through the gate. Danny's a nice enough kid, but overly rigid and formal, everything's *Yes, sir* and *No, sir,* and *I'll check on that, sir.* Probably hasn't been out of the academy more than a year.

Don't get me wrong, such courtesy would be perfectly appropriate if he was giving me a ticket, but we're all on the same team here and I get uncomfortable when people call me sir, especially fellow law enforcement.

"I'll unlock it for you, sir."

Jimmy starts to make small talk with Danny, who's unlocking the driver's door, then the passenger's door, then the trunk, while I walk around the exterior of the Hyundai. Ashley's car may have been nice years ago . . . many years ago . . . but it's a full-fledged doper car now. Every corner is bent or blemished, like a dog-eared book that's been loved too much or too little. The right rear taillight has red tape covering a gaping hole from an incident with a baseball bat; the windshield has a horizontal crack that runs the length of the glass; the rear bumper is held together by faded, peeling stickers; and the radio antenna is cockeyed. Its best feature is the two-tone paint job: faded silver and rust.

Sad Face is all over the vehicle.

His shine is in the driver's seat, on the

door, the steering wheel, the trunk, even the gas cap. *He drove it long enough to put gas in it.*

Ashley's all over the vehicle as well. The patch of shine in the trunk is particularly disturbing because it's shaped like a curled-up body; it's not a place one would willingly go. The original carpet is missing, as is the spare tire, leaving a filthy metal base with a tire-sized hole in the center. At some point the car was used to haul everything from trash to old car batteries and used motor oil, all of which have left their mark on the small space.

She was alive when he stuffed her into this nasty black hole.

I can almost see her struggling in the dark. She certainly would have been tied or duct-taped, but she must have slipped her hands in front of her because I see them all over the latch, groping for a handle, a knob, a button — something that would pop the trunk, something that would set her free.

She would have been smarter to rip the wires from the taillights, I think. That, at least, would've gotten the right kind of attention. Kicking the taillight out and sticking a hand through works even better.

There's no shine on the underside of the trunk, either; no fist-shaped glimmer where

195

she pounded and beat and pounded on the trunk, hoping someone would hear. Hoping *anyone* would hear.

No. She was quiet as a mouse; trembling in the dark; afraid.

Afraid *he* would hear.

Afraid of what *he* would do.

Ashley's shine is flat and dead; no vibration, no pulse, no life. Her fate was sealed when she was placed in that trunk. Better if she had kicked and screamed and pounded until the heavens shook. Her end may have been no different, but a mouse has two choices: it can walk into the lion's mouth and lie down upon its teeth, or it can bite and leap and claw and spit its last breath.

Better to fight than to lie down.

When Officer Coors is out of earshot, I whisper to Jimmy, "He's all over the car."

Jimmy nods his understanding and sighs. "I was hoping she was in Cabo."

"Me, too."

"Did he drive this one, or just leave his mark?"

"Oh, he drove it —" I begin, but Jimmy stops me with a furtive hand motion and indicates to the left with his eyes. I see Danny coming back toward us.

"You find what you're looking for?" Officer Coors asks, looking from me to Jimmy, then back to me.

"Typical doper ride," I say, giving him a crooked smile and thumbing toward the car. "Hard to tell how much of this mess was Ashley's and how much was Jacob's."

"I hear ya. The worst of it was cleared out when it was impounded — moldy hamburger, used syringes, used condoms, stuff like that. About twenty pounds of pure nasty. I don't know how they live like that."

"I don't call it living," Jimmy says in a tired voice.

"I just pulled the property sheet," Danny says, waving a lined and columned page in his hand. "It looks like they took about fifteen pieces of stolen property from the interior and the trunk. I don't think any of that had to do with Ashley, though. Most of it was linked back to several burglaries we had a few months back. A couple items that weren't claimed are still in evidence, including . . . let's see." He scans quickly down the list. "A ring — a dolphin ring, it looks like. Plus there's a package of brand-new unopened men's socks that were probably shoplifted, and . . . here it is, a TomTom GPS."

"The GPS might be worth a look," Jimmy says. "Remember Quillan?"

"Yeah, not a chance," I say. "We're not

that lucky."

We take a chance anyway.

Danny leads us into the main warehouse, where, with the help of an evidence technician, he retrieves the impounded GPS. The batteries are dead, so it takes a few more minutes to find and cannibalize a desk clock in the office that has the required AAA batteries.

"Try holding the button down for five seconds," Jimmy says after the new batteries have no effect.

"That only works on a frozen computer," I say, "and only when you're trying to shut it down, not turn it on." But I hold the button anyway.

Nothing.

And still nothing. Technology is a marvelous apocalypse of electricity. No wonder people sometimes lose their mind and pump some twelve-gauge slugs into their computer. In most cases it's justifiable.

Danny retrieves the clock batteries and seals the GPS back in the evidence bag. "I'll send it to the lab. Maybe they can retrieve something from the chip." I hand him my card — *Magnus Craig, Operations Specialist, Special Tracking Unit, FBI* — and he promises to call in a day or two.

Back in the car, Jimmy scribbles some

comments in his notebook . . . again. He hasn't even hinted at what he's working on, which has me curious, and therefore irritated. He knows it's killing me, but I'll let him do his thing, play his little game. He'll tell me eventually. He has to. I mean, it has to be something related to the case, he just wants to make sure he's right before he pops it on me.

I can wait. Sure I can wait. Patience is a virtue and the sign of a calm, mature mind. He'll tell me soon enough, no sense in getting all spun up over it.

"*What* do you keep writing in that notebook?" I blurt as he closes the cover and stuffs it back into his dark brown Fossil Estate leather portfolio briefcase.

Damnation!

Virtue — gone.

Patience — gone.

Jimmy doesn't answer right away, but pushes back in his seat, fishes the keys out of his pocket, starts the car, adjusts the radio, checks his hair in the mirror. After spending forever adjusting his seat — seriously, he could have built a new one faster — he lifts his sunglasses just enough so I can see his eyes and says, "Patience is a virtue," then throws the car in gear.

Damnation!

The rest of the day goes quickly. First to Weed for Sarah Wells, where we don't find any of Sad Face's shine on her car, but we do find his mark on her mailbox in pink crayon. Her body was dumped in the Shasta National Forest west of Weed, along a hiking trail but obscured by bushes. The park rangers were able to take us to the exact spot: a dim, oppressive patch of wood with violence spilled upon the ground in a rainbow of color.

I could feel the trees pressing in . . .

. . . leaning over me.

Whispering.

Always whispering.

We finally make our way back to Millville, a small community just east of Redding, for the first victim, Valerie Heagle, whose body was dumped in the Odd Fellows Cemetery off Brookdale Road. There was no attempt to hide her body and the story got a lot of local attention, probably more than Sad Face wanted.

He was more careful after that.

Since the body was found outside the Redding city limits, the case landed in the lap of the Shasta County Sheriff's Office. Everything in the case report shows a competent, well-executed investigation, but there was no DNA, no hair follicles, no prints, nothing to point to a suspect or even hint at one.

The killer had done his homework; forensics revealed that the body had been washed down in bleach. The interior of Valerie's car, a 1992 Jeep Cherokee, had also been wiped free of prints and spritzed with a bleach solution.

The only good news is the vehicle is still in police impound. It's locked away in a storage building protected from the elements, the same building that holds Alison Lister's Honda, but in a separate room. When we arrive and walk through the roll-up door, I see it tucked away in a corner, the sad relic of a heinous crime now collecting dust and years.

Sad Face is all over the Jeep: the driver's seat, the cargo area, the glove box, and, once more, the gas cap. Cut into the grime on the back window, almost indistinguishable now, is his mark. The eyes have blurred out to hazy smudges, but most of the circle is intact, along with the nose and half of the ugly, downturned mouth.

I see it all in neon amaranth and rust.

CHAPTER FOURTEEN

Redding, 8:13 P.M.
Jimmy has a theory.

He won't tell me the theory, but assures me it's valid and says it explains some of what we've seen. On the drive back to the hotel I press him for his thoughts. "Just a hint," I say, but he's stubborn and mulish when he's working on a theory, has been as long as I've known him. To make matters worse, he placed his briefcase in the trunk, so I can't even rifle through it when we stop for gas.

He's wise to me.

"Give it a rest, Steps!" he finally says as we're pulling into the parking lot. "It's not that I don't want to talk about it, I just want to make sure it all makes sense first."

Jimmy has a natural gift for crime analysis; give him a case file and he'll find a dozen things that need further exploration: questions that haven't even been asked, let alone

202

answered. He doesn't trust his instincts enough.

He should.

Back at the hotel, I convince Jimmy to eat something while he works, and we order room service. It gives me an excuse to camp out in his room, a constant reminder that he has a theory to explain.

"Seriously, Steps," he argues, "why don't you go to your room and get a shower or a bath or watch some TV? I'll call you when the food arrives."

"I'll just watch TV here," I reply. "Yours has more channels."

"They both have the same channels," he says with a sigh.

"My room's boring."

"This room is identical to yours, how is it less boring?" I shrug.

"Really? You're going to just sit here and watch TV while I work?"

"Unless you want me to help?"

Jimmy holds up both hands and shakes his head. "No!"

After that he just ignores me.

Retrieving the Bureau-issued Dell laptop from his briefcase, along with two pens, one black and one red, and the offending note-book he's been scribbling in for the last couple days, he settles at the small round table in the corner of the room and gets to work.

Clearly I'm just the eye candy in this brain trust, so I settle back on the queen-sized bed and start flipping through channels. The volume's a little loud, I admit, so when Jimmy casts an annoyed look my way, I turn it down a notch. Apparently one notch isn't enough, because his eyes narrow and he continues staring until I turn it down another five notches.

Touchy!

Room service arrives twenty minutes later, and I dig into a pepperoni calzone with extra sauce on the side while Jimmy pauses long enough to eat his eight-ounce steak smothered in A.1. sauce and a loaded baked potato the size of a large river rock. He's not normally an overly picky eater, but the first thing he does is scrape the chives off the potato.

"Those are good for blood pressure," I say between bites. "You just turned thirty-three a couple weeks ago; you should pay more attention to stuff like that."

"Thirty-three is not old," he shoots back, "and my blood pressure is nearly perfect." Pointing his fork at the little pile of green ringlets, he adds, "You're welcome to them, please. The sooner they're off my plate, the better."

"I'm just trying to look out for you," I say, trying not to grin.

He goes back to his potato.

"They've also got antioxidants that help fight cancer."

He looks at me now, fork in his left hand, knife in his right; I notice they're both pointing in my general direction. "When did you become an expert on chives?"

"We grew chives on the back porch when I was a kid. Mom loves them. Dad's not particularly fond of them but doesn't complain much."

"He doesn't complain because your mother would beat him with a dirty frying pan."

I'm about to object, but then realize there might be some truth to that.

In ten minutes I finish off the monarch's share of my calzone — the thing was huge — and dump the remains in the garbage can. I thoroughly rinse the plate and silverware in the sink and set them back on the serving tray. When Jimmy finishes, I do the same for him so he can finish collecting and sorting his thoughts on the case. As I go to scrape his plate, the only thing left is a lonely pile of chives nesting in A.1. sauce and butter drippings.

Sad. Just sad.

Meanwhile, Jimmy apparently has *a lot* of thoughts to collect and organize. So much so that I finish watching one episode of *NCIS* and I'm halfway through another before he speaks again.

Finally, the theory!

There's a great shuffling as he turns the laptop around to face me and returns the notebook, pens, and miscellaneous scraps of paper to his briefcase.

I hit the off button on the remote and the TV goes black; the room goes quiet.

Jimmy motions to the chair next to him at the table and I grudgingly extract myself from a stack of pillows and blankets.

"You remember your description of Ashley's car?" Jimmy begins. "About how Sad Face's shine was all over the inside, the steering wheel, even the gas cap, like he'd fueled up as some point?"

"Yeah, I remember."

"And it was pretty clear from Ashley's shine in the trunk, and her hands on the inside of the trunk lid looking for a latch or a release, that she was held there for a while, probably just long enough to transport her to wherever he keeps them, right?"

I nod.

"Which other cars looked the same?"

"How do you mean?" I'm puzzled.

"How many did Sad Face drive? How many did he fuel up? How many had the victim's shine in the trunk?"

I think for a moment.

"Other than Ashley there was . . . well, Valerie Heagle for sure . . . and the one from Susanville —"

"Tawnee Rich."

"That's right . . . and Leah Daniels. I think that's it."

"You're missing one."

I think for a moment, running the names, the cars, the shine around in my head.

"Jennifer Green," he says without waiting.

"Jennifer Green, right, I remember: Crescent City."

Jimmy pushes a piece of paper across the table. At the top of the page the victims are listed in chronological order of their disappearance, starting with Valerie Heagle. Jimmy watches me as I study the list; he doesn't say a thing, just lets me digest it.

"Do you see it?" He knows that I don't and loves every minute of it.

I hold my finger up, begging for more time.

"It's right in front of you, clear as day."

"If it was clear as day you wouldn't have

spent two days working on it."

"I had to do some research first."

"Research?"

"Yeah, I had to let you check for shine."

"So *your* research is actually *my* research?"

He grins. "Well, if you put it that way, I suppose so."

"Wonderful." I push the paper away. "And what did *my* research reveal?"

"*Our* research revealed a strange phenomenon hidden within the first five lines of the list." He pushes the paper back to me.

"Line number one?" he says. When I don't answer, he gets annoying. "Line number one, come on, Steps, what is it?"

I glance down at the paper. "Valerie Heagle," I growl.

"Number two?"

"I'm not playing this —"

"Line number two?" he persists.

"Jennifer Green," I snap. "And then Tawnee Rich, and then —"

Dammit! I see it. He's right.

"— and then Leah Daniels and Ashley Sprague, the first five victims."

"And," Jimmy says, "the only victims whose vehicles were occupied by and driven by Sad Face."

"But we're up to eleven victims; why only

the first five?"

"That's the big question. Something happened, something significant enough to cause him to change an established routine. We figure out what it was and we'll be closer to catching him."

"Maybe he didn't have a car during the first abductions."

"Maybe."

"But you don't think so? You think it's something else?"

Jimmy shrugs. "I think he liked using the victims' cars. I think it gave him a sense of power and added to the fantasy. It's not something he would give up easily. Besides, if it was working so well for him, as it appeared to be, at least for the first five victims, why switch to your own car? That just increases the risk. Now it's *your* license plate number someone might see as you're stuffing the victim in the trunk, or *your* license plate number attached to the parking ticket written outside the victim's apartment. That's how they caught David Berkowitz, you know."

"Berkowitz?" *I know the name.*

"Yeah, the Son of Sam killer."

"He got caught because of a parking ticket?"

"He did," Jimmy says.

I mull this over a minute. "So, what if Sad Face used the victims' cars because, like Berkowitz, he almost got caught for some other crime, maybe a burglary or a robbery, something like that, and learned his lesson about using your own car during the commission of a crime? If that's the case, what's he doing for transportation now? He wouldn't use his own car, or a rental — that can still be traced back to him."

"Maybe he uses his own car, but swaps out the plates for some that are stolen?"

"That's good," I say. Then I remember something from a conversation three months earlier. "Dex was telling me that a lot of their dopers buy cheap cars and never put them in their name. They just drive them awhile and then sell them to someone else."

"Don't they have to register the car in their name to renew the tabs?"

"Yeah, but you can drive up to a year before the tabs expire. And if the seller doesn't fill out a report of sale and turn it in to the Department of Licensing there's no way to find out who actually owns the vehicle."

"I like that one better than the switched plates," Jimmy says, "but that's not going to help us track Sad Face, if his real name's not attached to anything. And we don't have time to wait for him to screw up."

No, we don't, I think. I reach into my pocket and pull out the locket, Lauren Brouwer's locket. It still pulses, like a small heart beating in my hand. Jimmy watches me from the other side of the table. After a moment, I slide the locket back into my pocket.

"We need to work faster," I say.

Jimmy just nods.

CHAPTER FIFTEEN

I was ten years old when I lost my mind.

It was temporary . . . mostly.

When I emerged from the woods two years earlier — and recently dead — the shine was no more than a dusty hue brushed over the world with gentle strokes. A lot changed in two years. By age ten the shine had fully blossomed: an apocalypse of color that shoved its way through my eyes and bounced around inside my skull.

I hadn't yet learned to control it, to turn down the volume. That wouldn't come for a few more years, and then slowly; in the meantime I lost my mind. I remember my father cradling me in his arms when I sobbed, his eyes wet with a father's grief, not knowing what to do.

We kept it from Mom as best we could, though I heard snatches of conversation on occasion, usually late in the evening when they thought I was asleep, and often after those days that were particularly tough. She knew something was wrong, but never got the *why* or the *what* of it out of Dad. He would deftly answer her questions without answering and then redirect her concerns in a harmless direction.

It was best that way.

Meanwhile, Dad was determined to find a solution to the shine, so we started spending weekends on a variety of father-son outings. We consulted experts in various religions, in mysticism, in spiritualism. We visited several parapsychologists and one regular psychologist. We experimented with colored glasses and infrared lights.

Often we'd find ourselves on the waterfront looking out at the Puget Sound. There's no shine on the water, just beautiful waves of normalcy. It's here that we first started to learn how to control the shine, to mute it and hide layers.

Dad would place a ball in the surf with just two or three distinct shines on it. That ball, set against a backdrop of beautiful shine-free water, allowed me to focus on one shine at a time and, eventually, to turn the others low, like you would with a dimmer switch. I've never been able to completely shut it out, not on my own, but the relief that came from learning to turn the neon glow down is indescribable.

It came at a price.

The effort of it gave me headaches, real skull-pounders that throbbed at the front of my head. The first few times it happened I remember holding my eyes closed with my hands. The pounding was so bad I thought my eyes might pop right out of my head; I was determined to hold them in.

It was on a trip to a glass studio a month before my eleventh birthday that things changed, and for the better this time. Mom was with us; it was actually her idea. She had been talking about taking up pottery or some other hobby and wanted to see what glassblowing was like. This particular studio was having an open house, and though we had to drive an hour to get there, Mom determined that it would be quality family time.

Of course she loved it: the studio, in addition to the quality time.

The studio was in a surprisingly small work space with an odd assortment of metal tools and stands and three metal doors built into the wall, each opening into a separate furnace with a separate purpose. We soon learned that one was the main furnace, where molten glass waited to be collected and shaped. The second was the glory hole, a furnace used to reheat a piece as it was being worked on. Finally, there was the lehr, or annealer, used to slowly cool the glass over hours or even days.

When we first entered the shop, a glass-blower, or gaffer, was taking a raging-hot glob of shapeless glass from the furnace using the end of a long metal rod — which, I soon discovered, was hollow. The blob began to take shape as the glassblower blew air through the rod and then rotated it around and around and around like a piece of wood on a lathe. In no time at all it began to resemble a vase with bands of color, called caning, running from top to bottom.

That's about the time I lost interest and wandered into the gift store attached to the shop. Here was every manner of bowl and plate and vase and glass, a thousand colors shining and reflecting from ten thousand facets.

Near the front of the store was a magnificent platter propped upright on a wooden stand. The glass was clear, with a flourish of burgundy and blue on each end. I remember giving it a casual glance as I passed, the glance of a disinterested ten-year-old on an art outing with his parents.

But something in the glass caught my eye.

The glass was so crystal clear — ironically

because it *was* crystal — that I noticed a fingerprint on the backside. A single fingerprint on the upper edge, most likely left when it was placed on the stand.

Big deal, it was a fingerprint.

Only this fingerprint didn't have any shine. *Big* deal! Huge!

Walking around to the other side of the table, I stared at the backside of the platter. There before me was a fingerprint in dark walnut dappled with rose petals. It stared back at me; hell, it slapped me in the face. I couldn't take my eyes off it. Every fiber of the feltlike texture was on display . . . as clear as crystal. I moved back to the front of the platter.

Nothing: a fingerprint.

It was maddening, overwhelming, amazing.

I wanted to scream, *DAD, DAD, DAD,* and run into the other room, but I realized that would be unwise and hard to explain. Instead, I walked with excited steps back into the shop and tugged at dad's right hand, trying to pull him into the store while at the same time trying not to garner too much attention.

Dad resisted, caught up in the magic of glowing glass and dark metal tongs.

"Da-aaad," I whined . . . though I kept

the volume to a whisper.

He ignored me.

I tugged again . . . and again . . . and again.

"What is it, Mag—" The look on my face when he whirled around, or maybe it was the tears stretching down my checks, startled him, and he whisked me from the room, shepherding me in the crook of his left arm.

In the store, he knelt before me and held me at arm's length, looking me up and down. "Are you all right?" he asked. "Did you hurt yourself?"

I remember shaking my head and taking him by the hand. I led him to the platter and just pointed as the tears started to fall again.

"What, Magnus?" he practically pleaded. "What?" He glanced through the opening into the workshop and saw that Mom was still engrossed by the glassblower.

"Do you see the fingerprint?" I asked. I used my own small finger to guide his eyes, until the tip was just inches from the glass.

"I see it," he answered.

"So do I."

I burst into tears and threw myself into his arms. Over the next ten minutes he had me look through maybe a hundred different pieces of glass and crystal, always with the same result. Soon it all made sense. Glass had no effect; it was something we'd experimented with before with no luck, despite what colors might be added to it. But put a crystal in front of my eyes and every bit of shine was magically erased, as if it never existed. Move the crystal away, and the shine returned in all its hideous glory.

The glassblower found it a rather odd request, but within a week I had my glasses with their lead-crystal lenses: my special glasses.

And with them I reclaimed my sanity and my life . . . until some dozen years later when the FBI took both away. At least this time I have some say in the matter. I can quit anytime I like. Jimmy says so.

I can quit anytime I like.

CHAPTER SIXTEEN

June 28, 7:47 P.M.

"Diane, it's almost eight, what are you still doing in the office?"

"My boys are in the field," Diane replies. "Where else would I be?"

"At home reading a book," I suggest. "At the movies; bowling; Zumba classes . . . anyplace but the office. *Someone* on this team has to have a real life."

"This *is* my real life. Besides, I don't bowl . . . or Zumba."

"I'm worried about you, Diane," I say, but she just laughs. "So what's this interesting tidbit?"

Her tone changes instantly. "I know how he picks his victims," she replies.

My pulse quickens and I feel the sudden rush of adrenaline. "Hang on, Diane." I wave Jimmy and Walt over and search for the speakerphone button on the keypad. "Go ahead, Diane. You're on speaker."

"As I was saying, it occurred to me early this afternoon that the kidnap sites are sporadic: Susanville, Red Bluff, Oroville, Crescent City, even Medford, Oregon. His range is maybe a hundred and fifty miles in every direction, with Redding as the hub."

"So he's a delivery driver of some sort," Jimmy offers.

"Or a forest ranger," Sheriff Gant says. "Maybe a logger or a hunter. Most of the area you're describing is covered in national parks and national forests. You've got Shasta National Forest, Trinity National Forest, Lassen Volcanic National Park, Six Rivers National Forest, Klamath National Forest, and the list goes on. You can't go anywhere in this part of the country without tripping into a national forest or park."

"Or he reads the newspaper," Diane says patiently.

"What do you mean?" I say, leaning into the phone.

"Our victims were all pictured — pictured, mind you, not just named — in various newspapers and weeklies in the months prior to their disappearance. All but one: Valerie Heagle."

"The first victim," Jimmy says.

"Correct. Other than her, I have photos of all of them within weeks or months of their disappearance: Jennifer Green out of Crescent City, Tawnee Rich out of Susanville, Leah Daniels out of Eureka — she was singled out for her volunteer work with dementia patients. Some reward."

"So of the eleven victims, you found ten," Jimmy muses. "Lauren Brouwer included?"

"Lauren had her fifteen minutes of fame five months ago when she won a local writing competition — it had something to do with the personalities of dogs. Three months later she vanished."

"That's good work, Diane," I say.

"Well, someone has to do some honest work around here." I can almost feel her sarcastic grin on the other end of the phone and can't help smiling myself. "Oh, one more thing," she says as I'm about to disconnect. "I'm sure you geniuses have already figured this out, but the bodies recovered so far have all been found in Shasta, Trinity, or Tehama Counties — if we exclude Nevada — and not one of them more than seventy miles from Redding."

"So he likely lives or works near Redding," Jimmy says, "but he's willing to range farther afield when he finds a victim he wants."

"That was my assessment," Diane replies.

"I like it," Jimmy says. "It makes a bit

more sense now, and your newspaper theory explains his erratic pattern. Anything else?"

"Isn't that enough?" Her voice is heavy with feigned hurt — the old fraud. Jimmy gives me a grin. In the background we can hear her typing away, scouring the Web, continuing the hunt, kicking over one digital rock after another in search of the next clue. She loves piecing things together before we do — *piecing the puzzle,* she calls it. "Now, if you don't mind," she adds, "I'm late for my Zumba class."

CHAPTER SEVENTEEN

June 29, 6:15 A.M.

There's a buzzing in my head, some kind of alarm, persistent and irritating. Heather's gone — though she was just here. She was wearing royal blue and her long hair was swirling and lifting from the wind as it dipped in and out of the sunroof in my Mini Cooper . . . and the ringing, ringing, ringing won't quit. Each shrill intonation is like a crowbar on my eyelids, prying and pounding and prying again until I can't take it anymore.

"Hello," I grumble into the phone, barely lifting my head from the pillow. "Walt? Whoa, slow down! Which . . . no, don't tell them anything . . . I know . . . How many?" Sheriff Gant is spitting mad and yelling through the phone, then apologizing for yelling, then yelling some more.

"I'm sorry, Steps," he says, pausing for breath. "I don't mean to yell, but this is going to make things a lot more difficult, and quick. If I get my hands on the rat-bastard that did this —"

"It's all right, Walt," I interrupt. "It's not the first time something like this has happened, and it probably won't be the last. Let me grab Jimmy and we'll be down there as quick as we can."

"Yeah, I tried calling him first, but there was no answer."

Glancing at the clock, I say, "He's probably in the gym. I'll track him down. This is your show, Sheriff, but it would be a lot easier if you didn't talk to anyone until we can come up with a game plan."

"I'm not talking to anyone," Walt grumbles. "I might yell at a few folks, though."

Jimmy blows a gasket when I tell him.

He's just finishing his workout routine and insists on hopping in the shower for a minute. Even at that, he's dressed and we're on our way in fifteen minutes. It's a short drive to the sheriff's office and we're soon pulling into the parking lot. Lining the street are news vans from CNN, Fox News, and KRCR News Channel 7 out of Redding. As we park the car, a van from KRON out of San Francisco pulls up and parks behind the others.

Walt comes storming over as soon as our

noses breach the door. He's waving copies of the *Sacramento Bee,* the Redding *Record Searchlight,* and the *San Francisco Chronicle.* The one story title that's fully visible reads "Serial Killer Stalks Northern CA."

"Three so far," Sheriff Gant says, slamming the papers down on a desk in front of us. "Two front-page stories and a page-two. Plus, I've got voice mail from a dozen newspapers, radio stations, and TV stations . . . and the day hasn't even started. This is about as inside as it gets; they even list the victims by last name, first initial, and age. That came from someone familiar with the investigation."

"Why don't they just list their full names?" I mutter. "The damage is already done."

Jimmy snorts. "This way they can claim they're protecting the privacy of the victims' families." He looks at Walt. "Any idea who leaked it?"

The sheriff shakes his head. "I hope it wasn't one of mine; I'd like to think they have better sense than that, but I can't be a hundred percent sure." He suddenly squints his left eye until it's half closed, smashing down the corner of his mouth. There's a queer look on his face. "There was something . . . now that I think of it; it had to come from the source." He fishes through the stack of newspapers and retrieves the *Sacramento Bee.* Laying it flat on the desk, he quickly flips through to page A8, where the story continues from its front-page introduction. There, embedded in the text, garnishing the story, is a crisp and revealing black-and-white photo.

My mouth falls open. "You've got to be kidding me!"

Jimmy's fingertips are white from pressing into his temples. He stares silently at the image, an image showing two men in FBI Windbreakers at the scene of one of the body dumps.

"That's a good picture of you," I say in a soft, sarcastic voice. Then, with a frown, "My hair's all messed up. Why does that always happen to me when we're in the woods, yet you always look like you just walked out of a salon?"

"I go to an old-fashioned barber in Lynden, not a salon."

"Still, you've got that whole GQ thing going on."

The article doesn't name us, but our faces are plain to see and the pack of hungry hyenas cloistered in their vans out front won't have any problem putting two and two together; more specifically, the two faces in the picture and the two of us.

Looking closer at the image, I notice a fallen log in the background, ripe with fungi, sheared on one end where the wind had snapped the upper part of the tree off in some year past. The forest floor is thick with pine needles and last year's leaves. I remember the smell. "That's where Sarah Wells was found, just outside of Weed toward Mount Shasta."

"You're sure?"

"I never forget a forest. They're like nightmares with leaves."

Jimmy's thinking now. "We had to hike in a ways —" He snaps his fingers and turns toward me, holding his right hand like a gun and rocking it back and forth. "Remember that female park ranger? Her uniform didn't fit right, it made her look lopsided?"

"Really tall?"

"Yeah. She had a camera with her, but I don't remember her taking any pictures. What was her name . . . Harper . . . Harbor . . . ?"

I can picture her in my mind: mottled tan with a trace of turquoise and the texture of beaded glass. "Hooper, wasn't it?"

"Hooper! That was it."

"Where'd she get this level of information, though?" Walt asks. "Her only involvement was during the recovery of the body

227

last year, and then taking you two back to the scene."

I walk over to the bulletin board next to the coffee machine and extract a red pin holding a single-page flyer. Handing the paper to Walt, I say, "Every law enforcement agency in northern California, including the U.S. Forest Service, got a copy of this."

The flyer, issued by the Shasta County Sheriff's Office, alerts law enforcement to a possible serial killer — Sad Face — and asks for information on any similar cases. It lists victims and locations, and has an excerpt from a preliminary profile of the killer.

"Damn." Walt sighs. "How's this going to affect the investigation?"

"I don't know, Sheriff," Jimmy answers honestly. "These guys are going to be all over us from here on out. We'll just have to deal with it the best we can. You're going to have to talk to them at some point, though."

The room is silent a moment, then, in a beaten-down voice, Walt says, "Sorry 'bout the flyer."

"No need to be," Jimmy says strongly. "That's standard procedure. You wouldn't have been doing your job if you *didn't* send one out. The only one who needs to apologize — and lose her job — is the person who gave that photo and the information to the press, whether it's Ranger Hooper or someone else."

"It's just the media," I add. "We'll deal with it."

It's not the first time.

"Twenty-ounce mocha, single-shot, decaf, one percent milk with no whip," I say when I reach the counter.

"Single-shot *and* decaf," the barista chides, a quirky smile blossoming between her nose and chin. "Sure you don't want some coffee with your coffee?"

Before I can respond, I hear Jimmy pipe up behind me.

"He doesn't like coffee." It's a programmed response he's used a hundred times over the years to defend my honor, and my coffee. His voice is flat and the comment so ingrained that in three minutes he won't even remember having said it. His eyes are tight on his cell phone screen, never looking up.

That's Jimmy.

Mr. Multitask.

"That's a pretty complicated drink for someone who doesn't like coffee," the barista purrs, turning her brown eyes back on me. "How's that happen?"

"I was forced into a coffee shop against

my will . . . repeatedly." I tip my head toward Jimmy.

She has Heather's laugh and a beaming smile. Her name tag says Gail, but she seems more like a Susan or a Kathy . . . at least, more like a Susan and a Kathy that I know, I can't speak for them all.

"What's your name?" Gail asks.

When my eyebrows lift, she quickly jiggles the paper cup in front of me, saying, "It's for your order," but I notice she doesn't ask Jimmy for his name. *Mm-hmm.*

As we head out the door I say, "Good coffee," without having taken a sip. "We should come back tomorrow."

Jimmy's still scrolling through his messages, oblivious.

Halfway down the block my phone rings.

It's Diane and she's in a mood. I can hear it in her voice, like gargled gravel with a hot-tar chaser. Jimmy must have done something to irritate her.

"Officer Coors from Red Bluff PD called," she growls, "said he's working on a case with you?"

"Yeah, what'd he say?"

Silence.

"Diane?"

"Some joke. It's not funny . . . not even clever." *Gravel, gravel, gravel.* "It's actually sophomoric. You can't do any better than that?"

"Do any better than what?"

"Knock — it — off, Steps. It's not funny. And I've got better things to do, hon."

"Okay, let's try this again. Officer Coors. Red Bluff PD. Case. Message?"

"And I'll say *again* — it's not funny. Joke's over."

"Diane, you're not making sense?"

"You know exactly what I'm talking about, and I'm not falling for it."

"Uh . . . no, I don't. What do you mean? What joke?"

"Come on, Steps, I'm an analyst. I know when I'm being jerked around."

"Diane, I'm going to fly up there and take away your iPad, your coffee, *and* the chocolate-covered macadamia nuts you keep hidden at the back of your bottom drawer if you don't tell me what you're talking about."

"*Coors!* He's *working on a case* with you. Beer comes in a case. Coors is a beer. I even had him spell it to make sure I was hearing him correctly. C-O-O-R-S. I wrote it down."

"Wow!" I blurt into the phone. "*That* — is an epic fail, Diane. Epic. That one goes on the board." The "board" is the whiteboard in the conference room, the bottom right corner of which is devoted to a laundry list of significant screwups. Jimmy and I dominate the board, while Les has one entry and Marty has two. Diane has never made the board. Until now.

The phone is silent.

After a moment, Diane's voice grates through the earpiece, paving the way for the words that follow. "Explain. Please."

"Officer Coors is Danny Coors," I respond in a pleasant, oh-so-cheerful voice. "He's with Red Bluff PD, just like he said, and he's trying to get some data off a dead GPS found in Ashley Sprague's car."

More silence.

"Diane?"

Her voice is subdued — unusual for Diane. "Well, that partially explains the second part of the message."

"How do you mean?" I can't help smiling.

"He said, *'Memory's shot,'* and *'If beer can't fix it, it's hopeless.'* "

I chuckle.

I don't even try to hide it.

"Not beer as in B-E-E-R," I say, "Behr as in B-E-H-R. She's the lab tech."

CHAPTER EIGHTEEN

June 29, 12:07 P.M.

Tami pokes her head into the conference room and opens her mouth to speak, only to become transfixed by my fingers as they sort out the water chestnuts from a bowl of chicken stir-fry. "That's the best part, you know," she says after a second.

"Not in my book," I reply, glancing up only briefly. "They have the texture of raw potato and no flavor to speak of. Some starving person ate one five thousand years ago and didn't die of it, so now we're stuck with them as accepted cuisine. It's the same thing with snails, balut, and scores of other foods I don't care to think about while I'm eating."

"Balut?"

I look up from my stir-fry grudgingly. *Didn't I just say it's something I don't care to think about while I'm eating?* "It's a duck embryo that's boiled alive in its shell and then eaten, starting with the broth around the embryo, which is sipped from the egg before peeling."

Tami half gags. "That's disgusting!"

"As I said." My fingers are back to work on the water chestnuts.

In my peripheral vision I see her watching me, and then she slowly shakes her head. "I still say you're missing the best part."

"Not — in — my — book," I say, plucking a disgusting morsel with each word. The last one I toss in her direction. Instead of dodging it, she catches it and pops it into her mouth.

As the receptionist for the Shasta County Sheriff's Office, Tami's no stranger to odd behavior; she sees it every day . . . and not just from deputies and the occasional FBI tracker. To the public, she's the face of the sheriff's office; to the deputies, she's a chokepoint: a filter.

She's like an old 1940s switchboard operator, but instead of phones, she plugs people into the right slot. Sex offenders go to a Sex Crimes detective for registration, concealed firearms applicants are directed to the Records Division for fingerprinting and application submission, witnesses are handed off to detectives, those waiting for a polygraph sweat it out in a lobby chair until the examiner is ready for them, victims queue up to see the station deputy, packages are received, and Hershey's Kisses are handed out to anyone walking by with a need for chocolate.

Tami has the place wired, and with a willow-tree waist, black hair, and a smoky tan, she has the looks to match her natural talent and charisma.

"There's a guy in the lobby who says he needs to talk to the FBI. He wouldn't give me any details but said it's about Alison Lister."

"Another psychic?" I ask, though it's really not a question. "Maybe a mental?" I add, then pause and look up, not at her, but at the wall directly in front of me, as if it holds some secret revelation. "Or better yet," I muse, "a twice-convicted felon looking to get his charges dropped for some half-baked information? Yeah, I like that. Please let it be a half-baked felon," I say, turning toward Tami.

"Wow!" she snorts. "And I thought I was jaded." Her left eyebrow is perched high on her forehead, looking like some mutant hairy cobra about to strike. It's pointed in my direction. "Just my personal opinion," she says, "but this one seems legit."

Legit. That would be refreshing.

I stare disappointedly at the steaming stir-fry, my mouth watering. With an intentionally loud sigh I set my fork next to the unopened chopsticks. Placing the bowl in the community fridge — which smells like ten-day-old balut — I wipe my hands on a paper towel and follow Tami to the lobby.

Chas Lindstrom doesn't look like a psychic or a psycho — not that I know a lot of either type. He doesn't strike me as an ex-con, either, so I extend a hand, force a smile, and greet him like I'm ever so glad to see him. In twenty sentences that could have been two, he tells me he's a cell phone salesman for Verizon — Salesman of the Month in May — and is on his lunch break.

Lunch break, I think, forcing a smile. *Me, too.* Feigning an itchy eye, I remove my special glasses for a moment and quickly size Chas up: dirty purple with a stucco texture. Not even close to Sad Face. Still, I had to check. Serials, particularly the killers and burners, have been known to inject themselves into investigations. Some get an extra thrill out of it; for some it's just an extension of the fantasy they're making up as they go along; and for a few it's a way of muddying the water to throw off the investigation.

Three years ago I had just such a case.

The guy wasn't a serial — yet — but he was working on it. With two victims to his credit, he was a walk-in, like Chas, and claimed to have seen the second victim get into a tan Volvo wagon after the bar closed. We interviewed him for an hour before I happened to take off my glasses to rub my eyes, and there he was: all essence and texture.

I'm a little more suspicious of walk-ins these days.

Still, Chas seems to be on the level.

"About two months ago," he jabbers, "I go out to my truck to go to work and I notice this piece of paper lying on the seat. It stands out because I keep my truck neat — no garbage, no clutter. My sister, Peggy, she's got like six months of fast food bags, empty soda bottles, candy wrappers, and crap like that on the floor of her car. It's disgusting. I don't know how she can drive around like that. Know what I mean?"

He pauses, like I'm supposed to respond to that. I just nod my head in agreeable disgust.

"Well, like I said, the paper stood out and at first I thought it dropped out of my notebook — I keep a notebook to track my sales statistics, sales techniques that seem to work better than others, that sort of thing." He produces his leather-bound portfolio and flips it open to the indexed pages with their color-coded entries. "The note was folded into quarters, though, and I don't fold my pages, as you can see. The creases weaken the paper and distort the text. It's just not a smart practice."

I'm starting to like this guy.

"So then I'm thinking someone stopped by to visit while I was in the bathroom or asleep, and they just left a note in my truck — weird, I know. But when I open the note, there are just these fifteen entries, one to a line, and it doesn't take a genius to figure out that they're first initials and last names. The top eleven entries have a little check symbol next to the name, and the first ten have a line through the name.

"So now I'm thinking it's someone's fantasy football notes or something like that and I put it in the glove box in case someone comes looking for it — at this point I'm still thinking it belongs to one of my friends; one of my three friends, actually. I find that any more than three or four friends at a time is a bit of a burden, don't you? Anyway, there it sat. I completely forgot about it. And then I saw the newspaper this morning. J. Green, T. Rich, D. Grazier, A. Lister, they're all on the list. So now I'm thinking this isn't fantasy football. This is like a death list or something. Am I right?" He pauses. "Which means this is the killer's list and he was in my truck for some reason."

I suddenly feel that prickly sensation you get when the hair rises on your neck, and I hear myself asking, "Do you have the list?"

"Sure," Chas replies, "it's right here." He reaches for his shirt pocket and I shout, "No!" startling both of us. Holding a finger up, I say, "Don't touch it. Stand right here and I'll be back in a second."

Rushing into the reception office, I bark two words: "Tami. Gloves."

Without missing a beat, she tosses me a box of disposable latex gloves. I pull out a pair and toss the box back.

The latex groans softly as I pull them on, first the left, then the right. Gently, I reach into Chas's shirt pocket and retrieve the folded paper. With my left hand, I lift my glasses an inch and gasp aloud at the brilliant amaranth and rust. The paper is awash in it, almost as if the bastard had rubbed it over his body.

"Chas," I say, "I think you're my new best friend." I hold up that single universal finger, the one that everyone understands regardless of language or culture — no, the other universal finger. "Stay here for just a moment," I say. His eyes are fixed on my index finger like a drunk doing a sobriety test. Probably doesn't help that I have it six inches from his face.

Tami's on the phone when I rush into her office. After listening politely to the person on the other end of the line for twenty seconds — an eternity — she says, "Please hold," and directs the call to Detective Forgendirgenstern or something like that and smiles at me as she hangs up the phone.

"You called that one spot-on," I say, thumbing toward the reception window and the lobby beyond, where Chas is taking a seat and looking around at the plaques and pictures on the wall.

"You got something?"

"Just the Holy Grail, that's all." I hold up the paper.

She smiles and nods. "The Holy Grail looks different than I thought it would."

"Yeah, yeah. Can you *boop-boop* Jimmy for me? He wandered off somewhere with the sheriff and I need him to interview Chas ASAP. I'm running to the copy room to burn a few million of these." Pointing to the lobby, I add, "Don't let him leave! I don't care if you have to tase him and duct-tape him to a chair."

"I don't have a Taser."

"You'll think of something."

"I'll threaten him vigorously with my letter opener."

"See?" I say with a grin. "That's creative. I like that."

As I head down the hall, Tami's voice booms over the PA system requesting that Special Agent Donovan report to the front desk.

An hour later, we have everything we need, including Chas's white 1992 Ford F-150 pickup, which is impounded pending a thorough sweep by at least two crime scene investigators. Chas is gracious enough to sign a consent form allowing a search, so we don't need a warrant. It probably helped that Jimmy rented a new Mustang for him.

Jimmy has an expense account.

I don't have an expense account.

I once asked why I don't have an expense account and was told I don't need one. I don't need a pet whale, either, but it would be cool to have one.

Back in the conference room, Jimmy plops down in a deformed chair that looks like it fell out of a Salvador Dalí painting. When he turns to the left it *thu-thu-thu-thu-thumps;* when he turns to the right it squeaks like a miniature banshee; when he leans back it groans like some restless spirit with its finger in a vise.

I'm thinking Jimmy needs to take that expense account and buy the sheriff a new chair, one that's not possessed. Better yet, a dozen chairs, that way they all match.

"So," Jimmy says, "what are we thinking?"

I'm thinking I need a damn expense account.

I put the thought aside and say what Jimmy already knows. "He steals cars to commit the abduction and then returns them to the exact spot they were stolen from so the owner is none the wiser."

"Chas was adamant that he never leaves his keys in the ignition," Jimmy throws out, "and there was no evidence of tampering on the ignition — at least none I could see."

"So he's got some car skills," I say, "or an assortment of shaved keys."

A favorite among car thieves, shaved keys are nothing more than old car keys that have been ground down a bit. The locks and ignitions on older vehicles, like Chas's truck, tend to wear down and loosen up over time so that even an inexperienced thief can often start the car in twenty or thirty seconds with a shaved key.

"An auto thief turned serial killer?" Jimmy wonders aloud.

"Or a serial killer turned auto thief." I shrug when Jimmy looks up. "It's not like he's interested in the cars, right? He's just covering his tracks. Actually, it's pretty smart — and kind of scary. How else do you explain Chas's death list? We know Sad Face didn't toss it through the window as he strolled by; his shine was all over the interior."

Jimmy leans forward, sips at his coffee, and thinks for a moment. "You're certain the only other shine you recognized on Chas's truck was Lauren's? Not even a hint of Alison, or maybe —" He sees the look on my face and quickly holds up his hand. "Right, right. Sorry. It's just that Chas's truck looks a lot like the one in the Walmart surveillance video. It's even the right color."

"White's a popular color for trucks."

"It's not just that. You said it yourself, that he's probably using a shaved key. Doesn't a shaved key have to have started as the same make: a shaved Honda key to steal a Honda, Chevy for Chevy —"

"Ford for Ford." I see where he's going with this. "So maybe he only has one shaved key and has to keep stealing the same type of truck?"

Jimmy taps his nose with his index finger.

"That helps a little, but not much," I say. "The Ford F-150 is a popular rig."

"Yeah, but ask yourself this: *Why that type*

of vehicle?" He reaches into his back pocket, pulls out a wallet that looks like a booster seat, and extracts a $50 bill with his thumb and index finger. Dangling it in the air a moment, he places it gently on the table, slides the booster seat back into his pocket, and says. "Fifty bucks says that's the same make and model he owns. Probably had a copy of his own key made and then shaved it down."

I don't have a $50 bill in my wallet. I have a debit card, my driver's license, and a punch card for the place where I get my hair cut (three more punches and I get one free). No $50 bill, though. If I had a $50 bill it would probably elope with the expense account I don't have.

"I'd take that bet," I say boldly, for a guy with no $50 bill in his wallet, "but I think you're probably right." Then, in a somber voice, "I also think Chas's aptly named *death list* is exactly that. And based on what he wrote down, it looks like Sad Face preselects his victims well in advance." I hold a facsimile of the list up, but Jimmy only glances at it. I'm sure he already has it memorized. "The check next to each name indicates he's kidnapped them. Then, when he kills them, he draws a line through the name. So the last time he touched this note was right after he killed Alison Lister and abducted Lauren Brouwer."

"I know," Jimmy says in a quiet voice. He's silent for several long moments, lost in thought. Eventually he turns slowly in the moaning chair until he's facing me directly. "I think we need to focus on the last four names on the list, the ones without the lines or checks. If we can figure out who they are, we can break the cycle, throw him off his game. Save some lives."

"What about Lauren?" I want the words to come out calm, matter-of-fact, but when they leave my mouth they have an edge to them, an urgent and raw vibration that hints at distress. Inside I'm screaming, *I promised her mother. I promised!* Somehow that internal scream cuts through mind and matter and attaches itself to those three words: *What about Lauren?* I realize that I'm clutching the locket in my pocket — Lauren's locket — and rubbing it with my thumb as if it were a worry stone.

"We're not giving up on Lauren," Jimmy insists.

I wish I could be so sure.

CHAPTER NINETEEN

June 29, 2:45 P.M.

"I ran all four names through CLEAR," Diane says, referencing the massive public records database run by Thomson Reuters and used for corporate security, fraud investigations, skip tracing, and other purposes. It's a favorite tool of the FBI and other law enforcement because you can locate just about anyone.

Whenever you order cable TV at your new apartment, apply for a loan, get a new cell phone, apply for water and sewer service, or set up just about any other "public" service, the data is added to the tens of billions of public records stored in various corporate databases.

These are the databases that CLEAR calls upon when a query is run. And for those in law enforcement there's a special version of CLEAR that provides more and better information. It's a bit Orwellian, but the database is an indispensable tool and a favorite of Diane's.

"P. Nichols is most likely Peggy Nichols," Diane continues, "the twelfth name on the list; she moved to Florida last month. Looks like she just closed on a three-bedroom rancher in Punta Gorda — that's a bit south of Sarasota. I'll include her new phone number in the e-mail."

"Can you call the Punta Gorda Police Department as soon as you're off the phone and advise them of the situation? And if they don't have a PD, call the county sheriff's office."

"I called both before I called you. They tended to agree that the chance of Sad Face going all the way to Florida is remote but promised they'd notify Peggy and take the appropriate precautions until we give them the all-clear."

"Well . . . good, then. You're one step ahead of me."

"Of course I am."

The tap dance of fingers on the keyboard drifts through the phone and then Diane continues. "Number thirteen, M. Milne, is Melissa Milne. I'm close to a hundred percent on that because there haven't been any other Milnes pictured in any of the fifty-seven newspapers I've scanned, at least not in the last year and a half. Melissa lives in Redding; the address the sheriff's office has for her looks like it's still good. Same with number fourteen, Nikki Dearborn, and her husband Tyson. Their place appears to be a twenty-acre mini-ranch just outside Anderson."

"How about B. Contreras?" Jimmy asks.

"That one was a little tougher, but it's most likely Becky Contreras," Diane says. "I had four different addresses for her in the last two years. After some cross-referencing, which wasn't pretty, I was able to trace her to an apartment in Corning."

"Corning?"

"It's a small town fifteen to twenty miles south of Red Bluff, population less than eight thousand. It's also known as Olive City and is home to the Bell-Carter Olive Company. Wikipedia says it's the largest ripe olive cannery in the world."

"Fascinating," Jimmy replies dryly. "Do you have an address?"

"It'll be in the e-mail with the others," Diane replies a bit tersely, taking Jimmy's lack of interest in the mechanics of olive production as a snub against olives and, by association, olive lovers — which must include her.

"And when can we expect this e-mail?"

"I just sent it, didn't you hear the *click*?"

248

"I must have missed it."

"I thought as much."

"Bye, Diane."

"Mm-hmm."

Within the law enforcement community there are nicknames and acronyms for just about everything. It's much like the military in that sense. For example, a *holster sniffer* is a police groupie, a woman — or man — who loves the uniform and the authority it represents. At the opposite end of the spectrum is your standard *asshat,* a drunk or high knuckle-dragging degenerate looking for trouble.

Flip-a-bitch means to make a U-turn; a *fishwalk* is the ground-dance a suspect does when being tased, also known as *doing the funky chicken;* and *leering and peering with the intent to creep and crawl* is generally what an *Adam Henry* (asshole) is up to when you just can't figure out *what* he's up to.

Within this extensive cop vernacular is the term *law-enforcement-friendly,* which describes a citizen who generally appreciates the police and is cooperative; an upstanding citizen who is always ready to help.

Melissa Milne is not law-enforcement-friendly.

Melissa Milne hates cops.

Jimmy is nearly speechless. "Miss Milne, I just told you that a serial killer has you on his target list."

"And I told you to get off my porch, ass monkey."

Ass monkey? I mouth to Walt; he just shrugs.

"Ten women are dead," Jimmy practically pleads. "It's been all over the news."

"I don't give a — Hey! Where are you going?" she suddenly barks, pointing two cigarette-encumbered fingers at me as I start walking toward the side of the house.

"I'm just checking to see where that smell's coming from," I reply, glancing down the side of the house. "Smells like . . . fresh marijuana; a lot of it."

"The hell you say."

"The hell I *do* say," I shoot back. Jimmy's giving me a confused look and hustles off the porch and over to my side. "What are you doing?" he hisses.

"She has a grow-op upstairs," I say flatly. "The windows are covered with newspaper and she's got a pretty good ventilation system going. Plus, she's making eight to ten trips to the shed in the backyard every day. Nobody makes that many trips to their shed *every day* and still has a yard that looks this crappy."

Jimmy's impressed. He steals a glance at the second-floor windows to confirm the newspaper and sees that every single window is covered.

"How's that help us check for Sad Face's shine?"

"Watch."

Turning, I make my way back to the ass-monkey expert and lean on the bottom porch rail. She's just glowering at me, not sure what to think or say. "Here's the way I see it," I tell her. "You let us walk around the edge of the property, let us check the outside of the doors and windows to see if they've been tampered with, and we won't need to get a warrant to search the inside of the house . . . particularly the upstairs."

She catches my meaning immediately and the corner of her left eye gives an involuntary twitch. She stands there a moment — fuming mad; she knows I have her cornered. "Fine!" She spits the word at me, thrusting her head to add force. "But you better be gone next time I look out." Without waiting for a response, she turns and lets the screen door slam behind her.

It takes less than five minutes to give the place a thorough walkabout. There's no sign of Sad Face. Not on the ground, at the windows, on the cellar door — we even check the mailbox.

Nothing.

Still, she's on the target list, so Walt assigns a deputy to park discreetly on a parallel street that offers a good view of the entire property. It'll be that way with the other targets as well: a twenty-four-hour protection detail, seven days a week, until Sad Face is caught. It's not going to be cheap, but it's better than the alternative.

The next stop is the Dearborn Farm just outside of Anderson, California. After following I-5 south from Redding for about twelve miles, we exit onto Riverside Drive and make our way to Dersch Road. Three or four miles down the road we cross over Cow Creek and soon turn into the driveway on the left. A black metal arch stretches over the gravel entry announcing DEARBORN RANCH in large white letters.

It's not *really* a ranch. I know this because ranches have longhorn cattle and horses and five hundred acres of grazing land and a ranch house with a metal triangle that you ring when it's time to come in for lunch or dinner.

All I see is goats, hundreds of them.

It should be called Dearborn Goat Farm.

The sign at the road points to a small nine-hundred-square-foot store where they sell goat milk and goat cheese and goat ice cream, none of which sounds appealing. They also have a wide range of other goat products I didn't know existed, like lip balm and body lotion and soap, just to name a few. Much of it they produce at the farm, but some items are purchased elsewhere for resale . . . which means there are other goat farms masquerading as ranches.

Jimmy's already decided we need to get a goat-cheese pizza and make an early dinner of it. When I curl my nose, he starts extolling the many health benefits and the excellent flavor of goat cheese; personally, I think he's just making this stuff up as he goes. It doesn't matter. He can spout off all he wants; I'm not eating goat cheese.

The Dearborns are salt-of-the-earth people, and after we assure them they're not in any trouble, they immediately invite us up to the house for some lemonade, leaving the store in the hands of their only employee. As we make our way to the house, I give Jimmy a silent nod, letting him know that Sad Face has been here.

His shine was in the store, and it was recent. Apparently he was interested in the goat-based shampoo, because he picked up a bottle and handled it extensively, though this was probably a ruse so that he could watch Nikki while pretending to read the label. The intensity of the shine suggests he was here within the last week or so. Unfortunately, I didn't see any surveillance cameras in the store.

I'm guessing there aren't a lot of shoplifters targeting goat products.

Inside the house Tyson introduces us to Hannah, their two-year-old brindle boxer. While I'm not much for dogs, Hannah is under the misguided belief that I'm her biggest fan and shames me into scratching her behind the ears. She's a pushy little thing because whenever I stop, she sticks her nose under my hand and lifts it up, prompting more scratching and petting.

"So what's this all about?" Tyson says with a nervous laugh.

Jimmy takes a deep breath and then explains the situation in the most direct and thorough manner he can without compromising the investigation. Walt and I sit silently by. We watch the faces of Nikki and Tyson go from shock, to concern, to abject terror. By the time Jimmy finishes, Nikki's nearly in tears . . . and that was the sugar-coated version.

It's going to get worse.

After a well-timed and subtle suggestion, Walt stays with the Dearborns as Jimmy and

I walk the property and check the exterior of the house. In a low voice I tell Jimmy about the store, but as we work our way around the property, I see Sad Face everywhere. He's been in the barn and around the house; I even find his handprint on several windows and a couple doors. The prints are flat and lack any dermal ridge detail, indicating he wore gloves, probably latex. That's unfortunate.

The only good news is he never made it inside the house. It looks like he tried but failed, for some reason. My guess is Hannah scared him off.

On the outside of the master bedroom window, tucked down in the corner, we find a small wireless camera. It's well hidden by the bushes outside the window, as are the two wires going down the side of the house to a D-cell battery pack on the ground.

"He's got them strung together for longevity," Jimmy says, referring to the batteries. "He can probably run the camera for two or three weeks like that. Then all he has to do is park nearby and intercept the signal: instant Dearborn TV."

"Do we tell them," I ask, leaning my head toward the house, "or just remove the camera and not say anything? They're already freaked out."

"They should be."

"So you're going to tell them?"

"I think we have to." He studies my face. "You disagree?"

I shrug. "I think they already get it. There's such a thing as too much information and, frankly, a camera peeping into your bedroom is about as intrusive and unsettling as it gets. The thought of Sad Face parking nearby or crouching in the woods and watching them in the privacy of their own bedroom, well, I think that'll push Nikki into a bad place. They still have to live in this house and sleep in the bedroom and work in the shop."

"They'll have twenty-four-hour security," Jimmy argues. "From what we've seen, Nikki's high on the target list, so in addition to one of Walt's plainclothes detectives, we'll request an FBI surveillance team. We'll have our own cameras watching the house, the shop, even the woods and the road. There'll be three or four people here day and night."

"All the more reason not to mention the camera," I say. "We can loosen one of the wires on the battery pack so it looks like the batteries went dead. That way if Sad Face comes back he won't be able to get the signal. Maybe he'll think it too risky to replace the batteries. But even if he does, that gives us one more chance to catch him." I shrug. "Maybe we can chain up a noisy dog outside the bedroom window. That would keep him away."

We go back and forth a few more minutes before settling on a compromise: we'll tell the Dearborns that Sad Face has been to their property, that he's been around the house and barn, but we won't mention the camera.

Even at that, the news doesn't go over well and Nikki goes into full-blown meltdown. Who can blame her? Between comforting her and talking to us, Tyson makes a couple phone calls from the kitchen. By the time we leave, two of Nikki's brothers have arrived, each carrying a hastily-thrown-together backpack over his right shoulder — just the necessities: underwear, socks, a toothbrush, toothpaste, clothes, and five hundred rounds of .223 ammunition. The ammo is for the matching pair of AR-15s they carry slung over the other shoulder.

They're here for the duration.

It's good to have brothers.

Becky Contreras isn't home when we reach her place in Corning at 6:27 P.M. Her apartment is on the third floor, which narrows

Sad Face's abduction options considerably. Since there's no sign of him on the stairway, we focus on the parking lot and the laundry room and come up empty. No footsteps around the edge of the complex, no handprints on the back gate, no cameras in the bushes.

Looks like Becky hasn't made it to the A-list yet.

Either that or we have the wrong B. Contreras.

Since we're now outside Walt's jurisdiction, having left Shasta County and crossed into Tehama County on the drive south, Walt places a call to Tehama County Sheriff Paul Meeker, who he's on a first-name basis with, and fills him in.

Soon a Tehema County deputy arrives in the parking lot and backs into a free space that gives him an unobstructed view of Becky's apartment.

"Paul says he'll talk to Becky personally when she gets home, so he can explain the situation without terrifying the girl," Walt says. "She'll have whatever protection she needs and an escort everywhere she goes."

It's the best we can hope for in this, the worst of situations.

Still, Jimmy doesn't like the idea of parking a cop in plain view, arguing that we're tipping our hand, letting Sad Face know that we're on to him. But in the end, it comes down to the first rule of law enforcement: protect the public. In this case, that means Becky Contreras, regardless of the consequences to the case.

My eyelids are heavy as we head north on I-5. It's been a long day. Maybe I'll sleep well tonight. Maybe I won't dream . . . maybe. . . .

CHAPTER TWENTY

June 30, 7:42 A.M.

The hotel's complimentary breakfast is better than most and Jimmy's already halfway through a second helping of French toast when I make it downstairs. I grab a poppy-seed muffin and an orange juice and settle into the chair next to him.

Jimmy's intent on a crossword puzzle, so we eat in silence while the room around us murmurs with sleepy morning sounds: subdued voices, shuffling feet, coffee percolating, newspapers rustling, spoons rattling.

Most of the breakfast club consists of businessmen and businesswomen already dressed in their best attire, with briefcases and laptops at the ready. Even now you can see they're pumping themselves up for the day ahead. If they're staying in a hotel, it means they have an important meeting or sales pitch ahead of them.

Then there are the tourists. You can spot

them a mile away because they're wearing shorts, flip-flops, suntan lotion, and hallelujah smiles — that's the smile that plants itself on your lips when you realize you don't have to go back to work for two more weeks.

The businesspeople smile, too, but it's that polite smile we all wear when we're not really happy but have to pretend we're glad to see you or excited about the day ahead. It's a hi-how-are-you? smile, not a hallelujah smile.

"A tower," I say, tapping Jimmy's crossword puzzle.

"What?"

"Seventeen down, a group of giraffes."

"A group of giraffes is called a tower?"

"It is."

"That sounds like something you just made up."

"Google it."

He does — which is a bit insulting.

"How'd you know that?"

"I'm a genius."

He snorts and takes another bite of French toast.

Five minutes later the crossword puzzle is finished. I stuff what's left of the muffin in my mouth and chase it with orange juice as Jimmy wipes his hands on a baby-blue napkin and grabs his Fossil briefcase.

A smoky sky weeps as we exit the lobby, casting down a host of tears the size of cherry pits and sending us scurrying across the parking lot, our heads hunched low between our shoulders — as if that's going to stop the creeping wet. The forecast called for a partly cloudy day with a 10 percent chance of rain.

They were 100 percent right.

Our rental car is a blue Ford Escape and it looks miles away through the downpour. As usual, the rental agreement's in Jimmy's name, since he's the one with the expense account. He's also the only authorized driver, since it costs eleven dollars a day to add a second driver.

Jimmy assures me this isn't intentional, it's just that he wants me to be free to watch the road, the vehicles, the people, and the places; like I'm going to suddenly spot Sad Face thumbing a ride as we cruise down some backcounty road.

I suspect Jimmy doesn't trust my driving . . .

. . . which is ridiculous.

I've never been in an accident and I've only ever gotten one ticket, and that was for doing twenty miles per hour *under* the speed limit, which shouldn't even count. It was like a reverse speed trap: a slow trap. The speed limit changed from twenty-five to forty-five, and a half mile down the road Bubba Gump was waiting for me in a turn-out.

I feel edgy just at the thought.

It happens every time I see a traffic cop. Guilt sneaks up from behind and shanks me in the kidney. It doesn't matter that I'm in law enforcement; primal instincts take over. On that particular day I crept by Bubba at twenty-five, my eyes glued to the speedometer. I made sure I used my blinker well before the next turn, kept my wheels between the lines, and tried not to drift back and forth too much in my lane of travel.

Intense driving.

Religiously adherent to the rules of the road.

Suddenly lights were behind me, followed by a short *brrpt brrpt* of the siren. I was still swearing at my speedometer when he got to my window; and when he told me what I was getting pulled over for, I must have said, *You're kidding,* a dozen times.

I just paid the fine and told no one.

Something like that can ruin your reputation.

Jimmy's an alpha male, so I let him drive. Alpha males don't like the passenger seat because it doesn't fit well. If they're forced to sit in the passenger seat they just squirm and complain. I'm pretty sure I'm not an alpha male. I mean, I'll take charge of a situation if no one else steps up, but I prefer to be the guy in the background.

I'm probably a bravo male.

Bravo males are important because they help out the alpha males and say, *Bravo! Bravo!* whenever they do something right, even if it's infrequently. This positive reinforcement is vital because alpha males have large egos that constantly need refilling.

This morning the rain drives any thought of alpha males and bravo males from my mind, leaving only wet males in its wake. Despite a shielding hand, the morning storm consumes my special glasses and turns the world into a warped and fragmented kaleidoscope. Halfway across the unending parking lot I take them off and slide them into my shirt pocket. I'm ten paces from the Escape when something catches my eye.

No.

I stop abruptly; the rain beats me down. Jimmy's still hunkered down, eyes to the pavement, when he runs into me from behind. Like a pinball, he bounces off and tries to go around, his only thought to get out of the rain. I reach out and grab his sleeve, pulling him up short.

"What?"

The shine glows boldly through the rain, bursting forth with intensity. It's new, maybe three hours old. Jimmy sees it in my eyes, in the creases of my forehead, but I say it anyway. "It's Sad Face. He's been here."

In an instant his gun is out and at a ready position. Sweeping left, he clears the front of the vehicle and the bushes beyond while I sweep right. There are two distinct and separate tracks; one is coming and going from the landscaping at the front of the nosed-in Ford, the other is in the parking lot near the rear of the vehicle.

Neither track is connected, which is odd. I stare at the parking lot track for an eternity, oblivious now to the rain. All of a sudden it clicks. It makes sense.

I wave Jimmy over and raise my voice above the rain. "He must have our license plate number." I point to the pavement at our feet. "He drove through the parking lot looking for our SUV, then, when he thought he had the right Ford Escape, he got out right here and walked over in the dark to check the plate number." Pointing to the right, I continue. "He got back into his car and parked somewhere else, then came back on foot."

I open the Ford's passenger door and my gut convulses. He's all over the inside: in the seats, under the seats, on the visors, in the glove box. An ugly swath of brilliant amaranth and rust lays across the interior, a hideous beast asleep on the leather.

Inside the glove box, every document has been handled and searched. Most are irrelevant: owner's manual, satellite radio instructions, that type of thing. One piece of paper, however, is covered in amaranth.

"Jimmy," I say, holding the paper aloft, "it's the rental agreement; he was *really* interested in it. Looks like he was holding it with both hands, and he turned it over and over, like he was looking for —"

Of course

"— the renter's name." My words are a whisper.

I stare at Jimmy, immobile.

"Dammit!" Steam appears to rise off his body, as if something smolders below the surface, burning off the rain. "Dammit!" he repeats. "The bastard was watching us. He probably staked out the sheriff's office right after the media blitz. It wouldn't take much to single us out, especially with our picture plastered all over the paper. We're going to have to change vehicles — and hotels."

"Yeah, but what does he want? He already knows we're FBI."

"He wants names. He wants to know who his adversaries are, who's hunting him. He wants . . ." Jimmy's eyes glass over, and for a moment he assumes the thousand-yard stare.

"Oh, God." His voice is a whisper, a shiver.

"Let me see that," he says, snatching the wet paper from my hand. He flips it over and right side up. His eyes dart to the top and he exhales sharp and hard, like someone just gut-punched him with a lead fist. It almost doubles him over.

"My home address," he gasps.

"Your home add — Oh, no. Jane. Pete. No, he wouldn't. He can't."

Jimmy's on the phone; I'm pacing in the rain.

"He couldn't have made it to Bellingham," I say, more to myself than Jimmy. "There wasn't enough time. Not — enough — time," I emphasize. But there's no answer at Jimmy's house. He tries Jane's cell.

Nothing.

Jimmy keeps calling; over and over he calls, first the house, then the cell, pleading small prayers in between. Begging God. Begging Jane. Begging anyone.

We're jumping to conclusions, I tell myself. *Sad Face isn't interested in Jimmy's family, he's interested in Jimmy. He's interested in me.* But then I remember Alison Lister. I remember Jennifer Green and Dany Grazier and Sarah Wells. I realize that we know little about Sad Face and what motivates him.

Fishing the phone from my pocket, I flip to the contact list and scroll down, eyes searching. There he is. It's too early for the office, so I dial his home phone. It rings and rings, and then the answering machine kicks on. Just as I start to hang up, a voice cuts in. "Hello?"

"Dex. Thank God. I need your help."

Within four minutes the first Lynden officer arrives on Jimmy's doorstep. Within nine minutes two Whatcom County deputies, a state trooper, and two more Lynden officers, including the chief, are on site. With Jimmy's permission I guide them to the hidden key near the birdbath in the backyard. They enter through the front door, and I hear them sweeping each room and calling out, "Clear," over and over again as they work their way through the downstairs, then the upstairs.

It's empty.

No sign of a struggle.

A cell phone sits on the kitchen counter ringing and ringing, then stopping, then ringing some more. "There's a coffee mug with two inches of black in the bottom," the chief tells me. "It's lukewarm. She hasn't been gone long." A check of the garage finds Jane's 2008 Acura TL gone, and the chief calls dispatch and issues a BOLO — be on the lookout — for the car.

"Just a precaution," I tell Jimmy. "He can't have gotten up there that fast."

Time slows, and it's another hour before we know.

It's an hour of cursing as we pace.

It's an hour of rain bouncing off asphalt and traffic moving in surreal slow motion in the distance and bulging clouds weeping and weeping.

It's an hour.

You can never know the endless length of an hour until you walk it off by seconds and minutes. You can suffer a lifetime in an hour. Purgatory isn't a place, it's time.

The call comes at last; it's Dex.

"We got her," he says. "Pete, too. They're fine."

Seconds later Jimmy's phone rings. He's

sitting in the passenger seat of the Escape, soaked to the bone and shivering. The rain is finally letting up, so I leave him in the peace of his wife's voice and give him some space.

Sad Face's trail leads away from the Ford in a southwesterly direction, cutting through the mulched flower beds that define the edges of the hotel's property. It dips down into a depression of rocks and weeds now covered by two inches of storm water. I take little notice of the water as I trudge across the hundred-foot depression; my feet have been at risk of trench foot for the last hour, a little more water isn't going to hurt. My shoes make a wet squishing sound as I soldier on through.

On the other side the ground rises six or seven feet on a gentle sloop, leveling off into a sparse scattering of pine trees. Beyond is a strip mall with a gas station, a convenience store, a Domino's Pizza, and a custom nail salon.

Sad Face's trail ends in an empty parking space at the farthest corner of the lot. Any evidence he may have left — a cigarette butt, an empty beer can, signs of an oil leak, blood — has been washed away with the rain.

I turn my attention to the eaves of the

strip mall. There's nothing above the nail salon; nothing on the Domino's; nothing on the outside of the convenience store. The gas pumps. That's where I find them: three cameras watching the pumps from different angles, but not one of them points to the far end of the lot.

Still, I have to try.

My phone rings as I'm walking through the front door of the convenience store. It's Jimmy. He's exhausted and ecstatic at the same time — you can hear it in his voice. Like a man who just ran a marathon. I tell him where I'm at and ask him to bring the SUV over; my feet have managed to squeeze gallons of water from my shoes and socks and I have no intention of walking through the flooded ravine for a refill.

Jimmy says he's on the way and as I end the call I size up the tattooed clerk behind the counter. He's watching a YouTube video on his smartphone and barely looks up when I approach the counter.

"What can I get you?" he manages after a second, setting the phone to the side.

"I need to see your security footage for the last eight hours."

"You a cop?"

"FBI."

"Really? Can I see your badge?"

His tone tells me he's not trying to verify my credentials, he just wants to see an FBI badge up close. I pull the trifold wallet from my back pocket and hold it out so he can get a good long look.

"That's really cool," he says at length. "So . . . if I wanted to be an FBI guy, what would I have to do? You have to have, like, college for that, right?"

"In most cases," I reply shortly, while thinking, *You haven't got a prayer, buddy.* "You also have to pass a background check, a psychological evaluation, and a polygraph before you're even considered."

"Of course," he replies in a serious tone. "That sounds like the kind of change I need. Like, this is my fourth job in six months and they all pay minimum wage, which I can barely live on, even with food stamps. I bet you guys do pretty good, huh? Paywise, I mean?" He gives me an up-and-down look. "Yeah, you guys make bank. I can tell." He lowers his voice a little and leans across the counter. "So, like, if you've used drugs, would that be a disqualifier?"

"What kind of drugs?"

"Marijuana."

"You can sometimes get a waiver —"

"Well, and some Oxycontin, but my therapist says that's not my fault 'cause it was prescribed to me after my gallbladder surgery."

"If it was a prescribed medicine, that's fine —"

"It was just the first fifteen that were prescribed. I kinda got hooked 'cause I was crushing them up and snorting them. After that I had to score them wherever I could, which was mostly forty-dollar pills from this guy I used to get my coke from."

"Cocaine?"

"Yeah." His face suddenly scrunches up. "That's probably bad, right?"

I open my mouth to reply and nothing comes out. I close my mouth and then open it again. Still nothing. This guy is not much younger than I am and he probably spends a good amount of time complaining about how he never gets any breaks and how he's always stuck with dead-end, minimum-wage jobs.

Even if I took the time and explained to him that all of this — this train wreck of a life he's living — is his fault, he wouldn't believe me. It would always be someone else's fault: a high school teacher, his deadbeat father, his probation officer, his boss, the rich, his ex-girlfriend, global warming. The recipient of the blame would be meaningless because it would be ever-changing. The real culprit, the cause of this broken, dysfunctional life, watches him every morning from the other side of a mirror.

My father once told me that the easiest lie we tell is the one we tell ourselves, because we already know what we want to believe.

Just then Jimmy shuffles through the glass entry door, hands buried deep in his jacket pockets. I use the distraction to steer the conversation back on track.

"How about that security footage?"

Forty-five minutes later we finish reviewing the video from the last of the exterior cameras. Sad Face covered his tracks well. His parking spot was beyond the range of the cameras and his entrance to and egress from the back of the property went undetected. He was either incredibly lucky or he scouted the location carefully before making his move.

We have nothing.

Dex calls while we're on the way back to the hotel to dry off and change clothes. "Jane and Pete have a luxury corner suite at the Chrysalis Inn, courtesy of your boss, Mr. Carlson," he says. "They also have a security detail that will provide twenty-four-hour coverage. I think you can rest easy."

"You made sure they weren't followed?" Jimmy's voice is more relaxed.

"We changed vehicles twice; once at Lynden PD, a second time at the sheriff's office — inside the sally port where no one could see. We also had deputies running interference and blocking roads behind us. Unless this guy can fly without the benefit of an airplane and see through walls, there's no way he followed us. They're safe. They have room service and an incredible view of the water. Oh, and I think Jane's going to want her own Jacuzzi tub when this is over."

"Thanks, Dex," Jimmy says. "Anything you need, you let me know. I owe you for this."

"You owe me nothing. We take care of our own."

The bag is a mound of supple leather the color of chocolate. It yawns open at the top to reveal a consuming mouth that devours anything placed inside: clothes, books, notebooks, cameras, dirty socks, shaving cream, and the other accoutrements that accompany frequent flights and unpredictable stays.

A sturdy leather flap folds over the bag's top — a single massive lip to close the mouth. Three leather straps ending in brushed-nickel buckles serve to bind the mouth shut.

The mouth never speaks.

Though a thousand tales are folded into its creases and pressed into its chocolate, the bag remains silent. It bears the smell of leather that has too long marinated in adventure and misadventure, horror and joy. It's the kind of smell that thrills and satisfies in great gulps so that you find your nose lingering near the open mouth, hoping to be breathed upon.

On each end of the mouth-bag are pockets small and large, each with its own zipper or strap, and of course there's the main shoulder strap for lugging the beast around.

While the travel bag is only a replica of someone's idea of a vintage early-1900s bag, it manages to capture a certain mix of Indiana Jones, John Wayne, and Allan Quatermain.

That's not the reason I bought it, though.

As a young boy — before my misadventure in the woods — I remember playing in my grandfather's leather travel bag. It had a similar look and I remember the straps and particularly the sparkling buckles that *tink-tink-tinked* when you slapped them together. I was small enough — or the bag was big enough — that I could sit inside and pretend it was a submarine. When the captain gave the order to dive, I'd pull the flap over the top and plunge the inside into darkness, which usually lasted no more than four or five seconds before we resurfaced for air and light.

The smell was the same.

Adventure. Misadventure. Trouble and travel.

When I saw this particular bag on eBay five years ago, the lump in my chest decided for me. I probably overbid — I know I overbid — but I had to have it. When it arrived on my doorstep three days later, I was amazed at how it had shrunk since I was a kid. *But this isn't the same bag as Grandfather's,* I reminded myself.

But the smell; it was all over the bag.

Dusky. Musky. Earth.

Sweet and dry and sharp, tickling the nose.

Some, upon receiving such a memory-jolting item, a face-slapper, might have tried to once again sit inside the bag as they did in their earliest years. Others might have sat quietly in the dark during the longest hour of night and held the bag to their chest, breathing in the leather, a thousand memories of a grandfather lost too early rolling around in their head until finally condensed into a small company of soldier tears.

Some might have.

Pulling the bag from the half nook that the hotel tries to pass off as a closet, I set it on the bed, unbuckle the straps, and start fishing around at the bottom. I've become a Zen master of packing over the years, so it takes only seconds to find it.

It's light in my hand; heavy on my conscience.

Removing the Walther P22 semiautomatic from its plastic carry case, I set it naked upon the bed. Next I retrieve the holster, followed by two loaded magazines. Closing the bag, I stuff it back into the half nook. After checking the load on each magazine, I slide one into the grip and chamber a round.

There's something about the *shushing* sound of a slide ramming home, driving a round into the chamber, prepping it for a flight it may or may not take. It's both reassuring and frightening in one metallic *whump.*

Some of my compatriots in law enforcement laugh at my Walther P22. That's okay. I don't mind. Sure, a Glock has more stopping power, and it looks really cool and intimidating, but I like the feel of my P22. I'm comfortable with it. Yes, it only fires a .22-caliber round, but if you use the right ammo it can be a nasty little gun. And I always use the right ammo.

Like my life depends on it.

Fortunately, I've only had to fire the Walther once in the line of duty. Usually Jimmy's there to handle that sort of thing, but in this case he'd stepped away for a few minutes — too much coffee; another reason I don't like the stuff.

I remember it was early November, but the name of the area escapes me. It was in Vermont, though. I remember that. The air was crisp as glass, so cold that it burned your throat on the way to punishing your lungs. White mist poured from your mouth with each breath, followed by a sucking sound and then more white mist. You could feel the cold biting through one layer of clothes after another, working its way in.

I remember it well.

And the shine: calico tapioca. Like something a cat would *hhwoolps* up on the carpet. Though in this case the carpet was made of snow and the *hhwoolsp*ing cat was a six-foot-six Irishman named Pat Mc-Court.

The remote lakeside cabin might have been mistaken for abandoned save for the thin column of gray smoke pulling at the chimney. We hadn't expected to actually *find* him there . . . meaning our backup was an hour away . . . meaning we had to hunker down in the cold and just wait . . . and wait . . . and wait.

Good times.

Then Jimmy's coffee decided it wanted out — *and now, dammit!* — and about ten seconds after he disappeared behind a thicket to relieve himself, Pat McCourt trudged out of the woods with a recently expired pheasant dangling from one hand and an over-under double-barrel in the other.

He was so close I could smell the Jack Daniel's on his lips and the stench of his clothes, rank from cold perspiration.

For a slow-motion second we just stared at each other; each startled in a different way. I'm sure that's the only reason I was able to draw down on him and fire first, though I felt the air move over my head as the shotgun unloaded. When it was all over, I remember standing in snow pulling the trigger over and over again, but nothing was happening. The magazine was empty and Pat McCourt was sprawled motionless on red snow.

I later learned that my first shot took off McCourt's trigger finger, three more shots went wild, another found his right arm, another his left eye — that was the money shot, the death blow, the eye for an eye. Where the remaining rounds went I never learned.

It didn't matter.

Jimmy likes to tell people about my shoot-out with Pat McCourt, how I shot the guy's trigger finger right off. *A million-dollar shot!* he tells them, like I was Wild Bill Hickok or Wyatt Earp. I'm guessing Hickok and Earp didn't puke their guts out into the steaming snow after a shooting. Or maybe they leave that part out of the history books.

Regardless, my gun saved me that day.

Clipping the holster to my belt, I slide the Walther home and lock it down.

CHAPTER TWENTY-ONE

July 1, 10:39 A.M.

"It's a first-edition, first-printing," my brother's voice drones over the phone. "I asked him twice. He said it's got the six blurbs on the back and no price on the front flap."

"And it has the eighteen lines of text on the copyright page?"

"That's what he said," Jens replies.

I've been looking for a true first edition of *The Hunt for Red October,* Tom Clancy's debut novel and the book that launched a new genre of techno-thrillers. It was also the first work of fiction published by the Naval Institute Press.

The first printing consisted of five thousand copies, and the book quickly proved popular with submariners in particular, and sailors in general. As such, these early copies had a rough life. Ripped and stained dust jackets, broken spines, water damage, and missing pages were just a few of the horrors that awaited them. Finding a mint copy at a decent price has been a challenge since Clancy died.

"How much is he asking?"

"It's listed for six hundred fifty, but because you're his *faaavorite* customer — and he said it just like that," Jens adds. "*Faaavorite.* Like you're a candy bar or something. Anyway, he said you can have it for five-fifty."

"That doesn't sound very favorite to me. Tell him I'll give him four-fifty."

"You want me to PayPal the money if he agrees?"

"If you don't mind . . . and send me a text either way."

Jens is about to hang up when he remembers something. "Oh, you got a postcard today; it's from Heather. She's in D.C."

"What's it say?"

"Not much, just, *Wish you were here,* and it's got some giant phallic symbol on the front."

"Uh-uh. Stop it. What are they teaching you at that university?"

There's a pause and I can almost *hear* him grinning on the other end. "Okay, it's the Washington Monument," he confesses. "But if you're going to send *that* postcard with the words *Wish you were here,* people are going to talk. I'm just saying."

"I liked you better when you were ten," I say in a flat voice.

He's still snickering when I hang up.

The package arrives at 11:23 A.M., heralded by Tami's voice over the PA system: "Special Agent Donovan to the front desk, please." The announcement is repeated, and something in Tami's tone quickens my pace; Jimmy's on my heels.

"Did that sound a little edgy to you?" he asks.

"If you mean get-your-ass-up-here edgy, then yes."

Jimmy shakes his head. "What now?"

I recognize the delivery person as soon as I walk into the front office. Shawn or Shane, I don't remember for certain. He works the day shift at the hotel. Nice enough guy but timid and irritable. Not the normal sort to work the front counter at a chain hotel. He's standing at the lobby window holding something between his cautious left index finger and timid left thumb.

Something white, with one corner dipped in wet raspberry.

Not a scone.

It's the size of a small gift box, about three

inches on each side and two inches deep. It's wrapped in white tissue paper and tied off with two strands of narrow red ribbon. The letters *FBI* jump off the top in bold hues of deep burgundy — fat letters, as if written with lipstick or one of those foam paintbrushes.

Seth or Saul — the hotel guy — is holding a neatly folded brown paper towel several inches below the package, low enough that you can hear each drop hit — *tap . . . tap . . . tap* — but high enough not to splatter.

Red drops.

I suddenly remember the scene from *National Lampoon's Christmas Vacation* where Aunt Bethany shows up with a nicely wrapped gift that's sticky and wet at the corner. It's only after Uncle Eddie bravely — *stupidly* — tastes the seepage that they realized that feeble-minded Aunt Bethany has gift-wrapped her lime Jell-O mold. Something tells me the package in Steve's hand isn't Jell-O.

"Hey, Stan." I give him a what-up? chin-lift, like we're old pals.

"It's Sheldon, Sheldon Michaels." His voice is dry: sand blowing against sun-scorched wood; a rasping, scratching, etching voice.

"Sheldon. Right. I knew that."

"Please take this," he says, unimpressed.

"Uhhh . . . no. Not until you tell me what it is."

"I have no idea." He's impatient; irritated. "The manager ordered me to bring it down here. I refused, but he insisted. Please take it."

Jimmy snaps on a pair of latex gloves and approaches the tainted box like a snake charmer moving in on a king cobra. "Where'd it come from?" he asks.

"Some guy just walked up to the counter about an hour ago. I was going to give it to you when you returned to the hotel, but about fifteen minutes ago Tracy noticed it was leaking out one side . . . that's blood, right?"

"Let's not jump to conclusions," Jimmy replies, intent on the box. Taking hold of the ribbon, he lifts it from Sheldon's hands and gently swings it through the reception window. Tami is one step ahead of us and lays down a thick section of yesterday's newspaper on the counter next to the window, and Jimmy lands the box dead center with just one glitch: a single drop of viscous red falls and *splat*s next to a coffee mug full of pens just inside the window.

Tami's not happy.

Without missing a beat, she hands me a can of Lysol and a roll of paper towels. I'm kind of pointing at Jimmy and raising an eyebrow, but she doesn't get it, so I hose down the red dot with disinfectant and wipe it clean.

Sometimes it's just easier to *do* than to *argue.*

"What'd the guy look like?" Jimmy asks as his eyes walk over every side of the box, lingering long on the raspberry corner.

"I don't know . . . average."

"Could you be more specific?"

"Average height?" I suggest. "Average weight, average haircut?"

"Uh-huh."

That wasn't a statement, I think, but before I can say it Jimmy heads me off.

"How old was he?"

Sheldon screws up his face, his eyes drifting up and to the left. "Maybe forty. I don't know. He could have been fifty. Now that I think about it, his hair was funny, like a bad toupee or a wig, only real big in the front, like Donald Trump."

"Donald Trump, huh?" Jimmy mutters. "Hold that thought a minute." Turning to Tami, he says, "Can I borrow your scissors?"

She rises from behind her desk, a pair of

pink-handled Fiskars in her hand. Passing them to Jimmy, she takes a step back and watches from behind his right shoulder as he snips the ribbons one strand at a time and peels them back. The phone rings on Tami's desk, but she doesn't move. When I look at her, she just shrugs, saying, "If it's an emergency, they'll call 911."

Jimmy uses one side of the scissors to draw a slit in the white tissue paper and then peels it back in multiple sections, exposing a rectangular removable lid. With one gloved hand holding the box, the other on the lid, he mutters, "Hold your breath."

We do.

He lifts.

If there was a lexicon of geek-speak, a cumbersome tome dedicated to every term, phrase, and acronym devised by computer engineers, programmers, and users since the abacus was invented, it would include a word that is known, embraced, and practiced by only the most sophisticated of nerds; that word is *overclocking.*

It's a term used by computer geeks to describe the process whereby a computer's central processing unit, or CPU, is tweaked, allowing it to operate at a faster speed than intended by the manufacturer. Faster speed means more computing power, thus speeding up processing time and allowing the computer to do more work in less time.

The human brain also has an overclocking function. Unlike on a computer, where overclocking is achieved by adjusting the CPU's operating parameters, the brain goes into overclock mode when it detects the surreal, the dangerous, the shocking. When that happens, the brain begins to work so rapidly and thoughts are finished so quickly that those experiencing overclocking find that everything has slowed down and crystallized. They're more acutely aware of their surroundings and, after the fact, are amazed at the number of things they observed or thought about in the span of seconds or microseconds.

When people have a close encounter with death and talk about their life flashing before their eyes, they're talking about overclocking. Some researchers even speculate that déjà vu is a form of overclocking — though they don't use that term. They believe the brain operates so quickly at times that it remembers something at the same time that it's experiencing it.

Overclocking.

It's a good description of what happens in the front office of the Shasta County Sheriff's Office at 11:27 A.M. on June 29. In the time span of three eternal seconds, three distinct things happen simultaneously: First, Jimmy drops the box on the counter and cracks an Indiana-Jones-style whip of profanity, which is pretty impressive, since Jimmy doesn't swear. He's still swearing as he tosses the lid back on the box and cringes away, his face set and grim.

At the same time, Sheldon pokes his head through the counter window, his raspy, dry voice saying, "What is it?" though in the slow-motion of overclocking it seems to me the vowels are drawn out, sounding more like, "Whaaat iiiiis iiiiitt?" His beady eyes pry at the box, trying to disgorge its secrets.

And the third thing that happens: Tami faints dead away.

She drops like a bag of cement.

I'm right next to her when her knees buckle and she starts for the floor, which is both fortunate and miserably unfortunate. I manage to grab her by the arm and somehow prevent her head from hitting the desk and then the floor. In the process she takes me down with her, our legs and arms knotted together and falling in slow motion — overclocking.

We land in a frumpy pile.

It's not a good look for me.

Jimmy's eyes haven't left the box. "We have to get this to Evidence." He taps the counter with an arched index finger. "It's going to need to be refrig—" He turns and sees Tami doing the limp-fish sprawl on the floor and me trying to untangle myself from a nest of limbs.

Grabbing my hand, he helps me to a sitting position and then kneels next to Tami and shakes her gently by the shoulder, calling her name in progressively louder tones. She's unresponsive. Taking her left earlobe between my thumb and index finger, I pinch down for a second.

Her head moves.

"Tami," Jimmy says again.

This time her eyes flutter and open. A second later she's wide awake, eyes darting from me to Jimmy and then back. "What happened?"

"You fainted," I say gently.

Her eyebrows press together, confused. "I didn't faint. I never faint."

"Then you died," I reply, patting her hand. "Welcome back."

We help her to her feet and walk her over to a chair.

Now the box — what do we do about the box? More specifically, what do we do about the *contents* of the box? I've still got my special glasses on, so I can't see the shine on the lid or the base or on the contents within, but I don't need to see it to know who's behind this. The game has changed and Sad Face is playing by new rules.

And once more we're playing catch-up.

As the level of buzz-and-hum in the front office begins to pick up, I escort Sheldon down the hall and introduce him to Detective Courtney Smith, who's going to interview him — and babysit him — until a sketch artist arrives in an hour. Sheldon is less than pleased . . . until we make a call to his boss, who tells him he's still on the clock, still getting paid, even if it runs into overtime.

Now he won't shut up.

Somehow he's figuring out a way to stretch a one-minute contact in the lobby of a hotel, where less than a dozen words were spoken, into a five-hundred-page novel, and possibly a sequel. Only one word in ten is of any value: *bla blah, bla blah, bla bla blah,* box. *Bl-blaaaa, bla bla bla blah,* scar.

It's okay. His blather doesn't faze me in the least.

Detectives Division has thick walls . . .

. . . and I'm on the other side.

Jimmy's still fussing over Tami when I return to the front office. We kill another ten minutes taking her pulse, checking her pupils, that sort of thing, but the inevitability of the box is thick in the air. At last, we drag ourselves back to the counter, back to the raspberry-stained paper towel and the snow-white bleeding box.

I pull Lauren Brouwer's locket from my pocket. It's still pulsing. She's alive.

The lid is askew and upside down on the box where Jimmy had tossed it. You can see the edges of its gruesome contents through the gaps around the lid. It's the stuff of nightmares: a severed finger and two eyes still firm and a little wet from the plucking. Even the thought elicits an involuntary shudder. But there's something else, something I didn't see in the initial three-second examination.

Jimmy sees it, too.

Crammed into the underside of the lid is a neatly folded piece of lined paper stained in blood at the edge. Jimmy pries it gently from the lid and opens first one fold, then another, and lays the paper flat on the paper towel. I can see markings on it: numbers and letters in black pen, but I can't make them out.

Jimmy picks the note up and turns it toward better light.

"Fourteen seventy-three Bracker Street,"

he reads.

"That's all it says?"

"That's it."

"Bracker Street? Why does that sound familiar?"

"I don't know," he replies. "I was thinking the same thing."

Curious, I lift my glasses an inch and take a look at the blood on the fringe of the page. The instant I do, my stomach knots into a tight ball and my legs go wobbly.

"Oh, God!"

It's a prayer, not a curse.

I remember now.

CHAPTER TWENTY-TWO

July 1, 11:52 A.M.

The interior of the town house is orderly and spotless.

It's everything I expected . . .

. . . except for the body.

The foyer — if it can be called that — empties into the living room to the right, and up the stairs to the left. Straight ahead a narrow table adorns the hall, upon which are three items lined up in a row: a cell phone, a set of keys, and a name badge.

Two dark-wood bookshelves stand sentinel in the living room, equally spaced on either side of the TV. As a book collector and connoisseur, I'm always intrigued by the titles one finds on the bookshelves of others. It's almost a window into their personality, a peek behind the curtain and into the hidden clockwork of the mind.

I've always thought that every book tells two stories: one told by the author and one by the reader. The reason a person picks up a book in the first place is a story unto itself. One person picks up *Mein Kampf* because he's an anti-Semite, another because he wants to learn the origin of monsters.

The books on these shelves display the mind of their owner not just by their titles but by their order and symmetry. The books are arranged by height *and* by color, beginning with lighter colors on the bottom, such as oranges, pinks, and yellows, and working up to navy blues and blacks on the top shelves. As I stare at the books, I wonder if their owner at one time arranged them alphabetically by author, at another time by subject.

Probably, but it doesn't matter.

Visual symmetry won in the end.

My eyes drift to the body, to the paramedics, to the crimson-stained carpet that had recently been so clean. *Dammit! We should have taken precautions . . . but who could have known?*

In a neat line centered perfectly under the wall-mounted flat-screen in the living room is a row of DVDs, ordered alphabetically from left to right starting with *Æon Flux* and ending with *Zardoz.* Most of the movies in between are of similar genre, as are the books on the shelves.

Chas Lindstrom was a science fiction fan.

I say Chas *was* a science fiction fan because to say he *is* a sci-fi fan would be to imply that he's still alive, and, sadly, he isn't. His body lies in the breezeway between the living room and the dining room, cold to the touch and nearing rigor mortis, that clinical-sounding Latin term that simply means "stiffness of death."

He's been dead a few hours.

His hands are bound behind him with duct tape smeared wet and red, the same red that covers his face, his neck, his shirt. The outer edges have already started to dry, turning from bright red to carmine. Every inch of his face shows signs of a savage beating. His eyes are gone, of course, and his right index finger. They're still in the box tucked under Jimmy's arm.

I don't know why he brought them.

Probably in such a hurry that he didn't even think about it, just tucked and ran. And as we blazed through town to the shrill scream of a dozen sirens, there were many among us delusional enough to believe that Sad Face would cut out Chas's eyes, cut off his finger, personally deliver them gift-wrapped to the hotel, yet leave Chas alive so that we, his adversaries, could feel the gushing relief of saving him. So that we could smile and pat each other on the back and hold his hand while the ambulance rushed him off to a life of blindness . . . but a life.

I knew better.

I always know.

On the carpet next to Chas, written in his own blood, is a sad face . . . with no eyes. The sick bastard thinks he's funny.

"You did good, Chas," I say to the emptiness. It's a hollow sentiment, meaningless, too late. I don't know why I say it.

"He came because of the list." Jimmy's shaken. The words are heavy in his mouth, spilling into the room like bitter water, every syllable overenunciated. He thinks we should have foreseen this, prevented it.

He's right. We should have.

"There's nothing we could have done," I say, tasting the bitterness.

"Why his eyes, his finger?"

"I don't know. Maybe it's a message." I shrug. "Maybe he just didn't like the fact that Chas saw his list, so he cut out the offending parts. He's a serial killer; he doesn't need a reason."

"That's where you're wrong," Jimmy shoots back. "Serial killers are driven by reasons. Just because we find them unfathomable doesn't mean they don't exist." He pauses, staring at the empty vessel that was once Chas Lindstrom. "Trust me, he had a reason."

As we stand by Chas's body, empty of words, Noble Wallace comes through the front door with a young assistant from the medical examiner's office on his heels. Behind them is Sheriff Gant, looking beaten and weary.

"Helluva thing," he says as he comes up between Jimmy and me. He shakes his head, his big shoulders slumped. In a quiet voice he says, "We're getting our asses kicked here, you know that, right?"

"Sorry, Walt," Jimmy mutters.

"It's not *your* fault," the sheriff replies quickly. "You two have done one helluva job. More than we could have hoped for. I'm just stating the obvious." He buries his hands in his jacket pockets. "We're getting our asses kicked."

Nob does a quick inspection of the body, noting the bindings, the missing finger, the missing eyes; the obvious. With the help of his assistant, Mark, he tips the body on its side. The advancing rigor mortis holds the limbs in position, like turning a fiberglass mannequin. It's grotesque in its rigidity.

"No obvious puncture wounds," Nob notes, running his gloved fingers along the back. "No powder marks. The blood appears to be limited to his face, neck, and shoulders, except for some splatter." With a pair of scissors he cuts away Chas's shirt and peels it from the body. "Bag that," he tells Mark as he hands over the shirt.

"Lividity suggests he died right here, or was placed here soon after death." Nob points out the purplish red skin discoloration where the blood has settled to the lower portions of the body as it lay on the floor, pulled down by gravity and the absence of a heartbeat.

Lividity.

Another fancy word used in the death industry. It's Latin for "black and blue" and is related to the word *livid;* which is why you can say *He was livid,* or *He was so mad he was blue in the face,* and you're really saying the same thing.

The next half hour is a blur of activity as the crime scene investigators arrive and start setting up. The town house is secured front and rear and it's not long before a crowd develops and the media arrives.

For my part there's little to be done. Sad Face came in the front door and left the same way. He confronted Chas only feet from where he beat and killed him, and the only other place he went was into the kitchen, to the sink, where he washed the blood from his hands. He was careful to clean the sink thoroughly, and the shine on the bottle of bleach in the cupboard below tells me we won't find any DNA.

Smart.

Before leaving he opened the fridge and I can see where he grasped the plastic rings on a six-pack of Coke, holding it in place or picking it up, I can't tell which. One can's missing, though. And he was careful to wipe away any prints.

I'm standing just outside the living room when Dr. Wallace finishes his site work and sends Mark to the van for a body bag and a gurney. Nob collects his work bag and takes a seat at the dining room table, where he carves out some notes and a few reminders.

Chas is alone.

That bothers me, for some reason; it always has. In my mind I picture loved ones in anguish over the news of such a death; I hear the flurry of questions: *Did they suffer? Where are they now? Are they alone?* When we lose someone, there's something troubling about them being alone. We know they're dead. It shouldn't matter if they're alone. But it does.

I move close to Chas and kneel beside

him, muttering a small prayer. I stay with him until Mark comes back in and parks the gurney next to us. As he's unfolding the body bag, I say, "Give me a minute," and dig my iPhone from my pocket.

I snap a quick photo: another picture for the Book of the Dead.

Mark gives me a quizzical look.

"I collect them," I say in a flat voice.

"You collect pictures of the dead?"

"It's so I remember the ones I've failed." It takes him a second to realize my meaning and then his face goes ashen and he drops his eyes. He wants to say something but can't, and so I leave him to his task.

As I head for the front door, it catches my eye: a weeping wound on seasoned wood, but wood doesn't bleed. It's there for all to see, yet still invisible to the detectives and crime scene investigators milling about.

It's only a spot, but it's fresh . . . and it's all Sad Face.

My partner is engrossed in conversation with a detective near the stairs, something about Chas's eyes, something I probably don't want to hear. I have to prod him a couple times before I get his attention — and then he looks annoyed, like it's my fault I found evidence that could be crucial to the investigation.

"What?" Jimmy whispers forcefully after I drag him into the hall.

I tip my head to the front left leg of the hall table. He doesn't see it at first, so I crouch and draw a circle in the air around it. He crouches beside me, still looking, and then his eyes go wide.

"His?"

I nod.

We're like an old married couple that way: one-word conversations, gestures, the occasional grunt, and constantly finishing each other's sentences.

"We're going to need —"

"CSI," I say, pushing myself upright. "I'll get Palmer."

Terry Palmer is a twelve-year veteran of the sheriff's office and a certified CSI for the last five of those years. Like in a lot of jurisdictions, he's a deputy first. The CSI part of his job is a collateral duty, like a pair of fancy shoes you only wear on special occasions.

"I've already taken a dozen blood samples from around the body," he's saying as I lead him into the hall. "I don't think another's going to make much difference."

"This one's different," I insist.

"How so?"

There's the rub.

I can't very well say, *Because it has Sad Face's shine all over it.* He would instantly have two questions: *What's shine?* followed closely by, *What kind of meds are you on?*

It's the worst part of my job: keeping up the charade. I'm convinced that good lying is something you're either born with or not. I'm in the *not* category and it's usually Jimmy who has to come to the rescue with a good lie.

Still, I've gotten pretty good at the tracking lie because I don't have to say much, just look at the ground, shine a flashlight, outline a heel print with my finger, and generally pretend that I know what I'm doing. It helps that I've gotten better at *real* tracking skills. I try to incorporate them into each search as much as possible, but it's still the shine that shows me the way.

That doesn't get me any closer to answering Terry Palmer's question, though.

Looking down the hall to the front door, then to the kitchen, then down at the single red drop of abundant DNA, I race for the lie . . . only to be rescued by the truth.

It just pops into my head.

I don't know why I didn't realize it before.

"After killing Chas," I say without missing a beat, "Sad Face went into the kitchen. You found evidence of blood in the sink, right?"

"We did."

"Probably from him cleaning up; he had to have blood on his hands, maybe on his shirt, on his face —"

"— in his hair," Jimmy adds.

"He made a bloody mess of Chas and some of that had to transfer." I rest my hands on my hips and nod toward the kitchen. "So he's at the sink cleaning up, and after he's done he wipes everything down so there's no DNA to work with, no evidence of blood."

"He used bleach to wash everything down," Terry confirms. "You can smell it when you get close. It's everywhere."

I know.

"And why would he use bleach if all the blood came from Chas?" I press.

Terry pauses, confounded. After a moment, he says the obvious: "He wouldn't. He must have cut himself during the struggle."

"Or Chas cut him. Either way, he's now worried about leaving his DNA behind. Which means his DNA profile is already in the system."

"Or he thinks it's in the system," Jimmy adds.

I give Jimmy a nod and continue. "I'm guessing he didn't dump bleach on the carpet because it's one big blood spot and the chance of his DNA being pulled from a random, cross-contaminated sample is almost beyond calculation." *It's starting to make more sense now.* "He was worried about dripping blood across the kitchen floor, though, and in and around the sink, hence the bleach."

Taking a step backward, I gesture at the hall table. "Take a look at the blood drop. What side of the leg is it on?"

Terry frowns. "The side facing the kitchen."

"Right. So after cleaning up it only makes sense that he'd leave the kitchen, come down this hall —"

"— and out the front door," Terry finishes, "flinging a single drop from his hand, or maybe his forearm, as he passed the table. But that doesn't mean the blood belongs to the killer," he adds quickly. "He could have had some of Chas's blood on a sleeve or elsewhere that he just missed."

"He just finished cleaning every speck of blood from the kitchen sink and counter, then wiped it all down with bleach; do you really think he was careless enough to miss wet blood on his sleeve or arm?"

"It's possible. He'd be in a hurry, more likely to make a mistake."

I shake my head, now confident in my theory. "No. He bloodied his knuckles, or maybe Chas got a few blows in before he was subdued. Maybe a scratch, a torn fingernail, a bite; there are a thousand ways to draw blood in a fight, especially when you're fighting for your life."

Terry's still skeptical.

"So he does a big cleanup job to hide his DNA but doesn't realize he's still bleeding all over the place?"

"Not all over the place," I correct. "It's just one drop; just one. I've checked the rest of the hall, the entry, and the kitchen: nothing. Just the one drop."

Terry screws his mouth up, pushing his lips off to the left, then off to the right. After a few seconds he says, "All right." Retrieving a cotton swab, he dampens it and kneels next to the leg of the table, gently rehydrating the blood and gathering it in the cotton fibers.

"I'd like to send that sample to the FBI lab, if you don't mind," Jimmy says.

Terry snorts. "Be my guest. The state lab is so overloaded it'd take months to get a response, and that's if we're given priority status."

"We're seeing the same thing everywhere," Jimmy says. "Too much DNA, not enough qualified lab techs."

"What makes you think the FBI lab will get it done quicker? I heard you guys are backed up worse than the state labs."

"We are," Jimmy replies. "But the STU gets priority processing." Jimmy scratches down an address and hands the paper to Terry. "I wrote it down, but make sure you include the words 'STU Priority' and send it to the attention of Janet Burlingame."

"STU Priority . . . Burlingame," Terry says, glancing over the note. "And the results go to this Diane person?"

"Diane Parker. She's our intelligence analyst. I'll have her shoot you the original after she's finished with it."

"Roger that."

As Jimmy and I make our way to the front door, Terry calls out, "A hundred bucks says it's the victim's blood."

Jimmy and I stop instantly, like two bugs smacking the same windshield.

See, in law enforcement, a statement like that is the same as a double-dog dare. You're saying the results are going to be *this* way, the forensic guy is saying it's going to be *that* way.

As one, we turn in our shoes: two slow cogs on the same gear. Terry shoots us a big grin and then winks. The wink just makes it worse. I'm thinking that Jimmy and I are on the same page, which is to accept the bet and take the cocky bastard's bill.

Apparently I'm mistaken.

Instead of hearing, *You're on,* or *We'll take that bet,* Jimmy simply shrugs and says, "Professional courtesy. I can't steal your money."

Terry chuckles. "Yeah, you know I'm right."

Ooooo! Sometimes I could just smack Jimmy. Come to think of it, sometimes I *do* smack Jimmy.

Redding is wearing on me.

Don't get me wrong, the city is fabulous and I'd love to come back under better circumstances. It's surrounded by mountains and beauty and has wonderful architecture, including the Sundial Bridge, an impressive city hall, and the Market Street Promenade, just to name a few.

I see it all in passing.

You get a different view of a city when you're chasing a serial killer; it usually involves police stations, morgues, body dumps, and the seedier side of town.

We've only been back in Redding four days, but it feels like forty.

We've learned a lot and seen too much.

We're exhausted, our minds weighed down by the dead. After the scare with Jane and Pete, Jimmy just wants to see them and hold them. To say that we're unfocused and unsettled and that our mojo's been stolen by a serial killer who's as brazen as he is ruthless would be an understatement.

At five-thirty Jimmy makes the call.

We're heading home . . . but just for a day or two.

We're not done with Sad Face.

Not even close.

Chapter Twenty-Three

July 2

The view from Big Perch is magnificent year-round.

Each season has its own splash of color, but summers are particularly glorious. Today is no exception. By noon the sun starts baking the west-facing deck, and I'm forced to retreat under the awning to avoid an unpleasant case of sunburn. The Pacific Northwest isn't exactly known for its sunburns, but when you have northern blood, as I do, it doesn't take much to crisp the skin.

I'm about halfway through *Full Black,* a thriller by Brad Thor, and I'm determined to finish it by the end of the day. I've followed Thor for a number of years and have a signed first edition, first printing of his debut novel, *The Lions of Lucerne.* I'm a big Vince Flynn fan as well, and I was upset when cancer took him at such a young age.

I have a few of his books stacked up and ready to read and have sworn to read his entire works out of respect for the man: my own personal tribute.

There's just never enough time.

Today's the exception. I read and read and read some more, pausing only long enough to grab a glass of iced tea. The phone only rings once and I don't answer it. They don't call back, so I know it's not important.

By 4:15 P.M. *Full Black* is fully read, and I start in on Vince Flynn's *Extreme Measures.* I don't get very far before Ellis wanders over and suggests a barbecue. He has some two-inch steaks he's been wanting to cook but says it's a shame to enjoy such a treat alone. When I'm home, Ellis, Jens, and I tend to eat about half our meals together. It's good for all of us. We're like our own little three-man family unit, and Jens likes reminding Ellis that he's the grandpa of the group.

I make a run into town in Gus, my Mini Cooper, and pick up three decent-sized lobster tails so we can make it surf and turf. I also grab two dozen oysters, which are great on the barbecue with butter and garlic in the half shell.

Dinner's ready by 7:30, and at 9:16 we're still at the table talking and playing cards as the sun sets beyond the San Juan Islands, painting the sky a thousand shades of red and purple. It's beyond words; the afterglow of heaven.

As the night cools, we retreat to the hot tub with a six-pack of beer and melt into the soothing, caressing water. I'll sleep well tonight. There won't be any nightmares or the long parade of dead faces. The trailing shadow of a perfect day will carry me through the night.

Tomorrow evening we head back to Redding, but for now I sleep.

CHAPTER TWENTY-FOUR

July 3, 10:37 P.M.

There are certain situations in life where it's just not smart to take chances. A very public marriage proposal would be a good example. Before you propose on the Jumbotron during halftime at the football game, you'd better be certain she's going to say yes. And the more life-threatening the situation, the fewer chances you want to take. That's why you double-check parachutes, climbing ropes, scuba tanks, and landing gear. Some things you simply don't gamble on.

Serial killers: another good example.

Throw the dice all you want when you're in Vegas and it's just money on the line, but when a serial killer knows your name and isn't very happy with you, that's not the time to live loose and free. If said serial killer has sent you a nicely wrapped gift containing a pair of wet eyes and a severed finger, well, that ups the ante a bit. Now it's time to hold your cards close to the chest.

That's what Jimmy and I are doing.

Gulfstream jets are not an uncommon sight at smaller airports in northern California, but we decide not to take any chances and, instead, land Betsy seventy miles to the south, at Chico Municipal Airport. Even though FBI isn't splayed across her fuselage, and she looks like any other corporate jet on the tarmac, Sad Face is probably clever enough to get a tail number. Better to keep our distance so that our return goes unnoticed.

We rent a nondescript sedan at the airport — a Ford with tinted windows — and drop Les and Marty at a hotel a half mile from the control tower. They need to be ready at a moment's notice, if needed. There won't be any jaunts to San Francisco or Monterey this time around. The stakes have changed and the whole team is now at risk.

Les and Marty understand this; they've been through this drill before.

Before we pull out of the hotel parking lot, Jimmy slips Les a .40-caliber Glock and a black gun case. "It's loaded," he says, "same with the extra magazines in the case. Make sure you keep it close."

"No worries, boss," Les says, sliding the

Glock into his waistband gangster-style. He takes the gun case and hands it to Marty.

"Let's hope not," Jimmy replies. "I'm just starting to like you two." He grins and rolls the window up as the Ford glides away from the smirking, waving flight crew and merges into the stream of taillights on the parkway.

The pavement stretches forty-two miles from Chico to Red Bluff along Highway 99, also known as the Golden State Highway. I imagine it's a pleasant enough drive during the day, but there's not much to see by night and the drive seems to drag on and on; the end is out there somewhere, but it seems forever stuck just beyond the glow of the headlights.

"Red Bluff," Jimmy finally says in the darkness. The dim light from the dash highlights his cheeks, his nose, his eyes, and his chin as he stares into the dark tunnel of pavement before him. Beyond the tunnel of night, beyond the pavement, the glow of a city rises like yellow mist from the desert.

"Red Bluff," I say to myself.

With little talk and less enthusiasm, we check into a motel at the ragged edge of town. It's not a dirty motel, nor an unfriendly motel, it's just a worn-out motel. The tile in the lobby is faded and battered like so much wind-scarred granite. A million footfalls have coursed through the lobby over the years; ten million footfalls. The counter is retro-seventies Formica; the paint, the wallpaper, and the fixtures are all dated, and I suspect the last makeover was sometime in the mid-eighties . . . and it wasn't much of a makeover.

We have reservations tomorrow at the Hampton Inn, but they were full-up tonight, so we're slumming at Hotel California. That's not really the name of the dilapidated inn, but as we make our way to the sketchy elevator, Jimmy begins to hum "Hotel California."

"Nice," I hiss at him.

It's the perfect song for hunting serial killers.

Night . . . the woods. . . .

Cold shadow and black mist seep through the forest, filling every empty space, pushing out the light, the warmth, the hope. Somewhere above the canopy of leaves and pine needles the full moon is paused in space, lost to sight. Trees press close, leaning over me in a menacing, foreboding manner that suggests hatred and loathing. Gnarled and twisted branches jut from every trunk, clinging, reaching, grasping.

How did I get here?

I can't think straight; I open my mouth to call Jimmy's name, but a sound stops me. *Just a twig snapping behind me,* I think, but there's something else, some background noise, low and familiar. I press myself hard into the nearest tree and turn to stone, my ears pricking at the silence, poking it, but the thick night air reveals nothing.

A chill sweeps over me, a cold breath exhaled; I try to control the shiver. Raising my right hand, I rub my arm, but it's wet and sticky, so I stop. My hand hurts — a dull ache. *Where's Jimmy?* He can't be far. I don't remember how we got here or even where we are. Did I hit my head? Did someone else hit my head? I feel for bumps, but my hair is sticky and wet, so I stop.

The sound; it's closer now by a few feet: a low hiss, then a pause, then a slightly different hiss, then it repeats. It's right in front of me, maybe ten feet away, but the trees and the consuming darkness hide it. I don't like the sound; I know what it is, I recognize it, but I can't remember it. My thinking is fuddled. None of this makes sense; it's surreal.

Where's Jimmy?
Where's my gun?
Cursing myself for a coward, I push away from the tree and take a hesitant step

toward the sound. My left hand is out-stretched before me, feeling the way . . . guarding against . . . something. Another step, and then another. I see it now, a white mist in the darkness, hissed out in a small cloud, then dissolving, like steam ushered forth from the night.

Beyond is a shadow . . . a man-shadow.

I freeze — I'm no coward — and watch the blackness within the black. Realization comes to me slowly as I watch, unmoving. I recognize it now — the hiss, the mist — the sound that is so familiar: breathing, un-natural breathing; something not human. The sound of it chills my blood more than the cold mountain air.

I shrink back, raising both hands in front of me as he steps from the gloom. His head and face are hideous beyond words, feature-less and devoid of hair, with rocks for his eyes and nose and a mass of wriggling worms for his downturned mouth. He extends a hand as I stumble back and something drops to the ground from his gloved fingers. My eyes follow and I scratch furiously at my right hand as the dull persistent ache swells in the bone. The object bounces off the ground, scattering leaves.

I scream when I see it.

I scream at the pain in my hand.

I scream at the severed index finger lying on the forest floor — *my* index finger.

I'm sitting upright in bed when the scream wakes me — *my* scream. I'm clutching my hand and my eyes quickly scan the fingers, immediately feeling silly for doing so. My body is slick with a light sheen of sweat.

The clock reads 4:15 A.M.

"You look like hell," Jimmy says when he joins me in the lobby. "Rough night? Let me guess, bad dreams?"

"Nothing but gumballs and lollipops," I lie.

"Yeah, right," he snorts. "The décor in this place doesn't help. I was halfway through washing my hair this morning when the shower scene from *Psycho* popped into my head. I couldn't even open my eyes because of the shampoo, which made it even creepier. I kept imagining this shadowy figure with a knife on the other side of the curtain." He shoulders his bag and we start for the exit. "So you going to tell me about your dream?" he presses.

I don't reply and Jimmy leaves it alone.

He knows the routine.

After a short drive to Redding, we park at the Mt. Shasta Mall seven minutes after it opens. We're not here to shop, so we breeze quickly past Old Navy, Hot Topic, Radio-Shack, and the usual mall-squatters. We *do* stop long enough for Jimmy to grab an Orange Julius, and then we're on our way again, cutting straight through the mall. At the halfway point we split up; Jimmy goes to the left and I go to the right, popping in and out of random stores. When we reach the northern end of the mall, we don't exit but double back a hundred feet or so. Satisfied that we're not being tailed, we exit through the wall of glass doors to the north, back into sunlight and blue sky.

A dark blue Ford Expedition is idling in the parking lot but quickly pulls around to the sidewalk and stops. The front passenger door is thrown open and Sheriff Gant's smiling face says, "Hop in."

A surveillance detection route (SDR) is exactly what it sounds like. It's a twisting, stopping, doubling-back, turning, and sometimes dead-end course of walking or driving employed to help ferret out anyone who might be following.

While they're most commonly used by the intelligence community, SDRs are also a necessary tool for the FBI, for diplomats, for some private security firms, and even for the military in certain environments. It's best to have a second set of eyes, or better yet a second vehicle, when conducting SDRs. A chase vehicle a hundred yards back is better positioned to observe how other vehicles react to the target vehicle's random turns, stops, and stalls.

You can also do SDRs solo. It just takes some planning.

After a few random turns and sudden stops, Walt steers the Expedition down a preselected road that winds back and forth so that it's impossible to see what's right around each turn. At the end is a wide cul-de-sac with no outlet.

We park and wait.

Five minutes later Walt fires up the SUV and we continue to the station. It's doubtful that Sad Face has any intelligence training, or even knows what countersurveillance is, but he's surprised us before and we can't take any chances. We have to err on the side of overkill.

This is what happens when the hunters become the hunted.

CHAPTER TWENTY-FIVE

July 5, 7:45 A.M.
We've been back in Redding less than two days, and now this.

It's not good.

Sheriff Gant's house looks like a crime scene when Jimmy and I arrive. Four marked patrol cars, two unmarked SUVs, three unmarked Crown Victorias, and a crime scene van fill the street just beyond the ropes of yellow police tape that encompass the sidewalk, yard, and driveway of the sheriff's modest two-story. Uniformed deputies and plainclothes detectives move slowly about the property, studying every inch of ground, while two crime scene investigators process the sheriff's Ford Expedition.

Approaching the house, I see it immediately: brilliant amaranth and rust footsteps coming down the sidewalk from the north and turning up the driveway, one set coming and one set going. Waving Jimmy to follow, I pursue the amaranth trail north a block, then west two blocks, where the prints disappear.

"He got into a car right here," I say, pointing at the empty pavement.

Jimmy crouches a few feet away and dips his finger into a stained patch of road. Rolling the blackness between his finger and thumb, he smells it. "This oil was left recently . . . within the last twelve hours." He smells it again. "It's burnt. Probably left by an older car or truck, and one that's not well maintained."

Returning to the sheriff's house, we cross the yellow tape and make directly for the Ford Expedition. The amaranth steps pause next to the driver's-side front fender, then turn and leave the way they came.

"Bastard came to my house," Walter bellows as he bursts from the front door waving a standard #10 envelope in his hand. "Came to my house while I was sleeping, like some common sneak-thief, only he's not common, is he? My wife's in a state. I thought I was going to have to call paramedics because she was hyperventilating so badly. Now she's up there packing. Says she's going to her sister's in Sacramento until we catch this guy, and I don't blame her one bit."

"Is that it?" I ask, pointing at the envelope. *I know it is. I can see the amaranth.*

Walt hands it over. "He left it under my windshield wiper. Wanted to make sure I saw it first thing." He rubs his hands together as if they're covered in filth. "CSI is already finished with it. No prints. Son of a bitch wore gloves, which means there's little chance of touch DNA, either, but they swabbed it anyway."

Pulling on a pair of latex gloves, I open the flap slowly and extract the single piece of paper from inside. It's cut from newspaper print and folded in half. I unfold it on the hood of the Expedition, holding it flat. A woman's face smiles at us from the black-and-white image, a joyful moment captured and preserved and displayed.

"Oh, no," I hear myself say. Jimmy and I study the photo for a long moment.

"He's taunting us," Walt says in a calmer voice. "You know that, right?"

"He's not as smart as he thinks he is," Jimmy replies gruffly.

I don't say anything, but my mind is racing. I hope Jimmy's right; I hope Sad Face is as dumb as a rock in a riverbed, but my gut tells me otherwise. Right now it feels like he's winning.

Jimmy folds the square of paper and slides it back in the envelope, then places the envelope inside his briefcase. Rain begins to fall from an iron sky. "Call Les and have them bring the jet up. We may need it." He retrieves his own phone and punches a few numbers, then holds it to his ear.

"Who are you calling?"

"Diane. If anyone can do this fast, it's her."

The clock in the conference room at the Shasta County Sheriff's Office is typical of government clocks, meaning it's round, it ticks loudly, it has a black plastic case and a white face, and it can intermittently disrupt the space-time continuum to turn minutes into hours and hours into days. Just ask anyone who's spent an hour at the Department of Motor Vehicles and they'll tell you about the year they spent in hell.

It's the clocks.

That same torturous monotony is upon us now as we wait for Diane's call. Minutes drag. Seconds announce themselves over and over again, thumping their chests arrogantly: *tick* — I'm special — *tick* — I'm special — *tick* — I'm special.

Time is either your enemy or your friend.

Today it's the enemy.

Jimmy has his hands folded in his lap and his forehead resting on the edge of the table. He's not sleeping, though; his eyes are wide open and I can see them darting about as if he sees the case before him upon the floor, the pieces laid out from end to end.

This is the worst part: the waiting.

There's so much we could be doing right now, but most of it involves being on the road and chasing down leads. The envelope changed all that, at least temporarily. And so we wait for a call from Diane, a call that will launch us into . . . what?

Another clue leading nowhere?

Another shaken and shattered family?

Another crime scene?

"Come on, Diane," I breathe at the clock, my voice barely a whisper. She said an hour; it's been an hour and a half.

"She's not a miracle worker," Jimmy says softly, as if reading my mind.

"Yes, she is."

"The picture was closely cropped with no caption, no date, no text, nothing; just the girl. That's not a lot to work with."

"The backside had part of an advertisement with most of a phone number," I persist. "If she can figure out what business it belongs to, she'll be able to find out what paper they advertised in, and when."

"I'm sure she's doing exactly that," Jimmy replies. His eyes are closed now.

The clock from hell *tick-tick-ticks* from its perch on the wall as it eats another twenty minutes in small bites.

When the phone rings, Jimmy and I leap to our feet as one.

"You're on speaker," Jimmy says simply.

"Susan Ault out of Chico," Diane says flatly. "She was featured in the *Chico Enterprise-Record* just last week after she opened her third nail salon. I just called Chico PD and they're sending someone to her house. You should hear from them shortly."

"Good work, Diane," Jimmy says with a sigh.

"Really good work," I echo.

The phone is silent for a long minute, so long that I think we've been disconnected, then, as if from some hollow place where every word is a struggle, Diane's voice crackles from the cheap speaker.

"Save her," is all she says, then there's a click and the line drops off.

Les and Marty set Betsy down on the main runway of the Chico Municipal Airport less than twenty minutes later, and a white Ford Explorer driven by Sergeant Eddie Cooper of the Chico PD is parked on the tarmac waiting for us.

Introductions are polite but short out of necessity and we're soon rolling down the road on the way to 437 Hollow Wood Drive.

"We have units en route to each of her nail salons, and one to her kids' day care," Eddie recites. "Still no answer at the house."

"What do you mean, *no answer*?" Jimmy turns almost completely sideways in the front passenger seat. "They haven't made entry yet?"

"I think they're waiting for you," the sergeant says sheepishly. "We don't have probable cause to breach the —"

"I told your captain this woman is in *serious* danger!" Jimmy interrupts. "I made it clear we're dealing with a serial killer. What are they waiting for?"

Waving his right hand up and down the way you would urge an unruly dog to sit, Cooper says, "I'm on your side, trust me, but we lost a one-point-two-million-dollar lawsuit three months ago for a similar entry, and the powers that be are a bit gun-shy. That's money the city can't spare, and it cost us two commissioned positions."

"Unbelievable," Jimmy says, pressing both hands into his head as if trying to keep his cranium from exploding. "Let's just get there."

Hollow Wood Drive is a quiet, tree-lined road that pours smoothly off West Sacramento Avenue and winds its way to the east, then to the west, before reaching a large cul-de-sac at the dead end.

Susan Ault's rambler sits on a small lot in the northeast corner of the cul-de-sac. Only a few years old, the house still looks crisp and new, with a wall of river rock and elaborate windows covering the left front of the house and cement-board siding painted moss green and trimmed in cream with just the slightest hint of olive covering the rest.

"Nice place," I say as we exit the SUV. My eyes walk around the neighborhood, taking in the six homes in the cul-de-sac, with their big windows facing the road and their small trees. "Hard to get in and out without being seen," I observe.

"Yeah," Jimmy agrees. "Not too many places to hide. Let's take a look around back."

As we step onto the driveway and make for the house, a rather large Chico police officer at the corner of the garage spies us. Despite Sergeant Cooper's presence beside us, he comes barreling down the driveway with both hands held up in front of him yelling something incoherent. I can only make out the words *back, stop,* and *donut* — though I might be mistaken about the donut part.

He's wearing a captain's uniform with pretty gold bars on the collar that somehow complement the perspiration stains. His shirt has to be at least size 4X, and even with the extra yardage of shirt fabric, his buttons are straining at their threads — dangerously straining.

Captain Mudge's momentum nearly carries him past us, but he manages to stop at the last minute, his face splotchy red either from the ten-yard dash he just completed or because he's yelling at us about *his* crime scene and *his* investigation.

As he spews on, his finger jabbing first at Jimmy, then at me, then at the house, the sky, the road, a tree, and Sergeant Cooper's left ear, Jimmy calmly pulls out his phone, looks up a number, and dials. This elevates Captain Mudge into an even higher realm of hysterics. Spewing words that would make a rap artist blush, he manages to somehow jump into the air, though I use the word loosely, since the jump looks more like a mountain hiccupping.

My mouth hangs half open as I stare at him in a surreal daze.

"What's your problem?" I finally bark in horror and disgust.

Big mistake.

Mudge turns every ounce of his ire on me, solely on me. Spit flies as he gets in my face and vomits a stream of words I've never heard before; I swear he's making them up as he goes. I really don't know what we did to piss this guy off, but I'm starting to worry that he's going to have a coronary right here, right now . . . and I'm not doing mouth-to-mouth.

"Hi, Chief," I hear Jimmy say. He's got this index finger poised with authority in front of Mudge's face, but is otherwise ignoring the captain, his gaze directed at the house, the yard, the street; anyplace but Mudge's puffing red face and sweating forehead.

"This is Special Agent James Donovan, we talked a little while ago. Yes, sir. I appreciate that, Chief. Yes, we just got to the house, but there seems to be a misunderstanding. Captain . . ." He pauses long and intentionally as he reads the name on the sweaty shirt. "Captain Mudge is upset at our presence and has ordered us off his crime scene." There's a pause as Jimmy nods. "Of course, sir, he's right here."

Handing the phone to Mudge, Jimmy

says, "Your boss wants to clear up this little misunderstanding."

I don't know what the chief of police says, but Mudge's face goes as white as a powdered donut and he stammers, "Yes, sir," then "No, sir," then "Perfectly clear, sir." He hands the phone back to Jimmy with a stunned look on his face and without a word walks to a silver Crown Victoria parked on the street. He fumbles for his keys, drops them, and finally manages to unlock the car.

As he gets in, I throw him an olive branch. "Buckle up for safety," I say, bringing my hands together in front of me to demonstrate the proper way to fasten a seat belt. It was a small olive branch.

Mudge ignores me and starts the car.

Turning to Sergeant Cooper, Jimmy says, "How 'bout we take a look at the backyard now?"

"Yeah, sounds good," Cooper says, watching the car go. "Sorry about that." He gives a little shrug. "I won't make excuses for Mudge, he's always been . . . difficult. But he's going through a divorce and has some other issues going on; and he doesn't like the FBI, hasn't for about ten years now. Says you stole a homicide case from him. Lots of press that he thought he deserved."

"Well, that wasn't us," Jimmy says. "We

try to avoid the press when we can; it only muddies the relationship with local law enforcement. We help where we can, then go home. Serial killers are a bit different, though."

"I can only imagine," Cooper says.

The backyard of Susan Ault's home is more cluttered and less attractive than the front but still nice by most standards. A large deck sprouts from the back of the house, complete with railings, benches, a built-in grill, and a steel-and-glass table surrounded by six chairs and covered by a large green umbrella that pokes out from the center of the table.

The deck drops off to a patio, which in turn gives way to thick grass that was due for a mowing two weeks ago. There's no fence, just the neighboring yards on each side and a transition point between the grass and a wooded area in the very back.

I see it as soon as I come around the side of the house: brilliant rust-textured amaranth glaring at me defiantly, taunting me. The footsteps come in from the woods, cross the yard, and I see handprints where he peered through two windows before going to the sliding glass door.

The prints are fresh, only hours old, and they leave the same way they came, though joined by a second set of prints the color of bone marbled with violet: Susan Ault. Her footsteps are nearly sideways next to those of Sad Face, the way one would walk if struggling or looking back.

I kneel next to one of the prints and place my hand on the bent grass. "She has a daughter . . . how old?"

"Two." Sergeant Cooper pulls a notepad from his breast pocket and flips through several pages. "Her name's Sarah, Sarah Grace Ault."

Jimmy reads my face, knows what I've seen. "We've got to get inside," he says, pulling his Glock in one smooth motion. He fast-walks to the nearest window, but the curtain blocks his view. Moving to the sliding glass door with me and Sergeant Cooper close behind him, he tries the door.

It's unlocked.

I pull my Walther P22, check the chamber, and flip the switch from safe to fire. The trail tells me that Sad Face is long gone, so I don't expect a gun battle, but Jimmy and I have walked into too many surprises together to take any chances.

I follow him as he clears the house: first the living room, sweeping into the kitchen, checking closets as we go, then down the carpeted hall. Our feet make little sound as we shuffle through the familiar dance, a dance we call sweep-and-clear. Jimmy shouts, "FBI. Show yourself," or some rendition of the same, every ten or fifteen seconds, but no one does.

Ducking into the bathroom to check the shower, we continue on to the master bedroom on the right and find a brown and tan Coach purse spilled upon the pale carpet, its contents bleeding out in the form of keys, lipstick, a matching Coach wallet, and even a miniature flashlight. Three feet away from the purse rests a small unused can of pepper spray. *She tried to fight, but he was too fast.*

Sad Face's shine is on the door handle into the room; it's on the purse where he grabbed it; it's on the carpet in the shape of a knee print next to where Susan fell.

Did he strike her?

Push her?

Did she stumble back and fall?

If there are clues here, a story to tell, the shine is not giving them up . . . though it does whisper an even uglier truth — one more surprise for us to unfold. My stomach tightens into a clenched fist as my eyes follow the shine from the room. He's pulling her, dragging her, as she continues to struggle. I can see it in the placement of her feet, the drag marks, the sudden jerks forward as he wrenches her along.

And then the trail disappears under a closed door across the hall. The white six-panel door is like all the others in Susan Ault's home, with one difference: This one is adorned with a pink teddy bear holding a little plaque of painted wood that reads SARAH.

As Jimmy moves to the door, I hold my breath.

The house is quiet but for the tiny squeal of the hinge as the door opens wide onto an orderly pink and white room with a large bin in the corner bursting with toys. The only thing out of place is a set of wooden alphabet blocks on the cream carpet; they're shaped into a large circle with a single block for each eye, one for the nose, and five for the downturned mouth.

Sad Face.

Sarah is standing at the rail of her crib watching us, a small blanket clutched tight in her hands, a pacifier in her mouth, and the drying remnants of tears under each eye. She clutches me tightly when I lift her from the crib. My heart is breaking as she buries her face in my shoulder.

Chapter Twenty-Six

July 5, 12:15 P.M.

Jimmy is bent over in his chair when I enter the sheriff's office conference room; his back is to me and his face is to the floor. Pressed to his right ear is his cell phone, while his left hand cradles his forehead. His shoulders are doing the rhythmic up-and-down bounce of someone in the middle of either a hard cry or a suppressed laugh, I can't tell which.

Bad news. It's what I fear; it's what we both fear.

When he hears me behind him, Jimmy's face turns up and I see his crooked smile. The muscles in my neck, my back, my gut instantly let go, and I relax. It's good to see him smile. With the things we see and experience, like this morning's unfortunate events, it's often hard to laugh and smile. That's probably why cop humor is frequently dark; it's a way of taking the horrible, the unthinkable, and making light of it.

"Genna left me a message an hour ago. You gotta hear this," Jimmy says, placing the cell phone faceup on the conference table.

Genna is Jimmy's older sister in Houston. I've met her a few times, twice in Texas and three or four times on a cluster of trips she took to Bellingham over the last year. Divorced for five years, Genna wants to move closer to her brother so her son, Derek, will have a male role model. I was informed that the job of "role model" also applies to me, since Derek is somehow smitten by me and has set his mind on a career as an FBI tracker.

Smitten.

That's the word Jimmy used, which was slightly confusing to me since I thought smitten is what happens to co-eds when they see the school quarterback, or what happens to young moviegoers when they see this year's heartthrob on the big screen.

Smitten.

It's one of those words that we all think we know until someone uses it in a way that doesn't seem right. I looked it up, half expecting it to be some old Anglican abbreviation for "smacked with a kitten," and found that Jimmy may have used it correctly after all.

Derek isn't in love with me, nor have I struck him with my hand or a stick, nor have I afflicted him with some deadly disease . . . but I have affected him mentally, it would seem. So much so, according to Jimmy, that all he talks about is the FBI, man-tracking, and solving crimes. He's also gotten very good at tracking down information on the Internet, all kinds, shapes, and flavors of information.

"Listen to this," Jimmy says, jacking up the phone's volume, hitting speakerphone, and then pushing the play button.

Genna's voice is weary, slightly amused, matter-of-fact, and ho-hum all rolled into one. "Hey, Jimmy," she begins dryly, "you need to have a chat with your nephew. He's been self-diagnosing himself on the Internet again and thinks he has Exploding Head Syndrome." Jimmy's shoulders are doing the laughing dance again and I start chuckling, too, but more from Jimmy's reaction than from the call.

"Apparently he heard a ringing in his ear earlier today and started looking online to see what could have caused it. I've never heard of Exploding Head Syndrome, but I looked it up and it's real . . . not that your head actually explodes, it's just loud bangs and noises that people hear inside their head.

"I'm not taking him to the doctor, either, so don't even start. You convinced me to take him in on that other one and they 'bout laughed me out of the office, so you need to call him tonight and tell him it's perfectly fine to hear a ringing in your ear every once in a while. Okay, gotta go, Mr. Exploding Head is coming downstairs."

The phone clicks and Jimmy bursts into laughter.

"That kid is going to give her gray hair before she turns forty," he says.

"Yeah, and you're going to help him, right?"

Jimmy tries to look indignant. "I don't know what you're talking about."

"Sure," I say with a laugh. "What was that 'other one' that Genna was talking about?"

Jimmy looks surprised. "I didn't tell you about that?"

I shake my head.

"I had to have," he says, a perplexed look on his face. Then, in an instant, the lines on his forehead relax. "That's right," he says, smacking my left arm — *I've been smitten* — "we were on vacation . . . I can't believe I didn't tell you."

"You still haven't."

Jimmy grins. "Last summer Derek was complaining of hot flashes. Mind you, this was Texas in the middle of summer — I think hot flashes go with the territory. After doing some research online, he was absolutely convinced that he had menopause."

"Oh, no," I say, laughing. Then, in the next moment, my mouth drops open. "And you convinced Genna to take him to the doctor for it?"

Jimmy's shoulders are doing the laughing dance again.

Thirty minutes later, Jimmy's good humor is gone.

"Stop doing that!" he snaps, his voice strained, edgy. The command center is empty but for the two of us. Occasionally a Shasta County deputy will come in to drop something off or pick something up, but mostly they stay clear. They can sense the frustration, the anger.

I've been checking Susan's social media for the last hour, checking her friends list against registered sex offenders and looking for any odd or out-of-place comments. Susan has both a personal profile as well as a business profile, though most of the activity appears to be on her personal page.

She's an attractive woman.

Her various online photo albums contain more than three hundred images; more than half are of Sarah.

Pulling Lauren Brouwer's necklace from my shirt pocket, I look at it quickly and then return it.

"Will you *please* stop doing that?" Jimmy scolds. "You're becoming obsessed."

"I can't help it."

"You can."

"No, I can't. Think about it, Jimmy. He's got two of them now; he never keeps two at a time, not for very long anyway. We're running out of time." I reach into my pocket and pull out the pulsing locket, shoving it toward him. "This is all I've got. As long as it keeps —" I gasp and jerk my hand back, as if bitten. The locket tumbles to the floor.

Jimmy's on his feet. He can't see the shine, but he knows.

Lauren Brouwer just died.

I was holding her heart in my hand.

Walt bursts into the conference room like a whirlwind of energy, waving a thumb drive in the air as he turns on the computer connected to the large flat-screen monitor on the wall. He doesn't seem to notice the dejected look on my face, or Jimmy at the table with his head in his hands.

It's good he doesn't notice.

It would be hard to explain.

"Susan Ault had a surveillance system installed in her home just two days ago. According to her neighbor, Mrs. Eden, she had the feeling that someone was watching her, and at one point thought someone might have been in the house."

Walt plugs the thumb drive into the computer and opens a file named *Ault*. "Butte County detectives noticed the cameras while processing the scene and found the recorder on one of the shelves below the TV in Susan's bedroom. They just e-mailed a short video taken before the abduction, which shows a truck pulling into the driveway and then quickly leaving — maybe scared off by the motion-activated lights." He hits play, and the thirty-three-second video begins to run.

The time stamp reads 11:27 P.M. and the video is dark. There's no activity for a second or two, then a white work truck with a black decal on the door pulls into the parking pad. Its headlights wash out the camera for a moment, but then they're switched off and the camera refocuses. In the glow from the motion-activated light above the garage door, you can clearly see the Ford emblem in the truck's grille. What's more, you can read the license plate.

"Steven Paul Swanson," Walt says, pointing at the plate. "He lives here in Redding and owns an extermination business."

"Any history?"

"We're working that right now."

Jimmy retrieves his cell phone and hits speed dial. "Diane, I have a name for you: Steven Paul Swanson, DOB —" he turns away from the phone. "Walt, do you have his date of birth?"

"Five/twenty-seven/sixty-five."

"Did you catch that, Diane . . . ? No. May twenty-seventh, 1965 . . . Right . . . Will do. Call me as soon as you have something."

CHAPTER TWENTY-SEVEN

July 5, 3:47 P.M.

"Just let me go ring the doorbell," I plead with Walt. "I'll take some candy bars and pretend I'm raising funds for a mission to Haiti, or orphans in Bali."

"It's not my call, Steps." The sheriff is just as frustrated as I am and my pestering isn't improving his mood, but I can't help it. "Redding PD is geared up and prepositioned to hit the house in five minutes," Walt adds. "I've talked to Sheriff Mendall in Butte County till I'm red in the face and he won't back off. He's putting pressure on Redding PD to hit the house now."

"But the chance of Swanson being Sad Face is minimal at best. He doesn't have any criminal history, he has a happy marriage from all appearances, and three teenage boys at home. He sings in the church choir, for crying out loud — he's a choirboy. That's so ridiculously innocent that it's . . .

well . . . it's ridiculous."

"I've got nothing to give them except your hunch."

"Sad Face doesn't use his own truck. Period. It's not just a hunch." Jimmy puts his hand on my shoulder and I realize my voice has risen considerably.

Walt drops his head in defeat. "I know, Steps. I know. But there's nothing I can do. It's out of my jurisdiction. Mendall's getting a lot of pressure from his county council. Susan's a rising star in the local business community and there are a lot of pissed-off people down there demanding action."

"Even if it's the wrong action?" Jimmy says softly.

Walt nods. "Even if it's the wrong action." There's a long, uncomfortable silence.

"Well, we're FBI," Jimmy says. "We don't take orders from Sheriff Mendall, or Chief whatever-the-hell-his-name-was at Redding PD." To me he says, "Grab your vest."

"Where are we going?" *Like I don't know.*

"Swanson's. When the dust settles, you can go in and see if his —" He almost says *shine,* but then remembers Walt is standing next to him. He pauses. "You can see if his track matches Sad Face."

Slapping down the Velcro straps on my

body armor, I make sure my Walther P22 is easily accessible and then throw on my black Windbreaker with FBI in large letters on the back.

Jimmy pauses and turns at the conference room door.

"You coming?" he says to Walt.

"Hell, yeah, I'm coming," the sheriff growls.

"Shots fired! Shots fired!"

We're still three minutes from the Swanson residence when the call comes out over TAC 3, the short-range tactical channel used by Redding PD for raids like this. We've been running with just lights up to this point, but now Walt hits the siren and the accelerator at the same time. We race through traffic, blowing through red lights and past parted traffic, wondering what kind of soup sandwich awaits us at the end of the road.

It's bad.

The wail of an approaching siren sets the tone as we spill from the Expedition and onto the Swanson family's front yard. The house is a typical middle-class two-story painted in earth tones with white shutters. A two-car attached garage is on the left, and the covered porch is wide enough for a pair of wooden rocking chairs.

The impeccable landscaping has three recent additions: Mrs. Swanson and two of the boys are flex-cuffed and facedown on the grass, a mix of shock and horror on their faces.

Inside the house, on the living room floor, seventeen-year-old Matt Swanson is fighting for his life. A silver universal remote control lies on the carpet two feet from his right hand. Steve Swanson is flex-cuffed on the carpet ten feet away. He's in shock. His eyes are fixed on Matt, his eldest son. He's oblivious to the whirlwind around him, to the shouted questions, to the drone of the arriving ambulance.

His shine is a beautiful sky-blue with a texture as smooth as glass. It's lovely to behold; mesmerizing. Perhaps a reflection of the soul parked under the skin.

He's not Sad Face.

He sings in the choir.

But some of us already knew that.

July 5, 6:33 P.M.

Jimmy answers the phone on the first ring, expecting Walt with an update on Matt Swanson's condition. Jimmy made him promise to call before we headed back to the hotel. Shasta County isn't on the hook for the shooting, but everyone is taking it pretty hard nonetheless. You don't look down at a young kid bleeding out on his living room floor and not walk away with an empty hole in your chest.

"Diane? Yeah, hang on. Let me put you on speaker." He pulls the phone away from his ear, presses a button, and lays it down on the nightstand next to the alarm clock.

"Go ahead, Diane."

"Janet Burlingame tried calling you earlier this afternoon. She couldn't get through, so she left the message with me."

"Yeah, we were tied up."

"I know," Diane says.

"How do *you* know?" Jimmy replies.

"Please!"

"Right — the all-knowing super-analyst," Jimmy chides, trying to project some humor with his words. It doesn't work. He just doesn't have it in him at the moment. "What did Janet say?"

"The DNA from the blood sample doesn't match Chas, so it's got to be the suspect's. The bad news is she ran the profile through CODIS and didn't get a hit."

CODIS, the FBI's Combined DNA Indexing System, is a comprehensive repository of DNA data from across the country. It holds not just DNA profiles of certain convicted felons and sex offenders, but profiles from unsolved homicides and rapes. This allows the FBI to link cases that they otherwise couldn't.

Say a murderer in Hawaii leaves behind his DNA at the crime scene and then ten years later he kills again in Maine. CODIS would automatically match the DNA from Hawaii to the new DNA from Maine, and investigators would know with certainty that the two cases are linked, though separated by a decade, a continent, and an ocean.

But it's still just a database, and databases are only as good as the data within.

"No hit. You're sure?" Jimmy says.

"Well," Diane replies, "I didn't run the test myself, but it's a pretty simple hit-or-no-hit system, so, on Janet's behalf, I'm going to say, yes, I'm sure."

She's a little testy.

"That just doesn't make any sense," I say. "Why would he go through all that trouble cleaning up, particularly using the bleach, if his DNA isn't in the system?"

"No, think about it," Jimmy says. "Remember Valerie Heagle? He washed her down with bleach before dumping her in the cemetery, and I'm betting he did it to the others as well; we just weren't looking for it in the autopsies. And if Valerie hadn't been found right after she was killed, the coroner might not have picked up on it."

"That still doesn't explain why," I say. "He's obviously not worried about us linking the cases together or he wouldn't leave his twisted little signature behind."

"Right, but you know as well as I do that it's a lot harder to prove a case without DNA or fingerprints, and he's gone to great lengths to make sure we don't have either."

"I have a better explanation," Diane says through the speakerphone; I'd forgotten she was still with us. "There are, right now, hundreds of thousands of rape kits across the country that have never been processed for DNA due to lack of resources. Jails and prisons have also been collecting DNA for years, and the Supreme Court expanded that in 2013 when they ruled that DNA is no different from a fingerprint, and anyone being booked into jail on any charge can have their DNA collected. Of course, every jurisdiction is going to have different rules on how that's carried out, but my point is that there is a huge backlog of DNA that has been collected and never analyzed — huge."

"And you think Sad Face's DNA is in the backlog somewhere?" Jimmy asks.

"It explains the bleach," Diane replies.

"He thinks he's already in the system."

It's sobering; frustrating.

"Makes you wonder how many unsolved cases would be cleared if that backlog was caught up," I say, each word biting, heavy with disappointment. "Imagine; we'd have a suspect right now. We'd know his name."

Jimmy's quiet, working it around in his head, processing it. When he eventually speaks, it's classic Jimmy: "We'll have to just do it the hard way," he says.

At a quarter after nine Walt calls, and we brace for the news.

"After three hours of surgery and a couple hours in the recovery room, Matt Swanson has been upgraded to serious. The doctor says he should make a full recovery. It's just going to take some time."

"That's the best news I've heard in a long time," Jimmy says as we exhale a collective sigh. "Thanks, Walt."

Matt Swanson, an unlikely victim of Sad Face — and inadvertent victim. The serial killer may not have pulled the trigger himself, but he initiated the circle jerk that got the kid shot for doing nothing more than holding a remote.

And there are other victims: mom, dad, and the brothers.

There's also the Redding PD officer who pulled the trigger when he saw a flash of silver in Matt's hand swinging in his direction. He's a different type of victim. He didn't make the call to raid the Swanson house. He didn't even know all the facts. All he was told was that a woman was missing in Butte County and that the license plate of a supposed serial killer named Steven Swanson was caught on surveillance video. He acted on the information he had.

Regardless, his life will never be the same.

CHAPTER TWENTY-EIGHT

July 7, 9:47 A.M.

Days often fade into one another as a case unfolds; time becomes meaningless, unhinged. Jimmy says it's because we're focused on the mission, not on the clock, but it's still hard to believe it's been two days since Susan Ault disappeared so completely. Worse still, we're no closer to finding her — or stopping Sad Face.

On top of that, yesterday was a media disaster for Walt. He spent the better part of the day locked away in his office either talking heatedly on the phone or yelling at the TV as it broadcast repetitive, mind-numbing news stories about the Swanson family, Susan Ault, and the search for a serial killer who seemed impossible to find.

As bad as it was for Walt and the Shasta County Sheriff's Office, it was worse for Redding PD.

"How much longer are you going to be in D.C.?"

"Not long," Heather replies. Her voice is sweet in my ear, soothing. Though three thousand miles separate us, I can almost feel her lips near my cheek, projecting whispered words toward my ear. "I should be able to wrap everything up in another couple days; a week at the most," she adds.

"Then back to Seattle?"

"Yes, provided nothing else pops up. How about you?"

I open my mouth, but the words don't come. It's an easy enough question, I just don't know how to answer. Frankly, I don't want to think about it. Sad Face has us up against the wall; he's playing games with us, and the life of Susan Ault is the prize. It's not a game we can forfeit. The pause drags into an uneasy silence, and then Heather's voice is in my ear again.

"That bad?"

It's only two soft words, but the compassion attached to them is palpable. I feel a sudden ache inside my chest — an emptiness in my gut — and all I have is the sweetness of her voice and the three thousand long miles between us.

"Yeah." I barely manage to get the word out, but once I force it past my teeth it's like a logjam breaking loose and I pour out my hopes and fears in long breathless sentences strung together with angst. "It's like Leonardo all over again," I say at the end, then cringe at my own words.

"Don't do that," Heather says.

"Do what?" I say the words, but I know perfectly well what she's going to say.

I hear her sigh, and then her voice is soft again. "You break my heart sometimes, Steps. You have this yoke you wear around your neck with great bags hanging off each side and whenever you don't solve a crime, or don't find someone in time, it's like you pick up the biggest rock you can find and put it into one of the bags. You punish yourself for something that was never your fault to begin with."

"I'm not punishing myself —"

"You are." The words are more forceful, direct. "And the greatest punishment of all is that you won't let anyone help; not Jimmy, not me." She lets the words sink in. "Your dedication to the victims, to all of them, is admirable, but you have to know when to let go or it's going to break you. That yoke is going to drive you right into the ground and bury you. Remember where the blame lies, and that's with monsters like Sad Face, and Mohawk, and Main Vein, and . . ." She pauses. "And, yes, Leonardo."

Leonardo.

She's right, of course; about all of it. My obsession with Leonardo, in particular, has turned him into a sort of bogeyman over the years; the one who got away; the twisted enigma who leaves his calling card upon the ground. Heather knows about him from her time with the unit. Even then, she told me I was obsessing over him too much, letting him get under my skin. She was right, of course. But I couldn't let it go then, and I can't let it go now. The fact that Leonardo's shine keeps reappearing at Bellis Fair Mall only emphasizes my inability to identify and capture him.

The phone is quiet as Heather waits.

"Thanks . . . for listening," I finally manage.

"You'll get him," she says in that soft, soothing voice. I don't know if she means Sad Face or Leonardo.

It doesn't matter.

July 7, 1:13 P.M.

Tami enters the conference room and lingers near the door. I can feel her eyes on us, but Jimmy and I barely stir from our reading. We're determined to find some overlooked clue or seemingly innocuous

358

tidbit tucked away in one of the case reports. Something — *anything* — that will guide us to Sad Face.

The case narratives are starting to blur together and it seems I've read the same pages from the same reports a dozen times. Still, what else can I do? Lauren is dead, Susan is missing, and the Swanson boy is clinging to life in the hospital.

We have nothing.

As suspected, Sad Face stole the Swansons' truck to carry out the abduction and then returned it to the driveway where he found it, once again leaving no prints and no clues. It's maddening — frightening.

I haven't eaten much in the last couple days, and I'm just unwrapping a Snickers bar when my pocket rings. I set the candy bar aside and fish out the cell phone. There's an odd tone to Diane's voice when I answer. It's a tone I've heard before and, like Pavlov's dog, my heart responds to the stimuli, pounding — *thump, thump, thump* — louder and quicker in anticipation.

This is it: the end, the last piece of the puzzle.

I can tell.

Diane is half Vulcan when it comes to masking her emotions, at least when she wants to, but she fails when she succeeds.

When she solves a puzzle, the mask is ripped away and her emotions run raw and open, like a weeping wound. Her voice reflects every feeling: joy at solving the puzzle, sorrow for the wreckage of victims along the way, relief that the end is in sight, horror after staring too long into the abyss.

"What is it?" I press, my voice husky and low, while in my head I'm screaming, *WHAT IS IT, DIANE? WHAT IS IT?*

"I have something," Diane repeats, "something that changes everything."

She pauses, probably because she can't believe it herself, but my head is about to explode and I fight to control my words, my heart, my head as I say, "Go on," in a quiet, settled voice. "You're on speaker."

"I was staring at my ficus tree this morning," she says, every syllable ripe with the tone. "Just sitting and staring at it," she continues. "Not admiring its leaves or wondering why its trunk grows the way it does, not even wondering how many days it's been since I watered it last, but staring at it and not seeing it. Have you ever done that, stared at something even though you're not really looking at it?"

"Sure," I say. *More than she will ever know.*

"Why did he switch his pattern?" she blurts.

"What do you mean?"

"Sad Face," she says. "Why did he switch his pattern?"

"You mean the cars?"

"That's what I was mulling over while I stared at my ficus: the cars, Jimmy's analysis. Sad Face had a pattern going, an MO that seemed to work. The first five victims were abducted using their own vehicles. Then, after Ashley Sprague, he changes things up. How come? Why take the extra risk of stealing a car instead of using the victim's?"

Jimmy and I look at each other, and Jimmy says, "Well . . . there are probably a number of reasons —"

"That was just rhetorical, dear," Diane interrupts, and without pausing for breath she plunges on. "When he stopped using the victims' cars and started stealing them it made me wonder if something happened that made him change, something that scared him or put him at risk or was more convenient. You wouldn't believe the number and types of searches I've done over the last few days. I even checked all the new and used vehicles purchased in the Redding area during the three months between Ashley's disappearance and Natalie Shoemaker's disappearance, just in case he bought a car of his own to use before deciding to switch to stolen vehicles.

"This morning — after staring at my ficus for the better part of an hour — it hit me. I ran Ashley's license plate and there it was, right in front of me, where it had been all along." She pauses, but only for a second. "On the night of her disappearance, well after midnight, Ashley's car was stopped by CHP on State Route 36 about ten miles outside of Red Bluff."

"Did you find that in a citation, or an incident report?" I ask.

"A citation: ten over the speed limit."

"Does the citation say where she was going, or where she came from?"

"You mean *he.*"

"He?"

"He," Diane repeats. *"He* claimed he had just dropped his daughter, Ashley Sprague, at the Arcata Airport in McKinleyville and was on the way back to their apartment in Red Bluff."

"That doesn't fit," Jimmy says. "Ashley's father passed away when she was young."

"Good memory," Diane coos, "almost as good as mine. Ashley's father was Walter Sprague, who died in a boating accident when Ashley was seven. Her mother never remarried."

"So . . . who was in the car?" Jimmy's

voice is urgent, strained.

Diane lets the question hang in the air, savoring the moment. I sometimes think she missed her calling as a stage actress or a politician.

"Diane?"

"His name is Arthur Zell," she finally replies, "and he's a very, verrrry bad man."

"Tell us," I say.

"In 1990 he was arrested for the murder of a woman in New Jersey after her badly decomposed body — and I'm talking bones and some skin — was found in the crawl space under his house. The body had been there at least a year. We know that because of a suspicious circumstance report filed by several neighbors in 1989. They complained of a foul smell coming from Zell's property. Unfortunately, by the time they called the police, several of them had also complained directly to Mr. Zell."

"Let me guess," I say. "He covered the body in lime and the police didn't smell a thing. Case closed."

"Correct, and that brings us back to 1990 and the circumstances leading to Zell's arrest. It seems his car was linked to the abduction of twenty-two-year-old Katie Stahl after a male was seen stuffing a bound woman into the trunk and then fleeing at a high rate of speed.

"Police immediately respond to Zell's residence but find the driveway empty and the house dark. While they wait, someone runs an address check and finds the suspicious circumstance report from a year earlier. They put two and two together and start to wonder if they have a serial killer on their hands —"

"Which they do," Jimmy interjects.

"Which they do," Diane confirms. "Meanwhile, the officer at the front door claims he hears a scream from inside, the door gets booted, and everyone floods in."

"I smell a *but* coming," I say.

"But," Diane emphasizes, "the house was empty. Katie Stahl was found bound and blindfolded alongside the road about an hour after she was taken — claimed she never saw the suspect's face. After he grabbed her and stuffed her in the trunk, he apparently drove around for at least a half hour, then, just as quickly as he grabbed her, he dumped her alongside the road."

"No rape?"

"None. The report suggests he got cold feet."

"This guy doesn't get cold feet," I say quickly. "He's calculating. Something else made him abort."

Silence. Then I hear paper whispering and shuffling on the other end of the phone.

"There were several witnesses to the abduction," Diane says. "Three, to be precise. One of them actually chased after the car, but he was on foot — he's the one who got the license plate number. That could have been enough to give Zell pause," she offers, "particularly if he had a police scanner in the car. Meanwhile, the officers back at Zell's house started poking around — that foul smell from a year earlier still on their minds — and one of them decided to wiggle into the crawl space."

"Where they found Ms. Skin and Bones," I say.

Jimmy gives me a disgusted, reproachful glare.

"What?" I hiss.

"Where they found what little remained of Kathryn Wythe, a twenty-year-old part-time waitress and full-time student . . . and a brunette," Diane adds. "Cause of death was strangulation, according to the medical examiner's report."

"Fractured hyoid bone?" I ask, referring to the U-shaped neck bone that is broken in about a third of all strangulation homicides.

"That would be putting it lightly," Diane

replies. "The ME said it looked like someone tried to squeeze her head right off her body. There was also evidence pointing to rape, but no DNA. Zell claimed that she died during consensual, albeit rough sex, and he just freaked out and put her in the crawl space until he figured out what to do."

"Yeah, that's a perfectly normal reaction," Jimmy scoffs.

"That's only the half of it," Diane says. "He cried a long sob story about how he'd been sexually abused as a child by his brother-slash-uncle —"

"His brother-slash-uncle?" Jimmy blurts.

"Yeah, apparently his brother was also his uncle. Don't ask me how that works, because I really don't want to know."

"His bruncle," I say.

Jimmy gives me a queer look.

"Bruncle." I give him a shrug. "Brother-slash-uncle."

"The problem is you don't know what a jury's going to believe," Diane continues. "Just look at the O. J. Simpson trial. In this case, because the search of the house was questionable, the prosecutor's office got cold feet and offered a plea of twenty years with a minimum of fifteen behind bars and the balance on probation."

"Which the defense jumped at," I say disgustedly.

"Correct. And now he's killing women in California."

The phone is silent as that sinks in; the room is silent.

"So," Jimmy says at last, "where is he?"

CHAPTER TWENTY-NINE

July 8, 8:23 A.M.
Wayward Road is a remote tar-and-gravel two-lane dead-end road west of Redding that's maintained by Shasta County Public Works, but only just barely. Snaking its way north off Placer Road for the better part of a mile, the road branches off into seven secluded driveways, the last of which is 1407 Wayward Road, which has an eight-foot-high fence along the road made from a patchwork of worn metal siding and rippled metal roofing. A gate at the driveway is of similar material, though slightly shorter.

"It's a regular compound," Detective Troy Bovencamp says as he points to the overhead image and circles the ten-acre parcel with his finger. "Coming up the road there's no way to conduct surveillance without being exposed, so we humped in through the trees to the west and then circled back and came in from the north."

He tosses a number of eight-by-ten photos on the table and straightens them into three neat rows of seven. "On the west side of the property, where the driveway comes in, is a barricade wall that looks like something out of a Mad Max movie, so that's a no-go. The north, east, and south boundaries of the property, however, are unfenced." He points to each picture in turn. "Though the south and east sides have some formidable underbrush and a good stretch of rough terrain, making infiltration and exfiltration problematic." He points to several more photos.

"Leaving just the northern edge of the property," Sheriff Gant clarifies.

"Yes, sir. The property's a regular junkyard: dozens of old cars, piles of scrap, mountains of tires and rims, even a junkyard dog. The good news is all that junk should give us plenty of cover coming in." Picking up one of the photos, Detective Bovencamp holds it up so everyone can see. "This single-wide trailer is Zell's primary residence, but there are also four travel trailers on the property. The newest is probably twenty years old."

"Good places to hold someone captive," Jimmy says.

"My thought exactly." Troy swallows a mouthful of microwave-warmed coffee and sets his mug back on the table. His auburn hair is cut high and tight; his woodland camouflage fatigues are starched and look almost new but for the fresh dirt and grass stains at the knees and elbows.

You couldn't tell by the look of him, but he and two other members of the SWAT team had set up surveillance on Zell's compound the previous afternoon and hunkered down for the night. They didn't exfiltrate until eight this morning, and only just arrived back at the S.O., or sheriff's office.

Bovencamp likes those words: *Infiltrate, exfiltrate,* and *S.O.*

He uses them repeatedly.

I think he likes *infiltrate* and *exfiltrate* because they're military terms, and the acronym *S.O.* because it's short and it sounds cool. He's a former Marine, so I figure he can say pretty much whatever he wants.

"He didn't return to the house until almost ten last night and spent about twenty minutes off-loading a bunch of scrap metal from the back of the truck: old tire rims, a broken wood-burning stove, the rusted hood off some seventies- or eighties-model car, even an aluminum ladder, which I'm pretty sure was stolen." Looking right at me, he says, "No one throws away a perfectly good aluminum ladder."

Like I didn't know that.

"When he finished, he went into his trailer, the light came on for about an hour, and then it was lights-out until just before seven A.M. We heard his alarm go off and within maybe three minutes he was going out the front door looking like he'd slept in his clothes and combed his hair with a greasy fork. He went into the travel trailer nearest to his single-wide and we heard some banging about and a lot of clatter before he came out again with a bowl of dog food for Tumor." Troy shrugs. "I don't know if that's the dog's real name, but that's what he called him — twice, that I heard. I asked Alex and Jason and they heard the same thing. The guy's not right in the head . . . but I guess we already know that. . . ." His voice trails off.

Clearing his throat, the detective continues.

"After Zell cleared out, we waited a few minutes and went down to try and make friends with the pooch. He was your typical doper-bad-guy dog at first, barking and yanking on his chain so hard I thought he was going to snap it off the tree."

"Let me guess," Jimmy says. "Pit bull?"

371

Bovencamp is gulping down more coffee but manages to shake his head at the same time. "Some kind of Heinz 57 mutt," he says. "Probably part German shepherd, part rottweiler, and six parts something else. Jason had a leftover bologna sandwich in his pack — I swear he brings six or seven on every op — and he was able to calm Tumor down and make friends while Alex and I did a quick sneak-and-peek.

"The windows to Zell's trailer were mostly curtained, but you could see through the cracks well enough to tell that there was no one else inside . . . unless he's keeping her in the bathroom. The travel trailers were a different story. Newspaper was pasted to the inside of every window and we couldn't see a thing. We gave the rest of the property a quick once-over, but without a warrant, there wasn't much we could do about the travel trailers."

Over the next half hour, Detective Bovencamp covers additional details from the op, mostly minutia that would prove irrelevant to the takedown of Arthur Zell, but in the early planning stages, everything is relevant. We still have one big problem: no probable cause. And without probable cause, we can't get a warrant and we can't arrest Zell.

I suddenly realize that I need to see him

— in person. I need to see Zell's shine, see if he glows brilliant amaranth with a rusty texture. I need to see the aura of a monster. *Of course it's him,* I tell myself. *It has to be him; he was in Ashley Sprague's car.* But I've learned through bitter experience that just when you're sure of something, that's when it gets turned on its head.

As the briefing winds down and Troy gathers his pictures and slides together, I know what needs to be done. "Sheriff," I say, turning to Walt. "I need to get in there. I need to see it for myself."

Walt sighs and pats me on the shoulder. "My deputies are tactical thinkers, Steps," he replies, being kind with his choice of words. "I can promise you they didn't miss a thing. They're good at this."

This is immediately followed by a few testy words from Jimmy. "The place is under surveillance, Steps; you can't just stroll in there and have a look around."

I'm not finished, and I won't be put off. "Sad Face has some peculiarities with the way he walks," I lie, giving Jimmy a scathing look. "They're barely noticeable, but if I can just look at some of the prints around the trailer, I might be able to say for sure whether Zell is Sad Face or not. I know it's not enough for a warrant, but at least *we* would know that we're on the right track. After that, we can build a case and take him down."

Walt seems intrigued by the idea. "There's something to be said about being certain. I'd hate to waste time and resources on this guy and have it be some weird coincidence."

"And we don't want another Matt Swanson incident," I add.

"No, we don't," the sheriff replies emphatically.

Jimmy's not so enthusiastic.

CHAPTER THIRTY

July 8, 10:22 P.M.

"This is Jason Lanham," Walt says, placing his hand on the shoulder of the deputy beside him. "He's going to be your guide on this little scenic tour." Giving the deputy a sideways glance, he adds, "Jason, meet Magnus Craig and Jimmy Donovan. Oh" — he points at me with his right index finger — "you can call him Steps. If you have time to kill out there, have him tell you how he got that nickname. It's a good story."

We're parked on Placer Road about a half mile east of the turnoff to Wayward. Walt's Expedition, though unmarked, was deemed too risky for the drop-off. Even without the sheriff's office markings and the overhead light bar, it still stands out as law enforcement to anyone paying attention. The light bars in the front and rear windows and grille, as well as the landscape of antennae, are a dead giveaway. Instead, we stopped by the impound lot and picked up a Cadillac STS seized during a drug raid three weeks ago. Its tinted windows and twenty-inch wheels are decidedly *not* law enforcement.

"Just in and out," Walt is saying. "See what you need to see and get the hell out of there. I've got two guys watching the house from a distance. You won't see them, but they'll see you. I've got another man in the trees just inside Wayward in case the son of a bitch comes back early. Jason has his radio, so he's your ears."

"Where are you going to be?" Jimmy asks.

"I'm going to have coffee," Walt shoots back with a big grin. When Jimmy gives him a smirk, he just shrugs and says, "I can't stay here, someone might get suspicious. And I'm getting a little too old to go traipsing through the woods."

"Okay, then," Jimmy says.

The mile hike into Zell's place is less work than I expected. The trees, though constant, are not clustered together in thick patches like you'd find farther north, and the underbrush is light. We add a few minutes to the hike by following a ravine that cuts in a north-northeast direction. It keeps us tucked below the horizon, so even if someone *is* watching, we'll pass by unnoticed.

Twenty-five minutes later we come up a rise and Zell's compound is laid out before us. My first impression is that Bovencamp's photos didn't do it justice. The single-wide trailer is an early seventies model, bleached by decades in the sun. It has a makeshift addition off the back that looks like it's about to fall over, and a huge chunk of aluminum siding is missing toward the rear where someone — Zell, I'm assuming — had accessed some wiring or plumbing and just never bothered to put everything back together.

The trailer should have been condemned twenty years ago, but out here, in the middle of nowhere, who's going to see it — especially with Zell's *Mad Max* barrier wall? The travel trailers aren't much better.

"Follow me and keep low till we get down there," Jason says, and then he's off, moving quickly and using the trees for cover. A hundred feet from the trailer we reach the edge of the trees and stop. Jason is crouched in the brush, watching. We follow his example. "Wait for me to wave you down," he says. "If anything goes sideways, get the hell out the same way we came in, and don't wait for me. Remember, we've got two guys on overwatch."

Tumor starts barking and howling and yanking on his chain like a fiend as soon as Jason steps from the tree line. Fishing a brown lump out of his pocket as he crosses the distance to the trailer, Jason manipulates the package in his hand and then steps toward the growling, howling dog, stopping just beyond the chain's reach.

His back is to us, so I can't see what he's doing, but Tumor stops barking immediately and cocks his head sideways, sniffing. Though the dog only has a two-inch stub for a tail, I can tell when he starts wagging it because his rear quarters start shaking back and forth and he starts prancing his front feet up and down. He sniffs eagerly at whatever it is that Jason is holding just beyond his reach. When the deputy turns, I see it: a hot dog.

Smart.

Seconds later Tumor's chowing down on the uncooked hot dog and Jason's scratching him behind the ears and talking to him. Probably the kindest words the dog has heard in his short, miserable life — all of it, no doubt, spent at the end of Zell's chain.

After a quick walk-around, Deputy Lanham signals us forward and we spill from the trees in a half walk, half run. I already see it, everywhere and on everything: brilliant amaranth with rusty texture.

"It's Sad Face," I say to Jimmy. "It's him."

Jason introduces us to Tumor, who's more than happy to welcome new friends, especially the kind of friends who scratch him behind the ear and rub his belly — that would be Jimmy, not me.

"Five minutes," Jason says, "then we're out of here."

"That's all I'll need," I reply.

While Jimmy entertains Tumor, I check around the travel trailers. I'm looking for any shine from the victims. There's none on the ground, but the women may have been drugged or unconscious and Zell may have had to carry them. I check the doorframe around each travel trailer, as well as the single-wide, looking for that spot where an arm or a leg may have brushed against the frame on the way in or out.

Nothing.

I'm almost done when I notice Jason messing with his radio. He's halfway between the trailer and the barbarian gate calling for a radio check with no response. Jimmy notices it, too, and walks toward him.

"Something wrong?" Jimmy asks.

Jason shakes his head. "No. I'm just getting some random bursts of static, like someone keeps keying their mic. It happens." He tilts his head to the hand mic attached to his shirt at the left shoulder, depresses the button, and says, "Sam One-Seven-Two, Sam One-Thirteen, over." There's no response. "Sam One-Seven-Two, Sam One-Thirteen, do you copy, over?"

There's no response.

"Is your battery —"

The words die in my throat when I notice a bush moving on the hill to the northeast of Zell's property. I notice it because it's a large bush and it's over Jason's left shoulder. I stop and stare a moment, and then realize what it is: a deputy in a moss-green sniper-style ghillie suit waving his arms frantically and pointing . . . pointing toward the road . . . pointing toward the front gate.

And in the moment it takes my mind to put the pieces together, the barbarian gate begins to open in the middle, folding into the property like some great metal mouth preparing to eat its prey.

"Cover!" I bark, jabbing a finger toward the gate. Turning, I race toward the nearest travel trailer and dive behind it.

For Jimmy and Jason the call comes too late. They're caught out in the open, like rabbits in a great empty field, afraid to move for fear of attracting the predator's attention. Perhaps they're hoping to blend into the camouflage of scattered junk and piled scrap. In any case, their eyes are glued to the gate as the monster comes into view.

Zell sees them immediately.

"THIS IS PRIVATE PROPERTY!" he bellows through the gate opening, jabbing an accusing finger at them. His eyes dart to the gun on Jason's hip and the black FBI Windbreaker Jimmy insisted on wearing. You can almost see him working it out in his head. And just that fast he knows why we're here.

His reaction is shockingly swift.

He jumps back behind the barrier and at first I think he's going to flee, but as the gate continues to swing open it exposes a white Ford F-150 pickup with the driver's-side door flung open.

A stream of vulgarity flows from the truck.

Grunting.

Banging.

Jimmy and Jason are racing to join me when Zell leaps from the cab of the truck with a rifle in his hands. The first shot kicks up dirt at Jimmy's feet and he dives for cover behind a pile of scrap metal. *Pop, pop, pop.* The rounds keep coming, striking the pile and glancing off.

Jimmy returns fire with his Glock —

random shots in Zell's direction as he holds the handgun above the scrap metal and pulls the trigger over and over and over. The barrel spits lead in a roaring crescendo. It's enough to force Zell to take cover and he scrambles behind the pickup. Jason peels off in the other direction as soon as the shooting starts and hunkers down behind a naked truck frame; he's using the exposed engine as cover.

"We need him alive," I shout to Jimmy.

"I KNOW!" He's facedown in the dirt behind the scrap metal and inching toward the right to try for an angle through the open gate.

Zell has cover now.

More bullets fly. They bounce off the engine, the frame, and the right wheel where Jason is crouched; Zell knows exactly where he is. As the prickling spray of lead turns back to Jimmy, Jason pops up and dumps seven rounds into the front left tire and engine block of Zell's truck. The radiator explodes in a white cloud of steam, punched through the core by two rounds that shred the aluminum.

Zell roars with rage.

It's a chilling sound: barely human.

There's a sudden outburst of banging and crashing from the back of the pickup, an adrenaline-fueled spike of mayhem, followed by another spray of bullets. Then the monster goes quiet. No shooting. No shouting. No banging.

A minute passes, then two. My ears ache from the quiet. I hear only three sounds: the soft whimpering of Tumor hiding under one of the travel trailers, the quiet roar of air as it enters through my nose and leaves through my mouth, and the *boom-boom-boom* of my heart.

Nothing else.

In the eerie quiet I begin to wonder if Zell caught a round. Maybe he's lying behind the truck bleeding out, cursing us with whispered words through bloodstained lips. Either that or he's on the run.

Jason peers quickly around the side of the skeletonized truck and mouths, *Where is he?* in big exaggerated facial expressions.

Jimmy shrugs the best he can from his prone position and then raises himself to a crouch and glances quickly over the top of the pile. Looking around at the junk-strewn yard, he exchanges a rapid series of hand signals with Jason and then, simultaneously, they leapfrog forward to concealed positions nearer the gate.

Jimmy waves a hand at me and points to a position to his left behind the travel trailer nearest to him. It's times like this that I realize what a burden I can be. I don't have the tactical training for a high-risk takedown like this, which means that in addition to watching for the bad guy, Jimmy has to keep me safe and make sure I have the proper cover.

It bothers me.

It reminds me of how unprepared I am for this game.

Rising to a crouch, I'm about to bolt for the trailer when I hear it: the distinct *snap* of a twig. I don't have to guess where it came from. It's right behind me. I pivot around almost instantly, but the world has gone into slow motion and the turn seems to take forever. At the same time my mind is analyzing the sound. It wasn't Tumor; he's still whimpering under the next trailer. It wasn't Jimmy or Jason. Perhaps it's the surveillance team finally arriving, but then I remember they're in the opposite direction.

No.

In my gut I know the cause and consequences of the snap. And as my slow-motion turn brings me around, I see the barrel rising toward my face not ten feet away. The hole at the end of the barrel is impossibly large and black and I realize Zell has switched to a shotgun. *A damn shotgun!*

384

There's no time to duck, to drop, to scream.
A thunderous shot shatters the quiet.

"Stay with me," Jimmy shouts, tearing open a package of QuikClot and shaking it out over the chest wound to stop the bleeding. "What's the status on that medevac?"

"Five minutes," Jason replies.

"He doesn't have five minutes, this is arterial. I'm losing him."

Jason drops to his knees and checks for a pulse.

"Well?"

"It's weak — no, I just lost it. *Dammit!* His heart just stopped beating."

"Start chest compressions."

"What about an AED?"

Jimmy shakes his head. "Defibrillators are only for arrhythmias, to stabilize the heartbeat; they're useless when the heart flatlines. Do chest compressions until the medevac chopper arrives. They'll have Adrenalin and other options; if we can restart the heart we have a chance, provided I can get this bleeding under control."

The helicopter sets down in a clearing a hundred feet south of Zell's driveway. It's impossible to move a gurney on the rutted mud and gravel road, so the medics bring in a two-man stretcher. Rather than covering the distance back to the helicopter in one run, they stop twice along the way and do a series of chest compressions to keep the blood flowing.

With their patient onboard, the medevac flight wastes no time getting airborne and the bird quickly disappears to the east.

"Do you think he'll make it?" I say to no one in particular.

Jimmy turns and taps his finger into my chest several times. "That could have been you, Steps," he chides. "Watch your six next time." He pats me on the shoulder and then gives a thank-you nod to Deputy Bill Pascal, whose well-placed .223 round dropped Zell just as his finger was feathering the trigger.

I heard the bullet pass my left ear.

I think I felt it.

In the quiet as we crouched behind cover, Zell had worked his way south and skirted around the wall of metal siding and corrugated tin. It was just luck that Deputy Pascal entered the compound when he did. He made good time from his surveillance position on the hill and was breathing heavily, but there was no time to think; upon seeing Zell, he just shouldered his AR-15, sighted in, and fired a single round.

Don't hit the FBI guy.

The thought had to be going through Pascal's head as he squeezed the trigger. Even so, there was little chance of that happening. He's one of three certified snipers at the sheriff's office. And though he doesn't have his sniper rifle with him today — since this was supposed to be strictly recon — apparently he's just as good with an AR-15, albeit at closer range.

"All bets are off," Walt bellows a few minutes later. "Warrant or no warrant, let's check these buildings, all of them. Tear it apart if you have to. If there are victims here, we need to find them. Let's move! Use your training and watch for booby traps; this guy's sick enough to use them."

But the exhaustive search turns up nothing.

Lauren may be dead, but Susan Ault is still alive. How long she remains alive may well depend on our next move. I fully expected to find some type of hidden bunker dug out underneath the single-wide, or a steel cage inside one of the travel trailers, but we've searched and searched again and there's nothing.

Zell's property is a bust.

An hour later we're inside the trailer looking through stacks of mail, old receipts, bills, and other paperwork, hoping that Zell has a storage unit somewhere, or that maybe he rents a remote cabin — anything that'll give us somewhere to start searching.

And then Walt's phone rings; the conversation is short.

"He wants to talk to you," the sheriff says, giving me a small grin as he slides his phone back into his pocket.

"Who?"

"Zell, of course."

Jimmy's eyebrows rise up. "He's still alive?"

"Appears so," Walt replies. "They're prepping him for surgery as we speak, but he's refusing to go until he talks to the FBI."

I let my head fall back on my shoulders and just stare at the ceiling. "Thank God." The words spill from me in a rush. If Zell wants to talk, he has a reason. Maybe he wants to cut a deal; maybe he'll cooperate and tell us where Susan is.

Jimmy nods and even ventures a smile. Just like that, everything changes. A moment ago the walls of hopelessness were closing in around us.

Zell just opened a door.

Pulling his keys from his pocket, Walt says, "I'll drive."

CHAPTER THIRTY-ONE

July 8, 12:41 P.M.

A pair of chrome handcuffs fastens Zell to his hospital bed. It's procedure, though probably unnecessary in this case. The killer looks too weak to lift his arm, let alone mount an escape.

"It's about time," a disheveled and moppy nurse huffs as we enter the room. Her name tag reads STACY, and Stacy's not happy. "He's on a morphine drip to take the edge off the pain," she says pointedly. "He won't take anything stronger and he won't let us operate until he talks to you." She raises a contemptuous eyebrow just in case we didn't catch the snide overtones in her voice.

Nurse Stacy marks something on a clipboard and sets it aside. "I don't know what you think he did," she continues, this time eyeballing Walt, "but really, isn't it bad enough that one of your deputies *shot* him? What? Now he feels he has to wait to talk to you before he gets proper medical care. This isn't Gitmo."

"No one asked him to wait," Walt growls.

"Oh, and I can tell you what he did," Jimmy says, taking two steps toward Nurse Stacy. "Not what we *think* he did, but what he actually did." There's a raw, perturbed edge to his voice. "He abducted, brutally raped, and then murdered a dozen women." As the color runs out of Stacy's face, she seems to have trouble swallowing — either that or she's struggling to keep the vomit from rising in her throat.

A low chuckle escapes through Zell's lips.

"Why don't you stand over here?" Jimmy continues, moving up to the hospital bed. "You can hold his hand while we talk to him, that way he won't be frightened."

Stacy shakes her head and shrinks into a corner.

Point made.

There's a smug look on Zell's face as he studies us through fragile eyes. "Special Agent James Donovan," he says weakly. "Operations Specialist Magnus Craig —"

"Steps," I say stupidly, before remembering that I'm talking to a serial killer.

A wide smile blossoms on his face and his gaze lingers a moment before turning away. "Sheriff Gant," he finishes as he takes in the giant lawman. "Nice of you all to visit me." His voice may be weak, but his words are coated in sarcasm and contempt.

"You know why we're here," Jimmy says without emotion. "There are two women still missing and we need to find them, it's that simple. You know that Susan Ault has a small daughter; you saw her; you were in her room. Maybe you know that her name is Sarah and that she's two years old. Did you know that Sarah lost her father in a car accident when she was just three months old? No, I bet you didn't know that. Do you really want to make this little girl an orphan? This is an opportunity for you to help yourself."

Zell takes it all in; he's quiet a moment . . . and then he chuckles. "Help myself? Sure. Let's see if we can balance the scales. On one side we have the two women you're still looking for. On the other side are — count them — twenty-one bodies?"

"Twenty-one!" I feel gut-kicked, and it shows on my face.

His smile is sickening, gloating.

"You didn't honestly think you found them all, did you?" The sentence ends in a coughing spasm. Stacy jumps from her seat but then stops abruptly and slowly lowers herself back into the chair.

When the coughing subsides, Jimmy presses close. "Give them peace, Zell. Give *yourself* peace. Do the right thing here."

"Right thing," the monster scoffs indignantly. "I'll die before I tell you anything. I'm doing right by me, just like those women did right by me." He tries to shake his head, but the effort ends in failure. "You won't find them," he says, his voice weaker now. As he continues to speak, we lean in close for the words. "They're tucked away in a nice dark place . . . I wanted you to know . . . they're in a place you won't find. . . . You lose."

My head is suddenly splitting.

Taking my glasses off, I tuck them away, casting my eyes toward the window, the wall, the floor, anywhere but at Zell and his hideous amaranth shine.

"What kind of deal are you looking for?" Jimmy presses, refusing to back away. "There's got to be something you want in exchange for Lauren and Susan."

"I want my lawyer," Zells says, forcing an end to our conversation.

Just like that, it's over.

As I trail behind Walt and Jimmy from the room, Zell's voice rises up, stronger than ever. "Aww, why the sad face, Steps?"

Anger ignites every nerve ending in my

body and I whirl on him, my mouth already open to respond — and then I see it: movement near the ceiling. The colors blend and mix and then separate again in a slow-moving vortex of shine. It's something I've never seen before, and for a moment it stuns me to silence. I missed it during the short interview. I had my glasses on when we entered the room, and I was too focused on Zell.

Now, through unfiltered eyes, I see them waiting over the hospital bed, like ethereal vultures over otherworldly roadkill. Perhaps a better description would be vengeful spirits over the condemned.

I shiver — a long and deep tremble that shakes every extremity.

Above the gloating, unremorseful Sad Face Killer, waiting, I count six separate shines. Three of them I recognize: Valerie Heagle, Leah Daniels, and Natalie Shoemaker. The other three I've never seen before.

Zell fights off a hard coughing fit after his parting outburst. Regaining his breath and his composure, he stares at me and then grows curious and befuddled. His eyes follow mine to the ceiling and then back down.

"What?" he croaks.

My gaze falls to the evil before me and I smile.

Jimmy's watching me; he's just as puzzled as Zell. Before he can stop me, I stride across the room to the side of the hospital bed and place my words in the killer's ear.

"I have a special ability," I hiss. "It lets me see things that others can't. That's how I know you killed Lauren three days ago at exactly twelve forty-seven P.M. It's also how I know Susan Ault is still alive." The look on Zell's face is priceless, but I'm not finished.

Pulling back, I turn my face slowly to the ceiling, linger a moment, and then turn slowly back from the dead to the dying. "I know what's waiting for you," I whisper.

As Zell erupts in a violent coughing fit that sends his body into spasms, I turn and make my way to the door.

I don't look back.

July 8, 3:17 P.M.

Forty miles west of Redding and snug up against Interstate 36 stands the tiny community of Platina. Founded as Noble's Station in 1902 by local resident Dan Noble, it served as a stop for stagecoaches traveling to and from Red Bluff, Knob, Hayfork, and other destinations. A boardinghouse, general store, and post office completed the tiny settlement.

The Roaring Twenties brought a new discovery — and a new name — to Noble's Station when Dan Noble and others discovered platinum in Beegum Creek. Soon after, the locals took to calling the place Platina, after a native alloy of platinum.

It didn't change their fortunes much.

In 1968 a monastic community of the Serbian Orthodox Church founded the Saint Herman of Alaska Monastery. With its adobe walls and bulbous onion-dome spires, the monastery is beautiful and humble among the hills and trees.

Today the town is little-changed from these earlier days, except now a serial killer's hideout lies hidden somewhere in the hills to the north.

A little piece of luck led us here.

After the initial search of Zell's property turned up nothing, Jimmy found a cell phone on the seat of the shot-up Ford pickup. It was one of the pay-as-you-go phones — a throwaway phone, in cop vernacular — which explains why we never found a phone number associated with Zell. With throwaways, it's nearly impossible to link the number to the user, or vice versa . . . unless you have the phone.

It's the break we were looking for.

It took less than a half hour to get a telephonic search warrant from a federal judge, which has to be close to a record. Diane immediately faxed the warrant to the cell phone service provider and a personal call from Jimmy explaining that at least one life was on the line helped expedite the data request.

By the time we reached the hospital in Redding, Diane was already crunching data from three months' worth of calls from Zell's phone. The provider also included a map of all the cell towers those calls bounced off.

When a call is made from a cell phone, it uses the nearest compatible cell tower to make the connection. If the caller is traveling down the road, the call bounces from one cell tower to the next as the caller progresses. Most of the tower data we received was as expected; they were towers near Zell's home, around Redding, and along the main roads.

There were seventeen calls, however, that bounced off a tower north of Platina. And since that area is mostly empty land filled with sparse forests and rolling hills, it begs a closer look. The search area is massive, though, the proverbial needle in a haystack.

It doesn't matter.

We've got nothing else to go on.

Walt pulls into the parking lot next to the general store and we retrieve our gear from the back of the SUV. With Zell in the hospital, there shouldn't be any need for a vest, but Jimmy insists we bring them anyway. After my close encounter with the shotgun, I'm not going to argue.

"We'll set up base camp for Search and Rescue right over there," Walt says, pointing to the large empty parking area on the east side of town. "The command vehicle is on the way, so we'll have good comms, computers, Internet access, a bathroom, even a couple bunks if someone needs rack time. Deputy Ross Greene is our SAR coordinator. He's about ten minutes behind us. I had him swing by the shop and pick up a couple ATVs for you."

"I appreciate that," Jimmy replies. "I know it seems odd, but Steps and I work better alone. And the more mobile we are, the better."

"Your call," Walt says. "A few weeks ago I would have challenged you on it, might have even called you crazy." He hands Jimmy a black backpack. "You've got nothing to prove. I don't know how you do it, but the two of you get results. That's all I care about right now." Nodding toward the backpack, he says, "Bottled water, MREs, a couple thermal blankets, first-aid kit, pretty much anything you might need in a pinch." He grabs a second pack and hands it to me.

I just nod my gratitude.

"We'll search until we lose the light," Walt says, "and start again first thing in the morning. Some of us will be here all night, so if you need something, just come to the command post." He hands Jimmy a portable radio. "It's set to TAC 3, one of our tactical channels, which has a shorter range than our normal frequency, so you don't need to worry about interfering with dispatch."

"I'm not sure if I remember my radio procedures," Jimmy says, examining the Icom portable radio. "It's been a while."

"You don't need to worry about procedures out here. We'll be the only ones listening. The call sign for the command post is just *command.* Yours will be *FBI.*"

"That's what I like about you, Walt: You keep things simple."

Minutes later the command vehicle appears on the road to the east. It's a large motor home on steroids. The sheriff's office bought it with a partial federal grant three years ago as a mobile emergency command center. It has all the bells and whistles, even a large retractable awning on the passenger side so you can sit outside without getting blasted by the sun.

Behind the command vehicle is a black Suburban towing a small trailer and two Kawasaki Brute Force ATVs with matching camouflage paint. The Suburban pulls onto the gravel beside the road, kicking up a cloud of dust, and Deputy Ross Greene is out of the driver's seat seemingly before the SUV comes to a complete stop. In less than two minutes he has the ATVs off-loaded and begins to top them off with fuel. Jimmy and I make our way over to Greene as other vehicles begin to arrive. The place is soon awash with members of the Shasta County Search and Rescue.

It's a good feeling.

Reassuring.

Hopeful.

I've seen it on searches all over the country, neighbors coming out to help neighbors, even if they're total strangers. Sometimes they work as an official Search and Rescue team, sometimes it's just citizens stepping up. When you spend your professional life wallowing in human debris, it's a good reminder that the honest and decent people outnumber the vile and evil by wide margins.

Jimmy and I greet Ross Greene near the ATVs, shaking hands and bantering back and forth. We haven't officially met, but we recognize each other from Chas Lindstrom's town house. Ross gives us a quick lesson on the quads; I haven't ridden one in probably a year. Jimmy owns one.

"I've got an extra five-gallon can for each of you," Ross says, retrieving the gas from the trailer. He proceeds to strap one down on the back rack using a snake-nest of bungee cords. Jimmy grabs the other can and does likewise on the other ATV. Then he straps down each of the black backpacks and we're about set.

"Take care out there," Ross says as we fire up the Kawasakis . . . well, Jimmy fires up *his* Kawasaki; somehow I manage to flood mine and can't manage to clear it. After repeated failed attempts to start it — with plenty of input from Jimmy — I let Ross take over and it fires up immediately.

Figures.

We ride for a good fifteen minutes before reaching the edge of the thirty-six-square-mile search grid. Unlike SAR, our goal isn't to do a methodical section-by-section search. Rather, we're going to ride like a bat out of hell along every trail we can find, hoping for just one glimpse of Zell's shine that will point us in the right direction.

"You take the lead," Jimmy says through the earpiece in my helmet.

"Any suggestions?"

"Your guess is as good as mine." His voice is *right* in my ear; it's a bit unnerving. "We're either going to get lucky because he walked a long way in," he continues, "or it's someplace accessible by truck and he drove right up to it. That's going to be a lot harder to find."

I nod my understanding. "Cross your fingers."

"And say a prayer," he adds.

We stop for a chicken-and-rice MRE supper just after seven. I have a raging headache from staring at shine too long and pop three ibuprofens, chasing it with a couple gulps of warm water. While we eat, I wear my special glasses. The relicf is almost immediate when I put them on, though the headache doesn't entirely retreat; instead it lingers in the background at half strength.

Funny thing about the glasses is that the same thing happens if I wear them too long. It usually takes at least six or seven hours before I start to feel the low throb, so I've learned to alternate. I wear the glasses for an hour or two, then take them off for

401

fifteen or twenty minutes. It seems to do the trick.

Sunset is at 8:43 P.M., so we figure we can search another hour and a half before we start losing the light. It doesn't matter; not from my perspective. I can see shine without the light. It glows like neon; the darkness might actually help.

The problem is terrain.

One wrong turn, one miscalculation, could send us tumbling end over end down the side of a steep hill. Worse, the landscape is filled with small plateaus and ledges that could end with a sudden drop and a quick stop. Some are long falls ending in certain death, others are content to cripple and maim. In either case, the last thing we need to do is complicate the search by having to be rescued ourselves.

So we sit on the crest of a green hill with the sun wallowing in the western sky and eat chicken and rice while we weigh the risks of a nighttime search.

Caution loses; unanimously.

By 7:20 we're rumbling down the hill with new resolve. The trail is here; we know it; we just have to find it. My glasses are tucked away in my shirt pocket and my headache is making a stunning encore performance despite the ibuprofen.

At 9:07 we turn on our headlights.

They're little help against the darkness.

"See anything?" Jimmy says through the earpiece.

" 'Course I do, just not what we're looking for," I reply. "I'm having a hard time filtering out the other shine. I don't know if it's because of this pounding headache or because it's so dark out here. Everywhere I look is lit up like the Vegas strip on steroids."

"Can you go on?"

"I have to."

"No, Steps, you don't. We can head back anytime you like."

I just shake my head in the dark and keep riding.

By 12:30 A.M. the gas starts to give out and now I'm worried we won't have enough to get back to base camp. Earlier in the evening, Ross tracked us down on one of the many dirt and gravel roads that snake their way through the hills. He topped off our tanks and our extra cans, but that was hours and miles ago.

Jimmy's ATV starts sputtering two miles out from the command vehicle. Mine soon joins in and we nurse them along the last open stretch until pulling in and parking at the front of the command vehicle.

Our tanks are so empty you could drop a

lit match inside and all it would do is choke and fizzle.

As we approach the command vehicle, saddle-weary and numb from too many hours on the quads, a steady droning emanates from inside. The sound spills from the RV in waves as Jimmy opens the door; I recognize it immediately and every trail-jarred bone in my body sags as the prospect of a good rest vanishes like mist before the sun.

Walt's asleep on one of the rear beds, still fully dressed, snoring loud enough to wake the dead. And speaking of the dead, three bodies occupy the other bunks, each snoring in their own right, or at least breathing deeply. They're exhausted beyond death, much the way I feel right now.

A SAR volunteer is manning the communications gear at the front of the vehicle, but at this point it's almost symbolic, since Jimmy and I were the last ones searching. I give her a nod and notice she's wearing a large pair of ear-enveloping headphones that aren't plugged in. She sees me glance at the plug and shoots me a big grin, her eyes shifting quickly to the symphony of snoring bodies to the rear, then back to me. Despite my fatigue, a chuckle manages to clear my throat and I return her smile.

We decide to rack out in Walt's Expedition, but when I open the rear gate we find an overflowing mountain of equipment jammed into a hill-sized space. Walt's got it packed with random electronics, supplies, and tactical gear; everything from traffic cones to clipboards. He's even got a bag of stuffed teddy bears that he hands out to kids who've been traumatized by an accident or an assault.

"Damn," I whisper under my breath.

"Shotgun," Jimmy says after quickly assessing the situation. He climbs into the front passenger seat and reclines the back as far as it will go. The seats are large and well padded; he doesn't even say good night, just surrenders to fatigue, and in minutes he assumes the rhythmic breathing of slumber.

I curl up in the only other moderately viable spot, which is the second-row seat, and there I lie for the longest time with my feet pressed into one door and my head pressed into the other.

Slumber ignores me.

Slumber snubs me.

The longer I lie in this compressed condition, the more frustrated I get, and the more frustrated I get, the more sleep eludes me. Soon I'm more awake than I was when I first lay down. My mind wanders back over the spent day, over the scores of dusty miles already searched. I say a silent prayer for Susan, for Lauren; I think on the endless miles of road and trail that await us in the morning.

A distant pack of coyotes soon take up a chorus, yipping and howling at each other in their high piercing voices. I wonder if it was their fleeting shadows in our peripheral vision earlier tonight as we returned to camp.

Soon their howling and yammering is louder and mixes with the heavy breathing from the front seat. Then the ruckus quiets for a few minutes and I've just started to relax when I hear sniffing around the door by my head. I lay motionless, eyes wide, barely daring to breathe.

It's just a coyote, I remind myself. But the creature brings with it visions of a dark, snow-covered forest, of a distant time and a distant place.

Then another nose starts sniffing at the other door.

Two coyotes! Three!

Still, I tell myself, *if I sat up and opened the door right now, they would spook and be gone before I finished pulling on the handle.* I will myself to pull the handle and open the door, but logic loses and primal fear scores a point. Next, I will myself to just kick the inside of the door, with me still fully inside the vehicle protected by sheet metal and glass.

Primal fear wins again.

Maybe it's because they're close cousins to the wolf, or because their howling and yipping really is that eerie, or maybe it's just because they're large predatory animals and I'm on their turf; how else do you explain such fear? In the end it doesn't matter, I suppose. I'll think of an excuse later; right now I continue to lay rigid and still in the backseat. I know how the rabbit feels cowering in his hole.

After a few minutes, the sniffing fades, nose by nose, until silence seeps in and the night shakes off a sigh. Then, minutes later, the chorus picks up again, moving away from the base camp toward the hills to the southwest. The pack moves on. The rabbit is safe.

I take my first deep breath in perhaps fifteen minutes. It feels good; helps me relax. Now I'm exhausted, utterly and completely. Between the long day behind me, the coyote-induced adrenaline rush, and the fear of what tomorrow brings, I'm done. I'm spent in every way imaginable:

spent beyond measure.

It's in this state that sleep finds me. Blessed, contorted, uncomfortable sleep.

CHAPTER THIRTY-TWO

July 9, 5:53 A.M.

The sun peeks above the rim of the world just before six the next morning. The weight of the darkness seems to hold it down at first, strapping it to the horizon, pushing it and stomping it down. But the sun will not be denied. It shoves past the darkness, casting it into the abyss behind, and rises into the deep blue of earliest morning.

Shadows flee before it.

It brings a new day, a new hope. It brings a chance to add a new page and a new chapter to the story of Susan Ault, so that her life won't be a book half written and abruptly ended.

"Today we find her," I vow to the sun. "She goes home today." But it's not just of Susan that I'm thinking. I grasp the locket in my front pocket and hold it for a long moment. *Today we find them.*

Jimmy's got a half-gone mug of hot coffee

in his hands when I join him outside the command vehicle. I open the large blue ice chest next to the RV door and sort through the various beverages smothered in ice until I find an eight-ounce bottle of orange juice. Shaking off the ice water, I peel the top back and take a long drink that nearly empties the container.

"Thirsty?" Jimmy says with a small laugh.

I nod, take another drink that finishes off the bottle, and wipe my mouth. "I think I'm dehydrated," I say as I fish out another orange juice.

"I'm not surprised. You didn't drink much while we were out there yesterday."

"Aren't you supposed to remind me of stuff like that?"

"I did; you ignored me."

"Oh!" I say brightly, unapologetically. "I guess that's why I'm dehydrated."

Breakfast consists of two large boxes of fresh donuts and some leftover pizza retrieved from the small refrigerator in the command vehicle's kitchenette.

The donuts have been thoroughly picked through, but there's a single maple bar that was somehow overlooked; can't go wrong with a maple bar.

"Trinity County's sending us about thirty volunteers this morning," Walt says as he retrieves a large folded map and spreads it out on the picnic table. "We're getting close to the county line with Trinity, so it makes sense to bring them in. Besides, we can use all the help we can get."

He circles an area on the map using his index finger. "SAR did a thorough job on this area yesterday and Ross thinks we should head north from where they left off."

Jimmy nods and takes his turn at the map. "We covered a lot of ground in this section," he says, circling an area northwest of the SAR grid. "The cell tower analysis from the phone company only approximated ranges, and so far we've been searching at the heart of that area with no luck. I think Steps and I are going to try something different today."

That's news to me.

"Like what?" Walt asks.

Running his finger along a line on the map that juts out from Platina in a northeasterly direction, he says, "I think we'll load the ATVs up and truck them along Platina Road for eight or ten miles." He looks closely at the map. "Maybe to this Bully Choop Road. That'll take us into some pretty remote areas; we have to stop thinking like cops and think like Zell. He would have wanted to be as remote as possible, but still have access to passable roads."

Sweeping his hand over the map, Jimmy says pointedly, "If we grid-search every square mile within range of any cell tower that bounced his calls, we'll be out here for a week, maybe more. If Susan's still alive, she doesn't have a week. She probably only has what food and water Zell gave her and he would have controlled that in order to control her."

I know how Jimmy thinks.

I know that he's not so much trying to convince Walt and the others that have started to gather around the table, he's trying to convince himself. His instincts are right, of course; they usually are. We've done enough of these types of searches that we've become experts on serial killer behavior. We may not be profilers, but we know how they dispose of their victims, how they hide themselves in plain sight, and how they keep their victims either very close or far away. If Zell was in these hills, it was for one reason and one reason only.

"Steps and I will follow Bully Choop to the extreme northern end of our search grid and then we'll work our way south from there. Maybe we'll get lucky."

Walt nods. "Good. That's a good plan. We'll start where we left off yesterday and maybe we'll all meet someplace in the middle." He tips his head toward the Icom on Jimmy's belt. "How's the battery in your radio?"

"Still full. Barely used it yesterday."

"Yeah, well, let's hope today is different."

Bully Choop Road proves to be less of a road and more of a dirt byway, which is encouraging because it's the type of road Zell would have chosen. We follow it for the better part of two miles before parking the truck and off-loading the Kawasakis. I have no trouble starting the Brute Force this morning, having mastered every element of the ATV during our lengthy acquaintance yesterday.

We ride for an hour, then two.

We keep the speed between ten and twenty miles an hour: fast enough to cover lots of ground; slow enough to see all the shine. I can already feel a dull ache festering behind my eyes, a harbinger of the headache to come. When we reach a straightaway, I take my hands off the steering wheel and root around in my jacket pocket for the ibuprofen bottle. I can't reach my CamelBak, so I swallow the three pills without benefit of water.

They go down hard.

The terrain is little different from what we

saw yesterday: naked, shrubby hillside transitioning to pockets of forest, then back to naked hillside. The forests aren't as dense as those farther to the north, for which I'm thankful. They're also dispersed and small enough so that when we ride through, we're usually out the other side before my phobia starts to kick in.

As the trees and rocks flicker by, Jimmy and I banter back and forth over the headsets, small talk to keep our spirits up while time and futile miles slowly pull us down into despair. We talk about my book collection and Ellis's hat collection and Jane and little Pete. We talk about the upcoming kitchen remodel and our mutual lack of confidence that we can pull it off without destroying half the house.

We talk about Jimmy's mom.

She died when he was five. It's part of the reason he's so interested in the afterlife. Not that we all don't wonder what comes after, but when you lose someone close to you at such a young age, that question steps forward from the shadows and raises its voice. You can never put it back in the shadows after such a loss. It begs to be answered.

I know there's something after.

I've seen it.

I just don't know what it is.

We're halfway through hour three when I see it: Sad Face — Zell — spilled upon the side of the road in front of me in brilliant amaranth and rust . . . but there's something wrong.

"I've got him!" I bark to Jimmy as I come to a sudden, rattling stop and practically leap off the quad. "He parked a vehicle right here, and then walked off toward the northeast. His footsteps are staggered, heavy, like he was carrying something."

"Or someone."

"Exactly." I stare at the shine more intently, studying it, dissecting it, filtering it like I've learned to do so well over the years. "This isn't right, Jimmy."

"How so?"

"These tracks are old, at least a year — maybe two or three . . . and he was here on at least two separate occasions." I walk along the edge of the road twenty feet and stop. "The first time, he parked here, exited the driver's seat, walked to the back of the vehicle. After that he walked off and headed down that trail." I point to a lightly used animal trail that starts about ten feet off the road.

I make my way back to Jimmy.

"The second time, he parked right here. Same routine: out the driver's door, around to the back of the vehicle —"

I freeze. *Dear God!*

It's on the ground before me, just a brief touch no larger than a silver dollar. Maybe it was a heel, or an elbow. Maybe it was the palm of her hand as she tried to get away. Dead color, without pulse, faded by time. It's starting to make sense, and I shiver at the realization.

"Come on." I don't wait to see if Jimmy's following, I just charge after the shine. Sad Face's trail stays to the animal path a short distance and then turns to the west. It doesn't take long. A hundred and fifty feet into the scrub I find them, scars upon the ground, his shine all around them. The dirt covering the two graves has settled over the years, blending back into the surroundings by some degree, but the shine outlines them as clearly as yellow police tape around a crime scene.

Two graves, two distinct shines. I recognize them both.

I see where he laid their bodies while he dug the grave. One of them was still alive; she tried to get away. Bound hand and foot, she moved by the tiniest of increments as he toiled with the shovel. It took ten incremental moves to gain the first foot, less for the second foot, and soon she was ten feet from the monster at his hole. Distance gave her courage and she began in earnest, pulling with her bound wrists and pushing with her bound feet.

She found a rock.

It's an old piece of granite the size of a football, but with a large chunk broken off; it leaves an edge, not sharp but enough.

Enough.

I kneel beside it, run my fingertips over the jagged, broken edge where she tried to sever her bindings; whether she succeeded or not, I can't tell. The stain of old blood is on the rock where she cut herself in the frenzy of sawing and scraping, but there's no trail leading away from the rock, no shine running away from the hole and the monster, running away to a future.

This is where he came for her.

I see it all in my head as if it were played out before me.

"Command —" I jump at the sound.

"— this is FBI, over." Jimmy waits for a response. I don't hear it because he's using the earpiece, but Jimmy continues. "We have a crime scene at . . ." He checks his GPS unit for the coordinates and rattles off the latitude and longitude. "Looks like two shallow graves. One has been disturbed by predators, exposing a number of bones. They appear human." Silence for a moment, then, "Negative, these appear to be earlier victims." There's another pause, this time longer. "Copy that. We'll be standing by. FBI out."

Five minutes later, Jimmy's earpiece startles him. "Go ahead," he replies, fumbling with the radio. As Jimmy listens, he shakes his head slowly. "Copy that." There's a pause, then, "I don't know. I'm not sure of anything right now." Pause. "Yeah, I'll tell him."

"What? Tell me what?" I blurt as Jimmy lowers the radio.

"That was Walt. He just heard from the hospital. Zell's dead." Jimmy looks at the graves, then at the sky, then at the great nothing on the far horizon.

"He wasn't going to help us anyway," I say flatly.

"Still . . ." Jimmy leaves the word dangling.

"We'll find Susan," I insist, trying to sound confident. "We'll find her alive. And we'll find Lauren and bring her home. There's nothing else to be done about it. This is the way it is."

A half hour passes slowly before the first vehicle arrives. More follow. Crime-scene tape goes up around the graves, photos are taken, measurements, everything. A trail of small red flags marks the path from the dirt road to the crime scene. It's another hour before Dr. Noble Wallace and his understudy show up.

"You caught me just as I was about to tee off," Dr. Wallace says as he exits the coroner's van and shakes hands all around. He and Walt talk golf for a minute, which I find odd . . . and not just because we're at a crime scene. I've only ever played miniature golf, which probably doesn't count. Still, from my limited experience, Nob looks every bit the golfer, and I can easily picture him on the green driving a ball down range.

Walt's a different story.

The sheriff is a big man — which is great if you're a cop, but I'm not sure how that might translate to golf. From their brief conversation, however, I get the impression he's not half bad, but then they switch gears and we're back to bodies and shallow graves.

"I'm afraid this is going to be a slow process," Nob tells Walt. "We'll be digging them out one trowelful at a time, cleaning the bone with the tip of a brush as we go. Every scoop of dirt will get sifted for evidence. Anything that was lodged in the body is now part of the soil, so that's the only way we'll find a bullet fragment or the broken edge of a knife — evidence that points to manner of death.

"Any idea who they are?" Nob asks; this time he's looking straight at me.

Tawnee Rich and Ashley Sprague, I think to myself, but for Nob I just shake my head and say, "They'll be on Zell's death list."

Nob seems satisfied and helps his assistant retrieve several waterproof cases from the van. As a ten-legged group, we make our way along the red-flagged trail.

"I can't tell you how long it's going to take," Nob says in response to a question from the sheriff. "This isn't a normal crime scene for us; in fact, I don't think I've done a shallow grave for at least five years. Every bone is going to need to be photographed in place, tagged, and bagged. I'm also going to need to take some soil samples and who knows what else. Our actions, and the time it takes, will be dictated by what we find."

Nob, Walt, and the Shasta County Sheriff's Office still have a case to build. Zell may be dead, but they need to show the public that this was his work, that the real killer has come to ultimate justice, and that there's no more danger. That comes from evidence.

I don't need evidence.
I have shine.

CHAPTER THIRTY-THREE

July 9, 12:13 P.M.

"We're burning daylight, Jimmy."

"I know."

"Then what are we waiting for? Walt's got things under control here. We're not CSI, this isn't our show."

"We found them . . . I just want to make sure —"

I step in front of Jimmy as he tries to move past, placing my hand solidly on his chest. "It's — not — our — show," I repeat. That seems to pull him back. Jimmy's a cop at heart; I'm not. It's hard to step back from a crime scene when your nature is to dive in and help; and it doesn't matter what kind of help, you could be holding a flashlight for the world's biggest jerk of a detective and it would be enough; you would know that you were helping in some small way.

Pulling Jimmy away from a crime scene is like pulling an open bottle from the hands of an alcoholic: there's bound to be some resistance. But we've wasted too much time standing idly by while we should be looking for Susan.

"We save the ones we can." The mantra spills from my lips out of habit or just some misguided hope. "Susan's still out there and we're close. I can sense it. If he's burying bodies here, he must have a cabin or a bunker nearby that he's operating from. It only makes sense. As remote as this place is, there'd be no reason to pack a body out for disposal. This whole area is one big hiding place." I give Jimmy a light punch to the left chest; it's like punching an oak wearing a T-shirt. "Come on, you know I'm right. Let's go find her." Then, in a softer voice, I add, "Please?"

The word is long in coming: "Okay." Pulling it out of him is like yanking a rubber boot from ankle-deep mud. "I'll let Walt know," he says.

Jimmy wanders off and I wonder if I'm going to have to wait another hour before he breaks free again, but he's back in less than two minutes and we make our way with long strides back to the quads.

The dirt road is a logjam of emergency vehicles, with the Kawasakis hemmed in tight on the right shoulder of the road. It

423

takes some maneuvering, but we skirt around the barrier of cars and SUVs and soon the hum and vibration of the Brute Force ATV again becomes my world.

My eyes never leave the road, darting from the left to the right and back again, looking for any sign of Sad Face. Five minutes pass, then ten, twenty. I'm just about to suggest backtracking a few miles and taking a road that cut to the southwest.

Then I see it.

It's not shine; it's not even overly promising; but it's worth investigating. At the edge of the road are two parallel tracks heading due north — vehicle tracks. The two narrow strips are well worn, suggesting frequent usage, but the driver was careful to always drive exactly in the same path each time, keeping the tracks narrow and less noticeable.

I'm right next to the trail before I see it, and almost decide to just keep riding. Instead, I brake hard and hail Jimmy on the headset as I circle back.

"Whatcha got?"

"Looks like someone's been off-road," I reply. "You can tell the trail's been here awhile, but there are also signs of recent activity." I pull the quad onto one of the ruts and reach down. Picking up the crushed golden petals of a California poppy, I hold them up as evidence.

"Very recent," Jimmy confirms. He tips his helmet down the rutted way. "Lead on."

But there's little leading to do; the trail dies quickly.

Three hundred feet beyond the road, the earthen ruts suddenly sputter and fail. And spilled upon the ground at the terminus of this wayward spoor, as if in testament to the sudden death of the trail, a rust-textured amaranth shine lies upon the dirt. It paints the wild grasses and the low brush. Like the slime trail of a neon slug, it presses itself into the earth and leads north to a dense copse of trees.

Blackness lies within.

"This is it," I whisper. "It's all fresh." My voice mutates into a barely controlled staccato. "He was here within the last few days, and he's been here a lot." I look around and gasp. "He's all over the place."

The thicket is two, perhaps three acres, yet even in the midday sun, the belly of the small wood is cast in deep shadow. The trees are uninviting and the array of thorn-riddled bushes around the edge couldn't have been better placed. It's almost as if they were intentionally planted and culti-vated . . . and perhaps they were. This is exactly the type of spot Zell would have chosen; his own woodland fortress. What better way to protect it than to plant a wall of thorns around the perimeter?

"Over here," I yell, bolting forward, weaving past the thorns and into the center of the copse of trees, where I tear into a pile of brush, tossing aside dead bushes recently stacked there and nearly hitting Jimmy with one of the shrubs in the process. It doesn't faze him; he's as eager as I am and tears into the brush pile.

"I see it!" Jimmy shouts, kicking the last of the debris out of the way. It's the end of the trail; the Holy Grail. Laid out upon the ground is a rectangular black metal hatch about three feet by two feet, with a thick clasp on one end that's secured with a solid brass Master Lock padlock.

"Call it in!" I cry, searching my pockets for anything metal that we can use to pick the lock and finding nothing.

"Walt, this is Jimmy, do you copy?" There's a pause, then, "We found it, Walt. We found Zell's bunker." He rattles off the GPS coordinates. "Hurry, Walt. We don't know if she's got air down there — or when she last had water." As an afterthought he adds, "And we're going to need some bolt-cutters." Pause. "No, I think it's too big to shoot off." Pause. "Copy that."

Finding my pockets useless and nearly empty, I turn to the backpack and am just about to upend it and empty the contents on the ground when a thought suddenly occurs to me. Dropping the bag, I glance around, searching the ground.

Jimmy's yanking on the hasp to no avail and gives up in disgust. Like me, he begins to search the ground, but we're searching for two different things. Ten seconds later, he has what he wants and returns to the hasp with a two-inch-diameter branch in hand. He's trying to get an angle on the latch when he notices me and pauses, watching.

"What are you doing?"

I hold a single finger in the air; a signal for him to wait, a signal for patience. Following the various trails of shine drifting off from the main pool, I check eight locations before the hunch pays off.

Tossing the three-pound rock aside, I retrieve the small treasure hidden beneath and hurry back to Jimmy, dangling the single brass key between my index finger and my thumb. Placing it in Jimmy's palm, I close his fingers around it. "I was thinking like Zell," I say, trying to control the fear and adrenaline coursing through my body.

"If I had a place like this, I wouldn't want to risk losing the key or driving all the way out here and forgetting it."

Jimmy's quiet a moment, staring at the key. "Good work, Steps." His words are soft and I know he's feeling the same apprehension. We've felt it before on too many cases; sometimes it ended well, sometimes it didn't.

We save the ones we can.

It's an odd sensation. I felt the same prickly panicky rush when we were waiting for the results of my mother's biopsy last year. A mammogram turned up an "anomaly," and we had to wait nearly two weeks for the results. They told us when to expect the lab report, so on the big day we all gathered at my parents' place and spent the day playing cards, watching movies, watching the phone.

The call came just before four.

As my mother stood in the kitchen with the phone pressed to her ear, nodding and answering in one-word sentences, it felt like every pore in my body was open and sweating. My body tingled with panic and fear, and my stomach was a twenty-pound concrete ball.

And then she turned and smiled . . . and it all washed away like so much dust under a warm spring shower. It was as if my soul just shrugged and let it all go. That night I slept for fourteen hours.

"Are you ready?" Jimmy has the key in the lock.

I nod and immediately hear a *click* as the key turns. Jimmy twists the lock from the latch and then pulls back the hasp. Together we lift the lid and reveal a rectangle of darkness yawning in the earth, like the lair of some feral beast.

A foul smell oozes from the black hole . . . a familiar smell.

I cover my nose quickly and reel back. "Jimmy, that's —"

"I know," he says, trying not to gag. "Let it air out a minute."

"We're too late, aren't we?"

Jimmy just shakes his head; he won't look at me.

I look around on the ground for Susan's shine to see if it's still vibrating, but there's none to be found.

Decomp.

Even the truncated word is unpleasant — cop shorthand for decomposition. The smell is hard to explain and impossible to forget. The best description might be rank sweetness; a wretched stench that, if allowed to marinate, causes involuntary vomiting and seeps into every fiber of your clothes and every follicle of your hair.

The body begins to decompose almost immediately upon death through two distinct and separate processes: autolysis and putrefaction. Autolysis can best be described as self-digestion. The enzymes within the body begin to break down the cells and tissue, much like saliva and stomach acid break down food.

The uglier side of decomposition, putrefaction, is the process whereby bacteria in the body, particularly in the intestines, begin to break the body down. This causes massive bloating as the bacteria gives off gases that accumulate in the body's cavities and in the skin. The skin itself becomes discolored, marbling into a spiderweb of green-black veins on the face, the torso, the arms and legs. Eventually the skin blisters, fingernails slough off, and purge fluids begin to drain from the nose and mouth.

The speed of this process varies greatly depending on the environment. The most significant factor is temperature: heat speeds up the process, cold slows it down. Other factors come into play as well, such as whether the body is exposed, buried, or submerged. Bacteria react differently in each of these environments. The exposed body is also subject to a greater degree of predation — animals making a meal of it.

That's decomposition; the process is nasty, the smell is worse.

Moving close to the opening, I peer in. "FBI," I shout. "If anyone's in there, call out." I barely get the words out before having to force down the bile rising in my throat. At the same time, my body starts dumping saliva into my mouth, that telltale precursor to vomiting. I move back from the hole and gulp fresh air.

"It's pitch-black in there," I gasp at Jimmy. "We're going to need a flashlight or a torch or something."

Jimmy quickly shrugs off his backpack and sets it on the ground. I follow his lead and begin with the pockets in the front, working my way into the main pouch. We each find a small Maglite and numerous packs of twelve-hour tactical glow sticks.

There's something else.

At the bottom of the bag is a sealed container of light blue surgical face masks. Next to it is a small brown bottle that looks like it came from a kitchen pantry; it's peppermint oil. I hold them up for Jimmy to see. "I guess we don't have to throw up after all."

Some people prefer a dab of Vicks Vapo-

431

Rub when dealing with decomp; you see it in the movies all the time, detectives walking in on an autopsy and dabbing some Vicks or other menthol-based gel under their nose to deal with the smell.

The peppermint oil is a nice touch, a better option.

Unwrapping two masks, I pour out three quick drops of oil onto each, hand one of the masks to Jimmy, and pull the other over my nose and mouth. The result is instantly pleasant, even soothing.

Standing above the bunker opening, I snap two glow sticks and toss them in. They land on dirt ten feet down and reveal a metal ladder at a slight incline connecting to the metal frame of the hatch. I shine my light into the hole as Jimmy descends the steps with his Glock in hand.

He moves forward into the darkness and I see the scattered beam of his flashlight as it sweeps left and right and left again. His back is to me and his figure is cast in shadow, but I see him slowly lower his gun, then, just as slowly, he holsters it.

"Clear," Jimmy calls, his voice slightly muffled by the mask.

He comes back to a narrow wooden table to the left of the ladder and begins to fiddle with something as I make my way down two steps at a time. Just as I reach the bottom and turn around, a bright glow bursts from the table, and Jimmy turns around holding an electric lamp that casts light fifteen feet in every direction. It's the type of lamp designed for hunters and campers, and uses fluorescent bulbs powered by a rechargeable battery pack. It puts off a good glow, but even so the bunker is large enough that the corners are in shadow.

I pause to look around as Jimmy makes his way to the far left corner. The bunker is primitive by any standard: unpainted, stained cinder-block walls, a timber roof held up by a series of four-by-six beams, a dirt floor filthy with squalor.

There's a steady *tap-tap-tap* coming from the left and I turn to find the source: a six-inch puddle in the dirt. Above the puddle, sitting on a wooden frame, is a fifty-five-gallon white plastic drum about half full of water. The seal at the spigot is faulty and the water drips from it with a clocklike rhythm.

Jimmy's already in one corner and as I make my way over I notice he's standing on a makeshift floor of two-by-six planks laid down over the soil. No other part of the bunker has a floor, just this corner. A mattress rests upon a portion of the planks and a still figure rests upon the mattress: a rag doll cast aside after play.

Susan Ault.

She's covered in an old blanket with a quilt pattern, not a true quilt, just some knockoff made to look like one. A primitive, homemade manacle is around her scarred and bloody left wrist, secured in place by a small lock. A section of chain connects the manacle to the wall.

As before, a key is nearby, this time in plain sight. A nail protrudes from the cinder-block wall just beyond Susan's reach; a nail that holds the key. It's as if he put it there intentionally, on display, to taunt her.

A minute later she's free of the manacle but still not responding. Her eyes are closed, her lips dry and cracked, her pulse weak. Jimmy takes her in his arms, blanket and all, and lifts her from the filthy mattress. As he does, her eyes flutter and then open to a narrow slit.

Jimmy sees it. "We've got you," he says gently, his voice breaking at the edges. "It's all over. You're safe."

It takes a moment for her to focus on his face, and then on the FBI logo on his jacket. "Thank you," she says, her voice barely a whisper. "My . . . daughter?"

"She's safe," I say, taking Susan's hand

and holding it to my chest. My mind is suddenly overcome by the image of little Sarah burying her small face in my chest when we found her in her crib. The memory breaks me apart. "Your sister's looking after her," I manage. "She's a beautiful little girl and she's waiting for you."

"Thank you." Her eyes close, and for a moment I fear that she's letting go, drifting away, but then her breathing steadies.

"We've got to get her out of here," Jimmy says.

"Let me get topside. I can pull —" The words fall away, fractured and spent.

I stand rigid in the heart of the bunker, staring into the gloom of the right corner. *The smell!* My knees threaten to buckle and I stagger forward several steps. *Oh, God. I should have known — I should have guessed.*

"Steps."

Jimmy's voice does little to call me back.

"Come on, Steps, I need your help. STEPS!"

I don't answer him. My next words are directed elsewhere: difficult words that are hard to think, let alone speak. I push them from my throat, from my mouth, through my teeth. I force the words out and feel the sting of salt in my eyes as I address the silent shadow slumped in the corner.

435

"I'm sorry, Lauren. I'm so sorry."

Her naked body is bloated, discolored, and misshapen from decomposition. She's unrecognizable, but I know her. I know her shine, sweet girl. It's dull and flat now, with no vibration, like the locket, but it's her.

Seconds pass, minutes pass, maybe even hours. I feel a hand on my shoulder like someone reaching down from the rafters above. *No . . . not rafters.* I realize I'm huddled on the ground; folded over; broken. Jimmy takes me by the arm and helps me to my feet. He guides me away from the silent shadow and back to the light of the world above.

Susan has already been rushed from the bunker and spirited away in the back of an SUV. An ambulance is en route and will meet them somewhere along the way to Red Bluff.

Lauren is gone. I already knew that; I always know, I've known for days. But finding her body, seeing her . . . it makes it that much worse. My failure becomes tangible; in sight, in smell, in every way imaginable.

This is on me.

Jimmy will tell me later that it's not my fault, that we did everything we could to find her, to unmask Sad Face, but in the end his words are but wind and I'm left with the image of a once-beautiful girl on one side of my brain and a rotting corpse on the other.

My failure.

I feel hands on both sides of me now, Jimmy to my right and a giant to my left. It's Walt. He has tears in his eyes. They lay me down on the cool dirt in the shade of the copse of trees and I rip the surgical mask from my face and toss it aside. Jimmy forces me to drink some water; his forehead is hard and wrinkled, his eyes narrow with concern. He pats me on the chest and forces a bitter smile.

"Susan's alive," Jimmy says. "*You* saved her. She's going home to her little girl because of you, Steps."

I'm shaking my head and trying not to lose it again. "Lauren . . ."

"I know." He puts his hand on my shoulder, my brother in so many ways.

He doesn't say it; he doesn't have to. I hear the words in my head, the motto, the mantra.

We save the ones we can.

CHAPTER THIRTY-FOUR

July 9, 5:27 P.M.

The burgundy Chrysler 300 sits where I last saw it, still impeccably clean, still loved, still waiting. The well-groomed car is the embodiment of the Brouwers' sad vigil for a daughter too long missing.

I stand on the porch, Lauren's locket tight in my right hand, working up the courage to ring the doorbell. I can feel Jimmy watching me from inside Walt's Expedition. I insisted that they let me do this myself; I don't know why. It all seems so hard at this moment and I'm weary; weary beyond measure, beyond sleep.

My soul is weary.

I'm just about to turn and walk back to the SUV and let Walt and Jimmy handle this when I hear the doorknob turn, and then Alice Brouwer is standing before me. She sees the subtle streaks on my face and the watery glisten in my eyes and she knows.

She knows.

"I'm sorry." It's all I can manage to say as I gently place the locket in her hand. Her fingers hesitate to take it at first, but then she holds it tight. She collapses, broken, in my arms, sobbing, weeping; she wails a dreadful dirge that shatters the last of me into tiny pieces. I cradle her. I cry with her.

I don't know how long we stand there. There's no clock in purgatory. Eventually Walt and Jimmy join us and help guide Alice to the living room. Her pastor was notified before our arrival and is soon at her side. An assistant pastor is on his way to Redding to retrieve Martin Brouwer from work and drive him home.

Minutes turn to hours and word spreads among neighbors and family. They begin to arrive in ones and twos until the house is full to bursting. I'm on the porch, standing by myself at the rail and looking out over the California hills, when a young man arrives. He has Lauren's eyes and cheeks, and I immediately recognize him from her Facebook page — Larry, her brother. Beside him is another young man who can barely walk, his face tortured, his mind in a surreal fog. It's Lauren's fiancé.

Larry pauses on the porch and looks at me a moment. Letting go of the fiancé's arm, he walks over slowly and extends his hand. We've never met and I wonder how he knows me, but then I remember I'm wearing a Windbreaker with FBI in large letters on the back.

I take his hand; we shake. He puts his other hand over mine and just holds it for a moment. No words are said; there are no words for such a meeting. We just tip our heads at each other and share a moment of grief, an unspoken thank-you, an unspoken sorry. Then he's gone, guiding the fiancé into the house to face the sorrow within.

So much lost.

So much broken.

After a while, Jimmy and Walt join me on the porch and we make our way slowly back to the Expedition, Jimmy to my left, Walt to my right. Walt still has two crime scenes to process and three bodies to recover. For Jimmy, it's back home to Jane and little Pete. They'll wonder why he holds them so tight, as they've wondered a time or two before.

And when Jimmy kisses little Pete on the cheek, he'll say, "Stop, Dad. You're goofy. Boys don't kiss boys." He's said that a time or two before as well.

For me, it's back to Big Perch and Jens. It's back to Mom, Dad, Diane, an eccentric nudist neighbor who has too many hats, a pint-sized rodent who pees in my shoes, and . . . maybe . . . Heather?

Right now it's hard to hope for good things.

As I open the Expedition door, I hear a shout from behind and turn to see Alice racing from the porch. She slows a few feet in front of me and then embraces me hard. Her eyes are dry now, empty of tears. She stands on her tiptoes and whispers in my ear, "Thank you," and then holds me again. Stepping back, she places a piece of paper in my hand, and then says to the three of us, "Thank you for finding my girl, for bringing her home. You don't know what it means."

She turns without another word and walks back to the house. Larry's waiting on the porch and slides his arm around her as they come together and make their way back inside.

I feel it between my fingers — the paper. It has a silky smooth feel to it and I suddenly realize what it is, though I haven't yet looked.

I don't want to look, I tell myself. I'll just put it in my pocket, and later, much later, when the wound is not so fresh or so deep, then I'll look. But my eyes betray me, my hand defies me. I find myself staring at the four-by-six photo, and I can't look away.

Lauren smiles at me from a happier time not too long ago.

It's a good smile.

July 9, 9:41 P.M.

As we descend to Bellingham International Airport, a bloom of red and silver fireworks erupts over the bay, expanding to a large moon of sparkling light before dissolving into a storm of falling stars. Close on its heels, a second bloom of blue and gold lights the sky in a flash. Like the first, it quickly dissolves, and the night sky reverts to a dusky blue trailing into black. Independence Day has come and gone, but the revelers remain.

Marty's voice booms over the PA system, loud and as ridiculously obnoxious as he can make it. "Ladies and gentlemen, welcome to Bellingham International Airport. The temperature is a comfortable sixty-two degrees, with clear skies and a light breeze from the south. Thank you for flying Les and Marty Air, and remember that gratuities are always welcome." Marty peeks around from his seat in the cockpit and gives us a big grin.

I know how he feels; it's always good to

be home.

Hangar 7 is open and waiting as Les wheels the plane along the tarmac and expertly maneuvers it through the wide, though still tight opening. If the hangar is open, that means Diane is still here. I know that Jimmy called earlier to update her on the case, to tell her of Susan's rescue. I've noticed over the years that she waits for us on occasion. At first I thought it was because she didn't have anything better to do, or that she's just that married to her job.

I realized about three years ago that that wasn't the case.

She only lingers after the tough cases, the ones that take a while to solve and rip your guts out along the way. After those, Diane is always waiting, sometimes with cold beer, sometimes with Chinese takeout, sometimes with her homemade white-chocolate-and-macadamia cookies.

Diane waits because she needs to know her boys are okay. She, better than anyone, knows the dark path we sometimes walk. She's seen the damage it does, despite our efforts to hide it.

As I step through the Gulfstream's forward door and make my way down the ladder, two figures wait at the side of the hangar, silhouetted by the lights behind them. One is clearly Diane by her shape and posture, the other . . . is familiar.

Her face comes into the light as I move away from the plane, and now I can see her warm eyes, her high cheeks, her graceful hands. She steps toward me, trying to read my face, a gentle smile on her lips.

"Heather? I thought you were still in D.C."

"I finished yesterday," she says. "I just happened to be talking to Diane earlier and she mentioned that you were flying back tonight, so . . ."

I can't help but chuckle. "You just *happened* to be talking to Diane, huh?"

A smile spreads across her face, erupting into dimples at each end as her mischievous eyes beam with delight.

"Well, it's good to see you," I say. "Really good."

She moves close as I set my bag down and then her arms are around me and her head is pressed to my chest. Her hair smells of strawberry and I melt into it, forgetting Zell, forgetting Lauren, forgetting everything and taking each second as it comes.

EPILOGUE

Her name was Ally McCully.

She was born in Fairmont, West Virginia. Ally went to high school in Fairmont, fell in love in Fairmont, worked at a hair salon, performed with the local theater guild, and took night classes at the community college in Fairmont.

Ally McCully died in Fairmont.

An urgent early-morning call from the Criminal Justice Information Services complex in nearby Clarksburg, West Virginia, brought us to this dark and gloomy patch of earth. It's one of the most dismal forests I've set eyes on.

The trees are twisted and contorted, limbs bent as if they have elbows, leaves plentiful, though starved and ugly. The canopy overhead is thick with them, blocking out the sun and blanketing the woods in constant twilight. Even the underbrush is thick,

445

armored in spikes and thorns, barring passage.

This is the dark forest of fairy tales, a haunted wood out of fantasy . . . only worse, for here is the domain of real monsters.

The prints are before me, behind me, around me; their essence a hard ebony, barely illuminated by a fiendish, slow-pulsing glow. The texture is that of congealed blood, the stuff of nightmares. It corrupts her perfect essence of lilac.

As I stare down at the posed body of Ally McCully, an eleven-year-old crime scene — my first crime scene — suddenly shrouds my vision, and it's as if I'm staring down at the body of Jess Parker all over again.

In the wild hills of West Virginia, the beast has risen.

My nemesis has left his calling card upon the forest floor.

And as my eyes read the story before me, I can't help but wonder: *Is this Chapter Two, or Chapter Twenty-two?* Is this *murder* two, or murder twenty-two? I choke on the fear that it could be the latter, and shiver as I take in the shine of his hands upon her, every part of her, but most heavily upon her throat, where he squeezed the life from her. Simmering ebony oozes about her neck as she lies upon the ground both beautiful and terrible, as if nailed to an invisible cross.

Welcome to hell.

The white rises in the knuckles of my rigid fists and I force myself to release.

I stumble and nearly fall as my mind simultaneously devours and gags upon the scene, every dark impression of it. I see what the others don't. I see where he first placed her arms in a raised position before laying them perpendicular to the body pointing east and west. I see the lilac stains where her legs were likewise splayed before being pulled together pointing south.

I see Da Vinci's Vitruvian Man cast upon the ground in black and lilac.

All the elements are here, even the ring encapsulating the likeness; for the devil has walked in a near-perfect circle around the body, leaving a black trail in his wake.

Vomit comes easy and I feel better, but curse myself for looking the amateur.

My left hand begins to tremble, not from muscle spasm or chill but from something deeper in the bone. I shove it quickly into my pocket.

"What is it?" Jimmy asks furtively, pulling me away from the group.

I don't answer.

"Talk to me, Steps." His voice is urgent, distressed. Outwardly he's composed, but I see the alarm on his face, hear it skulking behind his words. "I've never seen you get sick at a crime scene, and we've been to some bad ones." Raising his hand toward my chin, he gasps, "Your face is as white as paper!"

I say but two words and he knows my meaning; two words that will set me upon a new obsession and change what we thought we knew; two words that may well destroy me before the end.

"It's Leonardo."

ABOUT THE AUTHOR

Spencer Kope is the Crime Analyst for the Whatcom County Sheriff's Office. Currently assigned to Detectives Division, he provides case support to detectives and deputies, and is particularly good at identifying possible suspects. In his spare time he developed a database-driven analytical process called Forensic Vehicle Analysis (FVA) used to identify the make, model and year range of vehicles from surveillance photos. It's a tool he's used repeatedly to solve crimes. *Collecting the Dead* is his first novel. One of his favorite pastimes is getting lost in a bookstore, and he lives in Washington State.